Praise for *When You Were Mine*

"I swooned. I cried. I loved, loved,
loved this delicious novel."
—Sarah Mlynowski, author of *Ten Things We Did*
(*and Probably Shouldn't Have*) and *Gimme a Call*

"By turns heart-stoppingly romantic and
heart-poundingly exciting, *When You Were Mine*
is a book you'll want to make yours."
—Emma McLaughlin and Nicola Kraus,
bestselling authors of *The Nanny Diaries*

"*When You Were Mine* is one of those wonderful
books that makes you feel like you're spending time
with friends. A sweet, fun, and utterly irresistible read."
—Deb Caletti, author of *The Story of Us* and
National Book Award Finalist *Honey, Baby, Sweetheart*

"A powerful story about the thrill of first love
and the devastation of first heartbreak."
—Leila Sales, author of *Mostly Good Girls* and *Past Perfect*

when you were mine

REBECCA SERLE

Simon Pulse

NEW YORK   LONDON   TORONTO   SYDNEY   NEW DELHI

⋀⋁⋀

SIMON PULSE
An imprint of Simon & Schuster Children's Publishing Division
1230 Avenue of the Americas, New York, NY 10020
First Simon Pulse hardcover edition May 2012
Copyright © 2012 by Rebecca Serle
SIMON PULSE and colophon are registered trademarks
of Simon & Schuster, Inc.
For information about special discounts for bulk purchases,
please contact Simon & Schuster Special Sales
at 1-866-506-1949 or business@simonandschuster.com.
The Simon & Schuster Speakers Bureau can bring authors to your live event.
For more information or to book an event contact the Simon & Schuster Speakers
Bureau at 1-866-248-3049 or visit our website at www.simonspeakers.com.
Designed by Mike Rosamilia
The text of this book was set in Adobe Garamond Pro.
Manufactured in the United States of America
2 4 6 8 10 9 7 5 3 1
Library of Congress Cataloging-in-Publication Data
Serle, Rebecca.
When you were mine / Rebecca Serle. — 1st Simon Pulse hardcover ed.
p. cm.
Summary: Seniors Rosaline Caplet and Rob Monteg, neighbors and best friends,
have finally become a couple at their Southern California high school. But when
Rosie's estranged cousin Juliet moves back into town and pursues Rob in an
unstable, needy, and vindictive manner, Rosie starts to worry not just about Rob's
emotions, but about his very life.
ISBN 978-1-4424-3313-7 (hardcover : alk. paper)
[1. Dating (Social customs)—Fiction. 2. High schools—Fiction. 3. Schools—
Fiction. 4. Family problems—Fiction. 5. Emotional problems—Fiction.] I. Title.
PZ7.S4827Wh 2012
[Fic]—dc23
2011032734

ISBN 978-1-4424-3315-1 (eBook)

For Ron and Ranjana Serle,
with limitless love

She'll not be hit

With Cupid's arrow. She hath Dian's wit,

And, in strong proof of chastity well armed,

From Love's weak childish bow she lives unharmed.

She will not stay the siege of loving terms,

Nor bide th' encounter of assailing eyes,

Nor ope her lap to saint-seducing gold.

O, she is rich in beauty; only poor

That when she dies, with beauty dies her store.

—Romeo, from *The Tragedy of Romeo and Juliet*, Act 1, Scene 1

when you were mine

Act One

Prologue

Shakespeare got it wrong. His most famous work, and he completely missed the mark. You know the one I'm talking about. Star-crossed lovers. Ill-fated romance. Torn apart by family and circumstance. It's the perfect love story. To have someone who loves you so much they would actually die for you.

But the thing people never remember about *Romeo and Juliet* is that it's not a love story; it's a drama. In fact, *Romeo and Juliet* isn't even the original title of the play. It was called *The Tragedy of Romeo and Juliet*. Tragedy. Everyone dies for this love that, in my opinion, wasn't all that solid from the get-go. I mean, their families hated each other, so even if they did survive, every holiday and birthday until the end of time would be a royal pain. Not to mention that they had absolutely no friends in common, so forget double dates. No, it would be Romeo and Juliet all alone, forever. And maybe that seems romantic at fourteen, or whatever, but it's totally not realistic. I mean, I can't think of a less romantic ending to a story. And the truth is, it wasn't supposed to end that way.

If you read closely, you'll realize that there was someone before Juliet ever came into the picture. Someone who Romeo loved very much. Her name was Rosaline. And Romeo went to the party that first night, the night everything began, to see her. Everyone always thinks Romeo and Juliet were so helpless to fate, that they were at the mercy of their love for each other. Not true. Juliet wasn't some sweet, innocent girl torn apart by destiny. She knew exactly what she was doing. The problem was, Shakespeare didn't. Romeo didn't belong with Juliet; he belonged with me. It was supposed to be us together forever, and it would have been if she hadn't come along and stolen him away. Maybe then all of this could have been avoided. Maybe then they'd still be alive.

What if the greatest love story ever told was the wrong one?

Scene One

"This is so *not* how it was supposed to go."

I crack one eye open and sneak the covers down over my head. Charlie is standing above my bed, arms crossed, a bag of Swedish Fish in one hand and a Starbucks cup in the other.

I blink and glance at the clock on my nightstand: 6:35.

"Jesus. It's the middle of the night."

Charlie lets out a dramatic sigh. "Please. I'm ten minutes early."

I rub my eyes and sit up. It's already light out, but that's not too surprising, given that it's August in Southern California. It's also hot, and the tank top I slept in is drenched. I don't understand why, after all these years, my parents still have not sprung for air-conditioning.

Charlie hands me the Starbucks cup, folding herself down

next to me on the bed and stuffing another piece of candy into her mouth as she continues to lecture me. Charlie never drinks coffee—she thinks it stunts your growth—but she still picks me one up every morning. Grande vanilla latte. One sugar.

"Are you even listening?" she asks, irritated.

"Are you kidding me, Charlotte? I'm *sleeping.*"

"Not anymore," Charlie says, pulling the covers off. "It's the first day of school, and I'm not letting you drag me down with you. Time to rise and shine, Ms. Caplet."

I scowl at her, and she smiles. Charlie's beautiful. Not in the way any old blond girl is in high school, but actually spectacular-looking. She's got strawberry-red, curly hair and bright green eyes and impossibly white, translucent skin. Sometimes she's so stunning, it's shocking even to me. And I'm her best friend.

We met on the playground in the first grade. John Sussmann had taken my peanut butter and jelly sandwich and tossed it into the sandbox. Charlie knocked him over, fished it out, and even ate half just to prove he hadn't won. That's real friendship, right there.

"So anyway, listen," she says as I swing my legs over the side of the bed and head into the bathroom. "Ben and Olivia totally just got together. Ben told me."

"About time." I stick a toothbrush into my mouth and root around in the medicine cabinet for my deodorant. I can tell from

Charlie's impatient prattle that there's no time to shower.

"This is, like, a big deal. He's my *brother*." Ben is Charlie's twin, actually, but they're nothing alike. He's tall and blond and lanky and he likes English, a subject Charlie thinks is frivolous. She's a history buff: "Why read about stuff that didn't happen, when you can read about stuff that did? Real life is way more interesting, anyway."

Olivia is our other best friend. She's been with us since the eighth grade, when she transferred to San Bellaro.

"Look," I say, spitting, "they've been flirting for decades. It was bound to happen."

"But now she's going to, like, what? Come over after school?"

"She *already* comes over after school."

"I know why you're so calm about this," Charlie says.

"Because I am still unconscious?"

"No, because Rob got back last night and you're going to see him today." She pops another fish into her mouth, triumphant.

My stomach clenches and releases. It's been doing that all week. The thought of seeing Rob is, well, making me ill.

It's been eight weeks, which I guess is a long time, although I refuse to see it that way. In the general scheme of things, what's two months? Like, a millisecond. Okay, so it's the longest we've ever been apart and, yeah, I've missed him, but I've known Rob my whole life. It's really not a big deal seeing him again. It's been a busy summer, and it's not like Robert Monteg is my boyfriend or anything. God, even his name flashing through my mind like that makes me nauseous. I don't get it. It *shouldn't*. We're friends. He's just the next-door neighbor.

"You guys are totally going to be the new senior couple," Charlie says. "I decided."

"Well, as long as you decided." I tug on a blue skirt and slip a white tank top over my head. Charlie looks like she just came from the salon, and I permit myself one glance in the mirror. Just as I suspected, total bed-head.

Charlie tosses me a bra, and it hits me in the face. "Thanks."

"Oh, come on," she says. "It's *Rob*. You guys finally kissed last year, and then he goes away to be a camp counselor the entire torturous summer and writes you all of these love letters saying how much he cares about you, and you think that now that he's back, you guys aren't going to get together? Please."

Of course this is how Charlie sees it. The problem is, that isn't exactly what happened. It's not even close. Let me explain.

The "kiss" she's talking about wasn't really a kiss at all. And the fact that Rob and I went to junior prom together has absolutely no significance. We're best friends, and neither of us had a date. Rob is handsome and smart, and I could easily list ten girls in our soon-to-be senior class who would have traded in their Gucci book bags to go to prom with Rob, but I think he's scared of the female species. Well, actually, Charlie thinks that. It's the only explanation, she says, for why he still doesn't have a girlfriend. The only explanation besides the fact that he's waiting for me (her words, not mine).

Anyway, we were on the dance floor and my hair got in my eyes, and Rob brushed it away and kissed my cheek. My hair is always getting in my eyes, and my *father* kisses my cheek, so I hardly think that counts as a make-out session. It just happened to be in public, to a slow song.

And those emails? Definitely not love notes. Example:

Hey Rosie,

Thanks for your letter. I'm glad to know Charlie is as crazy as ever, and thanks for the gum. I'm chewing it now. ☺

Camp is good but I miss home. Sometimes I think it was a stupid idea coming back here this summer, especially after the end of school and everything. It's good, I guess. I'm back with Bunk 13. Remember when we were here together? It seems like so long ago. I guess it was. Anyway, I really miss you. I guess that's what I meant when I said I missed home. It's not the same without you here. Last night I went out to the docks, and

I thought about that time we swam there after lights-out. Do you remember that? The water was freezing. It was that summer our parents had to send us more sweatshirts. Anyway, I'm thinking about you and hope you're doing well.

Rob

Charlie combed through that email and constructed a new one, which basically read: *I love you and I'm so sorry I went to camp and my heart is breaking being away from you and let's spend eternity together when I get back. Heart, Rob.*

It makes sense that she likes history, since she's constantly rewriting it.

Her fantasy is nice and all—it's just not accurate. It's the kind of thinking that gets girls into trouble all the time. And it's not just Charlie. For instance, last year when Olivia was dating Taylor Simsburg (and by "dating," I mean they made out twice and once was sort of in public at winter formal), he told her she looked nice in yellow, and she made him a playlist called "Here Comes the Sun." She also started carrying around sunflowers for no good reason.

It's not that most girls are delusional, per se. It's just that they have this subtle ability to warp actual circumstances into something different. And if there's one thing I'm really against, it is turning a blind eye to reality. What's the point? Things are the way they are, and the best thing for us to do is to just acknowledge that. No one ever died from having too much information. It's the misunderstandings that are the problem. And until Rob says or tells me otherwise, I have no reason to think he wants anything more than my friendship.

Except for this one thing that happened the night before he left. I haven't told Charlie or Olivia, because I'm not sure how I feel about it myself. But I keep going over it in my mind. I've been going over it for two months.

We were sitting on the floor in my bedroom watching an old DVD of *Friends*. This part isn't particularly unusual. We do that all the time. Rob likes to escape the chaos of his house, where he has three little brothers. But there was something different about him that night. When Ross made a joke, Rob didn't laugh, which was crazy, because Ross is his favorite character and Rob always laughs. He has this deep baritone laugh. It reminds me of Santa Claus.

We were watching the episode where Rachel moves out of the apartment she shares with Monica, and there's this scene where Rachel tries to steal Monica's candlesticks. Anyway, Rachel is grabbing them out of the box, and all of a sudden the television is on pause and Rob is staring at me in this really intense way he sometimes looks before a big basketball game.

"What's up?" I asked. He didn't answer. He just kept looking at me. He has these gigantic brown eyes that look like little teacups of hot chocolate. Not that that's what I think about when I look at him. I don't even like hot chocolate. I'm just trying to describe him accurately, here.

He didn't say anything, he just sat there looking at me, and then he reached over and cupped my chin in his hand. He'd never done that to me before. *No* boy had ever done that to me before. And then, with my chin still in his hand, he said, "God, you're beautiful." Just like that. "God, you're beautiful." Which is crazy because (a) it's not true. It's not that I'm unattractive; it's just that I don't look particularly different than anybody else. I mean, I have brown eyes and brown hair and what Charlie calls a button nose, so if someone were describing me, you'd probably think you knew me and at the same time never be able to pick me out of a crowd. Except for the fact that I blush like crazy when I'm embarrassed—but that doesn't exactly make me more desirable. So, (a) "beautiful" doesn't really fit, and (b) it's just so cheesy. So I laughed, because it was the only conceivable thing I could think to do, and then he dropped his hand and unpaused *Friends*, and when we said good night, he hugged me but not any differently than he usually does, and then the next morning he was gone. I've been turning that moment over in my mind ever since. For two months now.

"What time did he get in, anyway?" Charlie asks as we plod our way downstairs.

"Dunno. Late."

I want to say "Too late for me to see his light go on," but I don't. Charlie doesn't know that sometimes I angle myself out my bedroom window just to see if Rob's bedroom light is on. Our houses are separated by a barrier of trees, so you can't see much, but his bedroom is directly diagonal to mine, and I can tell if he's home because of the light. Most nights I wait for it to go on, to know he's next door, right here. I think that's one of the things I've missed most while he's been gone. Seeing that light go on.

"I'm surprised he didn't come over last night." She wiggles her hips and laughs.

I shrug. "He just texted me."

She spins on the stairs and grabs both my shoulders. "What exactly did he say?"

"'I'm back'?"

"I'm back," Charlie repeats, looking thoughtful. Then she gets this snarky grin on her face. "I'm back, and ready for action."

"Honestly," I say, "it's *Rob*. You're making something out of nothing."

"Maybe, maybe not." She links her arm through mine as we step into the kitchen. "But you know I always like to err on the side of caution."

"Drama," I correct her. "You like to err on the side of drama."

My mom and dad are in the kitchen dancing around with the orange juice, still in their bathrobes. She has it over her head, and he's tickling her.

"Sorry, girls," she says, her face flushed. "Didn't see you there." My dad just winks. Gross. Also, neither one of them is sorry. They do this sort of thing all the time. They are constantly making out in our living room and leaving each other love notes on the fridge—"Peas for my squeeze," that kind of thing. I guess it should make me happy, the fact that my parents are in love and still into each other after twenty years, but it sort of creeps me out.

"They definitely still have sex," Charlie says under her breath, like she's settling a debate. Trust me, it's not up for argument. Factual truth: They do.

I guess maybe it wouldn't be such a big deal if I had, you know, done it myself. It's not that I'm opposed to sex or anything. I mean, morally speaking. You want to know my problem, actually? It's that I *don't* feel particularly moral about the whole thing. It's like this girl I used to know, Sarah, who never ate meat. Literally, in her entire life, she never had a hamburger. Her parents didn't eat meat, and she was just raised that way. Anyway, one day her dad started eating it again, and all of a sudden it was in their house and on the table, and I remember her telling me how weird that seemed, how unnatural. Like all of a sudden she was supposed to just start eating meat and it was supposed to seem normal. She was a vegetarian, for crying out loud. It seems weird to just start. Like changing something fundamental about who you are.

It also might have something to do with the fact that I've never really gotten close. There was Jason Grove, who I dated last year. We made out a few times, mostly in the back of his dad's Audi and in his basement. It was okay, I guess, but he couldn't figure out how to unhook my bra, and after a few tries we sorta gave up.

Charlie thinks this is tragic. Olivia's and my virginity are like an affront to her values, or something. Mind you, she's done it with two people already. The first was Matt Lester, her boyfriend sophomore year. They did it after homecoming, and she said it was awful and they never did it again. Now there's Jake, her on-again, off-again boyfriend—and, as Charlie says, "I've lost count." Which I guess is what's supposed to happen. It's not like you keep counting the number of times you have sex. At a certain point it just becomes sex, I think.

"This year is definitely your year," Charlie told me last week. "You are not losing your virginity in a dorm room. Not an option."

"What are my prospects?"

"Just one," Charlie said. "Rob. You two are totally meant to be."

Meant to be. I'd be lying if I said I've never thought about that phrase in relation to Rob and me. It *has* occurred to me that something might happen between us. I haven't admitted too much of this to Charlie, though, mostly because I recognize the real possibility that these thoughts about Rob could have more to do with all those television shows she makes me watch than my actual feelings. I mean, yeah, I care about him. He's my best friend. Of course I love him. But do I want to kiss him? Do I want him to kiss me? And am I willing to risk our friendship on the off chance that a romance might really work out? Not to mention the fact that I don't even know what he's thinking. He probably regrets ever saying I was beautiful. He has probably already moved on. I mean, he's been halfway across the country for the entire summer, and just because I haven't managed to fall on anyone else's lips in two months doesn't mean he's hauling around the same track record.

My mom pries my father off of her and sets the juice down. "You girls ready for your first day?"

"Definitely," Charlie says, winking at me.

"Well, that's good," she says. She scoops some eggs onto a plate and hands it to my dad. "Rob back today?"

My mom would ask this. On top of everything else, my parents and his parents are also best friends. They've been neighbors for fifteen years. My parents moved to San Bellaro a few months before I was born. Rob's family moved here two years later. My mom actually used to be a movie star in LA. Not huge or anything, but I think she might have been headed that way before she met my dad. He was a community organizer with big plans for becoming a senator and got invited to one of her movie premieres. It was a screening of *The Last Stranger*, probably the biggest part my mom ever had, and my dad always says that he fell in love with her instantly, just by seeing her on-screen. That she was *his* last stranger. Six months later they were married, and a year after that they had me. My father never became a senator (he teaches history at our local college), but his brother did. I think it's still hard for my dad, the fact that his brother got to realize his dream when he didn't. They haven't spoken in years, and every time his name is in the paper, my dad takes the pages out to the recycling bin himself.

My mom is still looking at me, waiting for an answer about Rob, but I just shrug and stick a piece of toast into my mouth. Charlie immediately snatches it away.

"Bagel Wednesday," she says, dropping it down on the counter like it's radioactive. "Hello?"

My father smacks the back of his hand against his forehead dramatically, and my mother sighs.

"Well," she says, "have a great day."

"Oh, we will," Charlie says, slinging my book bag over her shoulder. "Don't wait up." She blows my mom a kiss and marches me outside.

Charlie has an old Jeep Cherokee we call Big Red. It's not as fancy as Olivia's car, but it doesn't matter. Charlie would look good on a tricycle. We climb inside, and the familiar smell of Charlie's perfume hits me. A combination of lilacs and plumeria she mixed for herself at the Body Shop last year. Her car is always stuffed to the brim, like she could take off at any minute and move somewhere else. There is a gigantic canvas tote in the backseat monogrammed with her initials, CAK, that contains absolutely anything you would possibly ever need. We were once at Olivia's beach house in Malibu, and I got a piece of corn stuck in between my teeth so hard that my gums started to bleed. Charlie marched me out to Big Red and performed minor dental surgery.

She starts the car and backs out of my driveway, applying lip gloss in the rearview at the same time. I risk a glance over to Rob's house, but it's hard to make out anything between the trees. Or see if there are any cars still parked in his driveway.

I pick up her iPod and put on Radiohead.

"Ew." She gives me a disgruntled look and yanks the iPod out of my hand. She puts on Beyoncé and turns to me. "What is wrong with you this morning? It's the first day of school. We need to be psyched up. Starting things on the right note is the only way to succeed."

This is one of her theories. Charlie is full of theories. She has a theory about everything. For instance, she believes firmly that you can only change your hair once over the course of high school. Olivia chopped all hers off when she broke up with Taylor, and Charlie told her she had used up her reinvention. "I hope he was worth it," I remember her saying.

"I'm psyched." I force my face into a smile and slip the lip gloss out from under her fingers.

Charlie sighs and turns onto the highway. "Come on. I'm serious. You should be psyched. Me and Jake, you and Rob, Olivia and Ben." She swallows after she says "Ben," like she has a bad taste in her mouth. "We're so ruling school this year."

Another one of Charlie's theories is that we live in a high school movie. Olivia seems to think this is true too. What I mean is that they can say things like "We're so ruling school" and not feel the need to add sarcasm. I guess we are popular. Charlie is formidable, attractive in a way that makes her feared and loved. Olivia, on the other hand, is basically the high school dream girl. Big boobs, blond hair, cute nose, and sweet tempered. There is literally no guy in school who isn't in love with her. Plus, her parents have more money than God. Her dad does something in the music industry. He's a producer or a record label owner. I think maybe both. To be honest, sometimes I'm not sure how I ended up in this mix. I shouldn't be popular. Conventional wisdom is completely stacked against me.

Which is why being friends with Rob has always felt so good. He's popular, sure—he's probably the most popular guy in our class—but he's also just *Rob*. I don't have to pretend around him or think about what I'm going to say next. Not that I do with Charlie or Olivia, but sometimes it feels like we're all—all three of us—in some kind of play. Like we need to get our lines right. Like the whole performance is depending on it.

"Want to hear about Len Stephens?" Charlie asks. "He's already being kicked out of school."

Len Stephens is this guy in our class we don't hang out with. Charlie calls him "toxic," but most people just call him an ass. He's sarcastic, and his hair is too long and messy, like he cuts it himself or something.

"School hasn't even started."

"Apparently he pulled senior prank early."

"What did he do?"

"Reorganized the online system so that it deleted every student transcript."

"No way."

"Swear." Charlie puts her hand over her heart like she's pledging allegiance.

"How is that even possible?"

Charlie shrugs. "He hacked into the school's computer system."

The only thing I really know about Len is that he used to take piano lessons before me from this German woman named Famke. I think I stopped in the sixth grade or something, and I guess he probably did too. That was around the time most people got serious with sports or dance and dropped other hobbies. I thought he was pretty good, but then again I used to think tube tops were cute, so what did I know?

"Whatever," Charlie says, moving on. "Let's talk about Jake."

"So you guys are back together?" I look out the window at the passing trees. It's not that I don't care about Charlie's love life. I do, of course. It's just that no one moment in time is very indicative of their overall relationship. If she's with Jake today, it doesn't mean she will be tomorrow. Or even by the time we get to school, for that matter. They have this very strange relationship. Charlie likes to act like it's all heartbreaking and disturbed. Like they *can't* be together even though they really want to. Honestly, I don't see the obstacles. Unless the fact that he wears baseball caps a lot and calls everyone "dude" is an obstacle. Which, maybe, it is. They broke up because he called her "bro" at prom last year, and then they didn't speak for a week. They've been casual all summer, but an official reunion doesn't surprise me. Mostly I think they hit so many speed bumps because Charlie likes injecting drama. And what is more dramatic, really, than heartbreak?

"Totally," she says. "He came over last night and said he wanted this year to be different." Jake has said he wants things to be different about forty-two times in the last year and a half, so I take this with a grain of salt.

"Cool."

"I'm serious, Rose. I think it's going to work out this time." I glance over at her, and her face looks set, determined. Celebratory, even. Which, if you know Charlie, makes a lot of sense. Deciding to do something and doing it are basically the same thing in her world.

"That's great," I chirp. "Super." I try to sound excited, but Charlie sees right through it.

"How am I supposed to work with you this year if you're going to be all mopey and dreary-eyed?" She passes me her makeup bag and flips down my visor mirror. "Apply, please. I need you looking your absolute best when we step into that auditorium."

Scene Two

We live exactly seven minutes from school, and when I say we've never been late, I mean it. We've never been late. Charlie has been picking me up since she got her car last October, but we've driven together since elementary school. First with her mom and then, when her mom got sick, with mine.

Charlie says the thing about being popular is that you can't push it. Meaning you can get away with a lot but you have to know the line you can't cross. For us that line is being late, and we never are. Even Olivia, who takes approximately four hours to get ready every morning. I don't think she particularly cares about being on time, but she's not one to be argumentative about much.

I've had a perfect attendance record since freshman year,

with the one exception of the time Olivia broke her foot and I had to go with her to the emergency room. I go along with the being-on-time because I plan on getting into and going to Stanford next year. I have an okay shot, too. I just need to focus and keep my eye on the ball for this first term. Which means I'll follow Charlie's never-be-late rule, even if I have different reasons for it.

Charlie swings into the upper parking lot, and for a second I open my mouth to correct her, but then I remember that we're seniors now, which means we really do park here. From the upper lot you can see down to the entire school. San Bellaro was named Most Beautiful Campus in some nationwide search last year, and for a moment, sitting in Charlie's car, I can see why. It used to be an estate, and Cooper House, our school's main building, is this former mansion. The teachers' offices are old converted bedrooms, and these Victorian chandeliers hang in a lot of classrooms. Jake wants to raid the girls' locker room and hang all our underwear, or whatever, from the chandeliers for senior prank this year. Charlie tried to explain to him that the senior prank is not supposed to be played *on* the seniors, but I don't think he really got it.

The rest of the school buildings are converted guesthouses and garages and even a horse stable. The building behind the quad is new, but it was built to look just like Cooper House, so you can't really tell. There is ivy growing up and over all the buildings, and if you look straight down past the soccer field, you can see the ocean. It would be a great place to spend time if it wasn't, you know, school.

Olivia is already there when we pull in, climbing out of her BMW SUV. It was a gift from her stepdad for her sixteenth birthday. It's white, and the license plate reads OLIVE16. Olivia's parents sometimes call her Olive. She says she can't stand it, but I think secretly she loves it. Her family is pretty close. Her mom had two new boys with her stepdad, and Olivia spends a lot of time with her little brothers.

"Heyyy," Olivia says. She has on basically the same thing Charlie is wearing: skinny jeans, purple ballet flats, and a gray tank top, except Olivia has a bright blue cardigan thrown over the whole thing instead of a hoodie. Her blond hair is up in a ponytail. She looks like she just stepped out of a plastic crate. Total Barbie doll.

The thing no one knows about Olivia is that she used to be chubby, way back in middle school. She lost it all the summer before eighth grade, when she moved here. We didn't know her then, but we've seen some pictures. It's strange to think of Olivia as being anything less than perfect-looking. But at one point, she was.

Olivia stretches, lifting her arms up over her head and

hiking her shirt, revealing a wide expanse of abdomen. Charlie would call this a power move. Her theory is that we all have one. It's the thing you do to show yourself off. For instance, sometimes Beth Orden sticks out her chest because her boobs have been sort of above average since the second half of sophomore year.

"Good luck with that," Charlie says, pointing to her belly button. "Contrary to appearances, we do have a dress code."

Olivia yawns, rolls her eyes, and hooks one of the buttons on her cardigan.

"Let's goooo," she says. Olivia has this habit of dragging out the last word of anything she says. It's annoying, but the thing about being that beautiful in high school is that your annoying habits don't matter. Kind of like how it doesn't matter whether you order a diet or regular Coke at McDonald's with a Big Mac. In the scheme of things, it really isn't affecting much. That's how Olivia's drawl is. It's irrelevant, and even if people notice, most of the time they think it's cute.

"Calm yourself," Charlie snaps. "It's still early. Did you get bagels?"

Olivia nods and produces a bag from the driver's seat. Grandma's Coffeehouse. Every Wednesday, Olivia has to drop her little brother Drew off at school and swings by the coffeehouse to get us stuff. We all order differently, but we know each other's orders by heart. Charlie gets an everything bagel with plain cream cheese, Olivia orders blueberry with butter and strawberry jam, and I get poppy seed with chive cream cheese. Sometimes Charlie and I share, half and half, but rarely.

Charlie opens the bag and passes around our respective orders. Along with my bagel she hands me a piece of gum she's produced from her jeans pocket. "For Rob," she says, and winks at me. I look away because I can feel my face start to heat up.

"How is he?" Olivia slides her bag over her shoulder and slams the door.

"How's Ben?" Charlie shoots back.

Olivia swallows, but then Charlie slings an arm over her shoulder. "Relax. It's fine. Anyway, Rose has the big romantic news of today. Tell her," she says, looking at me.

"Tell her what?" I tuck some hair behind my ear. It's not even eight a.m. on the first day of school, and I already don't want to be here.

"About the text."

"He just told me he was back," I say quietly.

"Oh my God," Olivia squeals. "You guys are totally together!"

I glance around the parking lot to see if I can spot Rob's silver Volvo, but he's always late, so I don't really expect to see anything, and I don't. Charlie just smiles and puts her other arm around my shoulder, and the three of us waltz toward campus.

✱   ✱   ✱

We're early, of course, but today there is good reason. We can finally take advantage of the senior lounge—or PL, as we call it, because technically it's the parents' lounge (they fund the vending machines)—a room off Cooper House that's reserved for seniors only. The three of us spent some illegal time there last year. In fact, it was the first place I let Jason attempt the bra unhook, but we've never been legitimately allowed in. So today is a big deal.

Olivia is babbling about how her little brother stole and hid her book bag this morning and how her mom promised her a new Tod's tote this year but she *still* hasn't gotten it.

"Can't you just get it yourself?" Charlie asks, looking annoyed.

"That's not the point," Olivia says, and stops talking.

By the time we make it to the PL, it's ten after seven, which means we have a full thirty minutes to spend here before assembly.

The PL has windows on three sides and an entrance that connects to what we call the breezeway. It's a walkway from inside Cooper House to the lower courtyard, where, since it's California, we generally have lunch all year long.

There are three vending machines against the fourth wall. One has coffee and cappuccinos and things like that, another has water and juice, and the third has snacks. Charlie punches in some numbers and hands around bottles of San Pellegrino. Charlie only drinks sparkling water. It's her thing.

Another one of Charlie's theories is that it's important to have "a thing." It makes you stand out. She calls it your seven, because that's her favorite prime number. Meaning it can't be divided, just like the thing that makes you *you* can't be separated. For instance, Olivia's seven is that she always has some item of purple on, even if it's just her key chain. Olivia wants her seven to be her hair, because she loves her hair, but Charlie says purple is way more interesting. My seven is that I don't drive. I mentioned to Charlie that that's sort of a negative thing, but she just brushed me off. "It makes you stand out," she said. "It's awesome."

I didn't get my license until my seventeenth birthday, which means I might as well have waited until forty. It's not that I don't like responsibility. I love responsibility. I'm a good student. I'm organized. I'm a good friend, most of the time. But driving freaks me out. Big-time. The possibility of an accident just seems so close. I mean, these massive metal tanks zooming around trying not to crash into each other? I could never shake the feeling that by driving I was taking someone's life in my hands. So I've just never done much of it.

My parents still bought me a car, though. An old white Camry off a colleague of my dad's who was moving. I think they thought it might provide some incentive for me to want to get behind the wheel. It didn't work. Every time I sit in the driver's seat, my hands sweat and my heart starts racing. It's weird, I know. I'm a *teenager*, for crying out loud. Driving is supposed to be the thing I love the most. Freedom, escape, independence. I get it, trust me. But for me it's way less excitement and way more terror.

There are a few seniors sitting on a bench near the right-hand windows. A girl named Dorothy who has been called Dorky since, like, the sixth grade, and Len, which is shocking. I don't think he's ever been on time to school. Plus, also, isn't he supposed to be kicked out? Charlie's rumor mill isn't always ironclad, but it's usually at least grounded in 10 percent truth.

"Hey." I wave to Dorothy. Len gives me a smirk, like I've just singled him out for a personal greeting.

"He is such a disease," Charlie whispers to me. Then she looks up and announces, "I'm shocked they didn't expel you."

"Who, me?" Len uncrosses his arms. They fall to his sides, revealing a purple T-shirt with a yellow lightning bolt down the front. Another thing about Len: He always wears long sleeves, even in the summer. It's bizarre.

He tilts his head, and a brown curl swings down onto his forehead. He's got this mess of curly hair that makes him look part mad scientist, part high school dropout. I think the only redeeming feature he's got is his eyes. They're big and blue and round, like gemstones stuck right in there.

"Why would they expel me?"

"Because you are a leper," she says. "You're, like, infecting this place."

Len's eyes flit from Charlie to me. "What do you think, Rosaline?"

It's not like Len and I speak regularly or anything, but he's got this habit of calling me by my full name. It's so patronizing. He can't even address someone without being annoying. Definitely his seven.

"I don't really have an opinion," I say. "Because I don't really care."

Charlie and Len look at me, impressed.

"Helloooo?" Olivia is waving a hand over her head, trying to get our attention about something. She's talking to Lauren, who is on the student activities committee with us—or SAC, as we call it. We had AP English together last year, and she lives a few doors down from Rob and me. I volunteered us to take her to school last year, but Charlie said it was out of our way. Which is ridiculous, of course, but not very surprising.

"You can see my *bra*," Olivia squeals, holding out her bottle of sparkling water to us as evidence. It's currently spraying all over her tank top, and Lauren steps to the side, presumably in search of drier ground.

"Not a bad way to kick things off," Len says.

"You're nauseating." Charlie grabs my elbow and drags me over to Olivia. "He makes me feel dirty," Charlie says. Olivia raises her eyebrows, and Charlie clarifies, "Not in a good way. Like I just showered in fish oil."

"You're going to make me lose my bagel," I announce, even though I still haven't consumed a thing.

"Watch that," Charlie says, reaching over to cap Olivia's water. "So what's the deal with you two, anyway?"

"Who?" Olivia fans out her tank top.

"My brother?"

Olivia stops, drops her shirt, and takes a huge gulp of sparkling water. "Three months," she squeaks out while swallowing. It surprises me. I figured they were getting close this summer, but this means they were together at the end of school. Before Rob even left.

"Three months?" Charlie's face is turning red. You can tell because she gets these little splotchy marks where she isn't wearing a lot of foundation.

"Yeah, but it was the summer," Olivia bleats. "You know, we weren't really around."

"What are you talking about, 'we weren't around'? We were at the beach together, like, daily," Charlie says.

Olivia scrunches up her lip. "I like him," she says.

"At least we know they're not sleeping together," I offer.

Olivia swats me on the shoulder, but it's playful, and even Charlie has to smile. Olivia is saving herself for marriage or until she can legally drink or something. Her mom got kind of religious after she married Olivia's stepdad. They all go to church on Sundays. We've never talked about why, exactly, she's waiting, but my guess is she has a better handle on all of it than I do. The moral part, anyway. So far as I know, she's only just made out. I would bet money that's all she has done with Ben, too.

Olivia starts adjusting her tank top in the glass window. I slump into a seat and open my sparkling water. I haven't even touched my bagel yet. Every time I try, my stomach launches a counterattack. Turns out, I'm completely terrified about seeing Rob. It's totally messing with my morning. My hands are tingling and my fingers feel numb. It reminds me of the way I used to feel when I was in *The Nutcracker* as a kid. Complete and total stage fright.

I see Len leave the PL and Lauren following out behind. He says something over his shoulder, and Lauren laughs. Probably making fun of us.

"Shall we?" Charlie comes over, chewing a piece of blueberry bagel, so I know she and Olivia have made up.

"Mhm." I stuff my bagel into my book bag and stand.

"Let's roll," Olivia says behind us, which makes Charlie

immediately snap to attention. She tosses her red hair over her shoulder and slides her book bag on.

"Do you think we should try to get Len to join SAC?" Olivia asks. Charlie shoots her a look like, *Don't even think about it,* and turns on her heel, the two of us following behind.

"I'm kidding," Olivia says. She mouths "Jesus" to me and rolls her eyes, miming her best Charlie impression. We walk out of the PL, across the breezeway, and down to assembly. The only thing I can think is that the second we walk through the doors, Rob will be there. And then, how completely and totally unprepared I am to see him.

Scene Three

If you're a senior, like we are, then you sit in chairs on the right-hand side of the auditorium during assembly, instead of up in the bleachers. Like by making it to senior year you have earned your right to *sit in a chair*. The whole thing becomes unbelievably political, with senior seats ending up like concert tickets. The chairs by the right far side and in the front are the most valuable and are reserved for popular people. The ones in the back and on the left are for everyone else.

Then there are the Trenches, which are on the other side of the bleachers, where people stand if they're late. The Trenches are mostly for kids like Corey Masner, John Susquich, and Charlie's ex, Matt Lester, who always smoke before class and just can't be bothered. It says something about you if you stand in the

Trenches—that you're not really a part of things, either because you can't be or because you choose not to be. And in high school, honestly, they might as well be the same thing.

I look for Rob and finally spot him. He's in the back row of senior seats, but on the right—solidly popular territory, his chair tilted backward—talking to Jake. The sight of him makes my heart and stomach do something very funny at the exact same time. He looks even cuter somehow. His brown hair is longer, a little bit shaggy, and although he's sitting down, I can tell he grew this summer. And he's tan. Probably from, you know, all the making out with other hot lifeguards on the boat dock. The image of Rob and some bikini chick locked in an embrace flashes on my frontal lobe, and I shake my head, trying to dislodge the picture.

"Loverboy looks good," Charlie says. "Who knew he was so . . . manly?"

I turn to tell her to keep it down, but in that moment he looks up. Our eyes lock, and neither of us moves, not even a facial muscle. But then he smiles and cocks his head, motioning to an empty seat next to him.

"Where are you going?" Charlie hisses as I make a move to head toward him. "We're doing front row this year, remember?"

"I'm gonna go sit with Rob."

Charlie looks hurt, but I know she isn't really. She just has this theory that we look "visually powerful" when we're seated together. She came up with that last year. I remember because afterward Olivia said, "That's totally true. It's the theory of collective hotness. One pretty girl alone is okay-looking, but, like, five pretty girls together, even if one of them is not that pretty, look way hotter."

I swear she looked right at me when she said "one of them."

"I'll sit with you tomorrow," I tell Charlie. "Don't worry."

Charlie makes a fuss of sighing, but she winks at me as I walk away.

Charlie and Olivia file into the front, and I hopscotch over book bags and backpacks. I almost trip on Megan Crayden's bag strap, but I right myself just in time.

Then, finally, I reach Rob. Jake gives me a nod and blows a kiss forward. I see Charlie catch it two rows up. 7:42—things with Charlie and Jake remain on.

"Hey," Rob says. He rights his chair, then takes my bag off my shoulder and puts it down on the ground. Then he looks at me, and for a second I think he's going to reach over and take my face in his hands again, he's looking at me that hard. But instead he just smiles and leans in for a hug. "I missed you, Rosie."

As soon as we touch, I realize how much I've missed him. He smells like green apples and soap, the best combination, and his arms are strong and tight around me. I could stay this way forever, I think just as he releases me.

I sit down next to him, and Jake turns back around. "Yo, dude," he says to me. "How was your summer?"

"I saw you this weekend."

"Awesome, right?" He snaps his fingers in front of Rob's face. "We gotta hit up the waves this weekend. They're supposed to be off the hook."

"Sure," Rob says, not taking his eyes off me.

He smiles with just the edges of his mouth, like we're the only two people in on some secret. *Are* we the only two people in on a secret? I guess if it was that he likes me, Charlie would be in on it too, so no. Plus, he doesn't like me. We're friends. Friends. I run the word through my head like it's on a conveyor belt. Just *friends.*

Everyone is wrapped up in their own first-day rituals. People are talking and hugging and squealing. Advisers are passing out schedules to kids who forgot the ones that were mailed out, and hesitant freshmen sit in the bleachers, looking white-faced and terrified.

"I can't believe we're seniors," I say to Rob. It sounds so lame—isn't that what everyone says on the first day of senior year?—but it's true.

"I feel like it was just us there," he says, nodding his head in the direction of the freshmen. Three girls in the front row are clutching their Trapper Keepers to their chests like life preservers. "Then look what happened." He laughs and points to Charlie and Olivia. Charlie is talking animatedly to no one in particular, and Olivia keeps pursing and releasing her lips, like she's practicing kissing, midair. Ben is next to them, and he has one arm over the back of Olivia's chair, but he's turned away from her, talking to Patrick DeWitt, who Olivia went to freshman banquet with. All of the chairs in front of us feel like tiny markers on a spiderweb, and I'm amazed at how connected we all are, how point A leads to point B and then all the way to Z, each of us spinning out into infinity but still tied together through birthday parties and drunken dances. Kisses and classes. For a very brief second it feels like we're all a part of something.

I shake my head, and Rob puts a hand on my shoulder. "Everything okay?"

"Oh, yeah," I say. "Just thinking."

"How are they, anyway?" Rob gestures with his head toward Charlie and Olivia.

"You really want to know?"

He gives me that cute corner smile again. "It's a toss-up."

I take a deep breath. "Well, Charlie and Jake are back on. Today." Rob nods sternly like he's taking this very seriously. "Olivia and Ben have started hooking up."

"And what about you?"

"What do you mean?"

"Any summer romances?" My stomach drops. I was right. He is asking so he can tell me all about his hot lifeguard. She's probably Olivia's look-alike from LA or New York or somewhere where being pretty is no big deal.

I shrug. "I was busy."

"Is that a no?"

I look down at my tank top and fiddle with the edge of it, not sure what to say. What exactly is he asking me, here?

He clears his throat. "I didn't see anyone either. If that helps any."

Instantly I look up, and I know we're thinking the same thing. It's like how in movies there's this music clip when the truth is being revealed so you just *know*, without anyone saying anything. Like someone in the corner of this auditorium is playing our theme song. Which, by the way, is "Fly Me to the Moon" by Frank Sinatra. Rob really loves old music.

"Anyway," I say, looking away, "new year." I'm convinced my heart is visibly beating out of my chest.

"Absolutely," he says. But he's smiling. A different smile. A funny little smile like he's going to laugh. Like he's telling himself a joke and the punch line is coming.

"What are you doing tonight?" he asks.

"Dunno. Homework?"

"Want to go to dinner?"

"Yeah, sure. Come over."

"No, I mean go *out* to dinner."

I know what Charlie would say here. Charlie would toss her hair over one shoulder and singsong, "Are you asking me out, Mr. Monteg?" But I don't have the nerve. Or the talent for such games. Instead I say, "Umm, sure." Rob opens his mouth to say something, but Mr. Johnson, our principal, comes onto the stage, and everyone stops talking.

"Good morning!" Mr. Johnson says in this fake boomy voice he uses for every single assembly. I know it's fake because when you go in to meet with him for office hours or to tell him we're out of sparkling waters in the PL (which, because of Charlie, we always are), he's actually superquiet. Also, he looks a little like a rodent. Half-bald, pointy nose, and tiny beady eyes that look perpetually frightened. But who am I to judge? If I was a principal, I'd probably look the same way most of the time.

"Good morning!" a few sophomore girls yell back. Mr. Johnson looks delighted, and does it again. This time a few more people join in on the return call but obviously not enough to warrant a third time, because he just holds his hands up like, *Silence.*

"It's a new year," he begins, "and over the course of the

summer I have been thinking about changes I can make here at San Bellaro so that we can continue to grow in the directions that we want to. I have thought about the way we structure our days here, how we fill our time . . ."

And then, just as I'm about to completely zone out, something spectacular happens. Rob's knee brushes mine and he doesn't move it. He just leaves it there, against mine, so that *our knees are touching*. My face has already turned the color of a tomato, so I keep my eyes fixed on Mr. Johnson, but I can feel Rob glance at me.

Then Rob's hand moves across the back of my chair. *Our knees are touching and Rob's hand is on the back of my chair.*

I try to remember what my mom's yoga DVD is always saying about hyperventilating. That it can be prevented by deep breathing. Inhale and exhale. Inhale and exhale.

"I see you as a forest," Mr. Johnson is saying. "We are all trees, and we compose a large wooded area. Without us, there would be no life."

Jake yawns next to us. Then he crosses his arms and closes his eyes. In two seconds he's breathing loudly, his mouth open.

Rob's knee has been next to mine for a full minute, I think. So long that my leg is starting to sweat. I wiggle in my chair, careful to keep my knee steady. I don't want Rob to think I'm purposefully ending our contact. The whole thing reminds me of the staring contests we used to have in middle school, seeing who could go the longest without blinking. Except I don't want to win this one. I want to lose. I want Rob to keep his knee there forever. But just then Jake snores next to us, and Rob jabs him, breaking us apart.

Jake sits up, startled, and wipes some drool from his mouth. It's a good thing Charlie isn't back here right now. 7:59—they'd definitely be off.

Mr. Johnson finishes, and the students start clapping, although it's mostly freshmen and a few very eager juniors who are quickly silenced by their friends. And Len, of course. He claps a few times, steadily, from the corner. Charlie and Olivia and a few other girls turn to look at him, but he doesn't seem the least bit fazed. Then the auditorium erupts into a sonic boom of sound as everyone gathers their backpacks and heads off to first period.

Charlie is waving her arms at me and pointing to her watch. Rob has gotten lost in the shuffle, and he gives me a quick, apologetic wave, following Jake out the side entrance.

"He's so cute," Charlie says when I reach her. "We should totally double date."

I'm still sort of reeling from such close contact with Rob, and I don't tell Charlie about our date tonight. I want to keep it my secret for just a little bit longer. Ben is tickling Olivia next to us, and she's laughing, her tank top riding up. It's actually kind of cute, if you squint a little. Charlie looks over at them and then declares, loudly, "I'm already over this," before tugging me, arm first, out through the double doors.

Scene Four

We all meet in the courtyard at lunch. Olivia and I are coming from calc, where I'm pretty sure she was flirting with Mr. Stetzler. I mean she *was* flirting, definitely, but the part I'm not sure of is why. Mr. Stetzler is old. Like, forty. I mean, when she flirts with Mr. Davis, I understand, because he teaches PE and he's just young enough to still wear his hair long. But Mr. Stetzler? Really?

"You're super," she says to him before we leave class, tossing her hair over her shoulder. I don't even know what that is supposed to mean, and apparently neither does Mr. Stetzler because he just takes off his glasses and kind of blinks a few times in rapid succession. I grab Olivia's arm and drag her out, and she waves and wiggles her shoulders the way she does with Ben. The way she used to do with the Belgian.

The Belgian is this kid in our class who moved here from Brussels. This happened sometime around September of last year, and he and Olivia spent the entire fall together. She started eating a lot of brussels sprouts and eating Belgian waffles whenever we went out. She even chose them over bagels, which Charlie was not okay with. It was when Olivia and Taylor were on a break, so she never called the Belgian her boyfriend. She never even called him Jhone, which is his real name. He was just "the Belgian." It's still crazy to me that Olivia has managed to date three guys—Taylor, the Belgian, and now Ben—and not go too far with any of them. I think part of the reason I ended things with Jason is that I was scared that if he ever successfully unhooked my bra, we'd have to keep going. It's not that I think you have to sleep with whomever you're seeing. It just seems kind of difficult, after a while, to explain why you're not. Especially if you don't really know the reason yourself.

"You are seriously disturbed," I say to Olivia.

"God, I'm like *flunking*," she says. "Give me a break."

"It's the first day of school," I point out. "You aren't flunking yet. We're good students." We are, it's true. I don't really have one subject I'm great at like Len and Lauren, who are amazing at science, or Charlie, who is a star history student. She likes to come over and ask my dad questions about wars

I've never heard of. That's how into it she is. But my GPA is pretty good.

"*You* are," Olivia says. "I don't even know why I'm in calc. I should have taken stats like a sane human being."

We trudge up to the table where Rob and Ben are sitting with Jake. The three of them are pretty close, although Ben is more of a recent addition. He didn't really join our group until sophomore year. Charlie tried her best to keep him away longer, but he and Rob became superclose. If you ask me, Ben is actually a really stand-up guy. Charlie gives him a hard time about being nerdy because he doesn't surf like Rob and Jake. I suspected something was going on this summer, and I'm not surprised Olivia and Ben are together, but the match is still funny. I always saw Ben as one of those guys that would end up a writer living in New York, sitting in cafés drinking black coffee and owning old Moleskine notebooks. Olivia drinks iced chai tea lattes and owns a Louis Vuitton book bag with the word MIAMI bedazzled on the front. So you can see the disconnect there.

We drop our bags down near them, and I see Charlie's; brown leather, worn and classic—totally her style.

"She inside?" I nod to Rob. Casual, cool. Like my heart isn't beating three million miles a minute because *we are going on a date tonight.*

"Yeah." He tilts his head to the side and squints at me. Since this morning everything he does seems like flirting. "How are you?" he asks, like it's the most important question in the world, like he's asking me how to defuse a nuclear bomb. I shrug, and he picks up his sandwich, offering it. "Want a bite?" Turkey and mustard. No tomato. He's been eating the same thing from the school cafeteria since we were freshmen.

"Sure." I take it and peer around the courtyard. Lauren is sitting with Dorothy Spellor. John and Matt are in a corner, playing Hacky Sack. Charlie is right. Everything is, I guess, in order.

"Another year," Charlie says, waltzing up behind me, "and they *still* don't have the good peanut butter." She smiles at Jake and sits down next to him.

Olivia has collapsed herself down next to Ben and is complaining about the fact that no one cares about seniority at this school, which basically ends up being an argument for why she should be allowed to cut in line in the cafeteria. Ben puts an arm around her shoulder and gives her an affectionate squeeze.

"I agree," Charlie says, waving an apple around. "It's totally absurd that we have to wait."

"Should we even bother getting food?" Olivia asks. She's craning her head over me to look into the cafeteria.

Sometimes we spend our lunch periods off campus, which is

legal if you're a senior. We used to do it last year too. I think the teachers knew, but I can't be sure because we never got caught. Mr. Davis just used to make really pointed statements like "I could really go for a Subway sandwich right about now," after we had just thrown the wrappers away.

The way lunch works senior year is that you can go off campus for your free period or lunch but not both, and if your free period happens to be before or after lunch, so that they're right up against each other, you can leave for an hour and fifteen minutes. It turns out this will happen to everyone once in the school week, so it's fair, I guess, but it still makes no sense. Why wouldn't you get to just take off two full periods? Why deny us those extra fifteen minutes? This is the stuff about high school that I don't understand.

I think that since we can legally do it this year, it holds less appeal, but it's only the first day of school, and no one leaves on the first day of school.

Rob's sandwich is kind of soggy, and as I hand it back to him, a piece of turkey falls onto the table.

Jake has Charlie in a headlock, and she's squealing loudly, and Ben and Olivia seem to be immersed in conversation, although about what, I really couldn't say.

I look at Rob. His shaggy hair is falling down in front of his face, and he looks so painfully cute, I just want to put my arms around him right here in the courtyard.

"I have to go," he says, "but I'll see you tonight?"

I nod, and he smiles. He leans in, but then Charlie and Jake break apart and so do we. Was he going to kiss me? Not possible. No way. Not here. Tonight?

"Later," Rob says to the table, and then takes off toward Cooper House.

"Dude, the cove, after school," Jake calls out after him, and Rob turns around and gives a little salute. It's not directed at Jake, though. It's straight at me.

"All you guys think about is surfing." Charlie leans her head briefly on Jake's shoulder and exaggerates a sigh.

"That is not all we think about, yo," Jake says, tickling her.

I am still buzzing from Rob being so close and the promise of tonight that it takes me another minute to realize I'm actually hungry. "Come on," I say to Olivia, and we both stand up and start walking over toward the cafeteria.

"Can you get us sparkling water?" Charlie calls, and I give her the thumbs-up over my shoulder.

The cafeteria is pretty small for a high school of our size. There are only about fifteen tables, given the fact that everyone, or at least upperclassmen, eat outside. When it's raining, we usually take our food into Copper House or the PL. The inside of the cafeteria is depressing, and it's basically all freshmen.

Taylor is in line, and Olivia scoots up to him, shimmying her hips in between him and Dan Jenkins so she's smack up against him. Taylor, I mean. Dan notices, though, and starts tapping Steve Gesher on the shoulder to get him to see that Olivia's hip is touching Taylor's hip.

It's not really all that surprising. She still flirts with Taylor a lot.

"Grab me a veggie," I say to Olivia. "I'm gonna go get the water."

Olivia is ignoring me, and Taylor. She's just casually making her salad, seemingly immune to the hysteria she's causing around her. At least she solved the problem of waiting in line.

I turn around and head toward the vending machines, where I pass Brittany Fesner, who everyone calls Brittany Fester because she's always had the most horrible skin. I think Charlie came up with that. I really hope Brittany doesn't know.

Brittany half waves at me, and I half wave back, and then I feed some dollars into the machine and stand around as San Pellegrino bottles dislodge and land with a *thump*. I pull them out and try to balance them in my arms, but there are six of them and they keep sliding.

"You need some help, Rosaline?" I spin around, and the bottles scatter to the floor. They're plastic, so they don't break, but I'm still annoyed. I bend down to pick them up and squint upward to see who is talking to me. It's Len, of course, and he's got that stupid smirk on.

"Is it your goal to just make life miserable?"

"I make your life miserable?" He puts his hand over his heart. "I'm flattered."

"Don't be."

"It's the first day of school, Rosaline. Whatever happened to a fresh start?"

"I'm not trying to start with you, Len."

He bends down and picks up a sparkling water, lining it up next to two others like little toy soldiers. "Why are you so hostile? Is it because you're not getting any from that boyfriend of yours?"

In a flurry of revolt my face flushes red. "Boyfriend?"

"You two seem totally sexually frustrated."

"Rob is not my boyfriend."

"So what's with the puppy-dog looks you two are constantly exchanging?"

He picks up another bottle and tosses it into the air, then catches it and hands it to me. His thumb is covering the label, and I notice his skin is red. Crimson, actually. A mark like spilled paint runs from his thumb up to his wrist and then disappears under his shirt sleeve. I don't remember ever seeing it before. He has a folder tucked underneath his arm.

"What's that?" I ask. Less because I care and more because I think he just caught me staring at his thumb.

He looks amused. "What?"

"The folder?"

"Grass," he says, shrugging.

"Grass?"

"Project for bio at the Cliffs," he says. "It's due the first of the year, so it's not exactly a priority."

"The Cliffs?" Immediately my mind flips to Rob. The Cliffs have always been our go-to place.

Len eyes me. "Do you run there or something?"

I shake my head, pushing Rob out. "What? No. I'm just shocked you'd do any work of your own accord."

"Bravo," he deadpans. "Senior year Rosaline has some spunk."

I take three of the bottles by their tops and stick the others against my chest. Olivia is waving to me from the doorway, informing me that she's going back outside.

"Excuse me," I say.

He moves to the side, letting me pass. "Great doing business with you, Rosaline."

I teeter outside and follow Olivia back into the courtyard, where I dump the San Pellegrino bottles onto the table. "You guys so owe me," I say. "I'm going to need physical therapy from that. Regular therapy too."

"Poor baby," Charlie says, sticking out her lower lip.

"Why does it feel like Len has it out for me this year?"

"He's always had it out for us," Charlie says. "He's nobody. We're *popular*." She really will take any excuse to use that word.

Olivia starts chomping on her salad, handing me a sandwich. She opens a bottle of sparkling water, and the entire thing explodes over the table and all over Charlie.

"For the love of God!" Charlie shouts. "This is, like, the fourteenth time today."

"Second," Olivia corrects, grabbing napkins off Ben's plate. She starts mopping up Charlie's shirt, and Charlie swats her, and then they are tossing napkins back and forth, water flying everywhere.

Jake leans way back in his chair and surveys the scene. "Goddamn, I love high school," he announces.

Charlie gives him a wilting look and drops the napkins onto the table. "What do you have after lunch?" she asks me.

"Bio," I say. "I have no idea why I'm even in this class. I should be taking physics." Like stats versus calc, everyone knows AP Physics is way easier than AP Bio. Mostly because it's taught by Mr. Dunfy, who is about eighty and forgets to show up to class half the time. He's been at San Bellaro for, like, fifty years, so they're not firing him or anything, but he gives As out like candy.

"Yeah," Charlie says, "weird move."

"I'll see you guys at SAC, though?"

"We have our first meeting today?" Olivia wails. "I wanted to see Ben."

Ben looks up from his sandwich and grins. "She totally digs me," he gets out before Charlie throws her sopping napkin at him.

Scene Five

When I get to bio, most people are already in their seats. That's the thing about taking AP classes. You're forced straight up against all the other übercompetitive kids, so that even if you're early, you still end up being late. Just being in the room gives me hives, and we haven't even started yet. Lauren is already there, and Jon Chote and Stacy Tempeski, who have taken the SATs every year since the tenth grade. Jon is, like, a musical prodigy and is for sure headed to Juilliard next year. Stacy won a national essay competition last year and got to spend a week at the UN in Switzerland. That's the kind of thing I'm dealing with here.

Mrs. Barch, our teacher, is the kind of woman you don't want to mess with. I think she actually used to be a research doctor. She's probably in her late forties, and as far as anyone at school can tell, she doesn't have a husband or kids or anything. So you can see why biology would be really important to her. If she likes you, you're in, no problem, but if she doesn't, she'll make your life impossible. And I don't think I'm exactly at the top of her list. I've had her before, and it hasn't gone too well.

I sit down next to Lauren, who already has her notebook open. It's filled with all of these charts and graphs and things written down in color-coded pens.

"Was there homework?" I ask her.

She squints at me. "Homework?"

I gesture to her notebook.

"Oh," Lauren mouths. "Nah, just getting a jump start." She takes out a pen and starts copying down the schedule Mrs. Barch is putting down on the whiteboard.

"Hey, babe. Miss me?" I whip around to catch Len sliding into the seat next to me.

"What are you, stalking me now?"

"Don't flatter yourself." He holds up his course schedule and points to bio. "See, I'm legit."

"I heard you forged those."

"Forged?"

"Or changed, whatever."

Len raises his eyebrows. "Been asking about me, huh?"

"You're perverted."

He sighs and takes out a spiral notebook. "Must we always fight?"

"Must you always be so intolerable?"

He does seem to have gotten more toxic over the years. Not that Len and I have ever been friends, but he doesn't usually single me out for quite so much special torture. I'd worry he's getting obsessed with me, but I can't imagine him caring too much about anything.

Mrs. Barch likes to start class off with a clap. I remember this from when I had her for chemistry in the tenth grade.

"This class is not about the exam," Mrs. Barch begins.

"Yeah, right," I mumble.

"We're here to learn advanced concepts of biology, not master a three-hour test. It will be tough, but anything worthwhile is. I expect you to be here on time and ready to work."

Jon and Stacy are scribbling furiously in their notebooks. I pick up my pen, but I have no idea what they could possibly be writing down. "Don't be late to class?" Isn't that sort of an obvious one?

Mrs. Barch claps again and tells us that whomever we are sitting next to will be our bio partners for the year. She counts us off, and I end up with Len. *You're kidding me,* I think as Mrs. Barch sends me an apologetic look. Fun fact: Even teachers think Len is a leech.

"This is a nightmare," I whisper.

Len smiles at me and knits his hands behind his head. "What's that?" he says. "You're going to have to speak up, Rosaline."

"Nothing."

"I for one am really looking forward to this arrangement."

"I'm sure you are."

I start filling out a handout Lauren is passing around. It's easy stuff, mostly name, class year, etc., and it allows me the opportunity to let my mind wander. Okay, so it's not really wandering. It's more like power walking. Power walking straight over to Rob. I'm trying to think of what I should wear tonight, whether I should put my hair up or down. Usually I'm fairly low maintenance. Olivia and Charlie are the ones with all the products—sprays, mists, and one disconcerting powder—but I want tonight to be perfect.

"Hey, daydreamer," Len says. He's leaning over me, wearing that annoying entitled smirk.

I snap to attention and realize I've missed the first half of what he just asked me. Damnit. Now he's going to think I'm an even bigger idiot than he already does. Not that I care. I just don't want to add any fuel to his fire, as my dad would say.

"What?"

"First day focus issues, huh?" He tilts his head to the side and gives me a sympathetic nod.

"Should we just divide the assignment, or what?"

He hands me a sheet of paper, his pink thumb lifted toward me.

"It's a birthmark," he states.

"I didn't ask."

"You didn't need to."

"Anyway," I say, "which should I take?"

"Why don't you do the first five," Len says, frowning and nodding. "We can discuss them all during class tomorrow."

"Didn't know you were so organized."

"Add it to the list," he says. Then he's out the door before I even have time to think up a comeback.

The student activities committee is for seniors only, but Charlie has been on since the tenth grade. Olivia and I were voted in at the end of last year, with Lauren, so we had a few sessions in the spring already. I saw pretty quickly that the whole thing was going to work because of Lauren. Her older sister joined when Lauren was a freshman, and Lauren has basically been taking notes ever since. Even though Charlie would probably disagree, Lauren is the fulcrum. Making SAC work is definitely her new seven.

We're trying to be involved, I guess, but it's hard to get anything done when Olivia wants to use the hour to talk to Charlie about the current drama with Jake and whether Mr. Davis was really suspended for flirting with Darcy. For the record, I think that one is definitely true. Her tops are even smaller than Olivia's, and she was constantly saying things to him like "Is that *really* what you want?" in response to him asking us to run laps.

"Can we start?" Charlie asks. We're all sitting in the PL, and it's a quarter after three, which means we are ten minutes behind schedule. Which means Charlie is irritated.

"Mhm," Olivia mumbles. She's on her phone, working the keypad, and she doesn't look up.

"I was thinking we should do a back-to-school dance this Friday," Lauren says. "Something fun."

Olivia stretches. She's lost the cardigan, and her belly button is practically poking out of her shirt. Lauren notices too and gives her a *Please put that away* look. Olivia ignores her and takes out a lollipop. Black licorice. Like Charlie's Swedish Fish, she always has them on hand. "I already checked with Mr. Johnson. He said it's fine," Lauren says.

"I think that's good," Charlie says. "Let's call it Fall Back."

"I don't get it," Olivia says. She is sliding the lollipop over her teeth, a move that she knows majorly bugs Charlie. Apparently Olivia's trying to get a rise out of her, probably payback for making a fuss about Ben this morning.

"Like the time?" Charlie says, although what she means is "Duh." She sends me an exasperated look that Olivia doesn't catch. I shrug it off. I generally do when Charlie puts me in the middle of her current Olivia annoyance.

Truth be told, I'm not paying much attention either. I'm thinking about Rob's knee next to mine this morning. How being close to him, even the *thought* of being close to him, makes my palms start sweating and my heart feel like it's going to beat right out of my chest. What would have happened if we were the only two people in the room this morning? If he had leaned a little closer?

"Hello, Rose?" Charlie says. "What do you think of Fall Back?"

I blink. "I like it, I guess."

"Does anyone know what our budget looks like?" Charlie snorts and mutters the word "attention" under her breath.

Lauren pulls out a folder and hands it to Charlie, and they start talking about money.

"So what's going on with Rob?" Olivia asks, lowering her voice so Charlie can't hear. She slips her phone into her bag and squints at me.

"I don't know. I mean, we're friends."

"Yeah," Olivia says, "but you guys looked kind of cozy this morning."

I shrug, trying to prove I don't care. I can tell my nonchalant act is fooling no one.

"This is a nightmare," Charlie announces, turning to us. "And why is no one helping me here?"

Olivia wrinkles her nose. "I'm hungry. I can't think when I'm hungry."

"It's barely three o'clock, O." Charlie holds up her watch to prove it.

"I know, but I didn't even get to eat my salad. Ben was . . ."

Charlie waves her hand in the air and cuts her off. "Listen, guys. I thought being SAC this year meant we were going to take it seriously." She crosses her arms. "Or I'd have asked other people to do it with me."

"Yeah? Who?" Olivia rotates her lollipop and smiles pointedly.

"Whatever." Charlie hands Lauren the folder. "This Friday. Fall Back. Let's email to divide up the supplies and ask Mr. Johnson if eight o'clock is okay." Lauren gives Charlie a little salute that I can tell really annoys her. She does this thing with her mouth when she's angry. She kind of sticks out her chin and sets her jaw.

"See you guys tomorrow," Lauren says. She slings her backpack over her shoulder and gives us a quick wave, tucking the SAC folder under her arm and disappearing out of the PL.

"That went well." Olivia tosses her lollipop into the trash can. It misses, and she has to go pry it off the carpet.

"Seriously?" Charlie says, watching her. "Can we just get out of here?"

"What have I been saying?" Olivia looks at me for confirmation.

The three of us start toward upper. The parking lot is practically deserted. Soccer practice hasn't started yet. It won't until next week, and Rob and Jake skipped last period to go surfing. I think about mentioning dinner with Rob tonight but decide against it. For just a little while longer, I want to keep it to myself.

"Cal Block?" Charlie asks when we've reached the cars.

California Blockade is a restaurant near school that we have been going to since the seventh grade. It's Mexican, the best in town, and they have this *queso* dip that we all love. We call it "the special *S*," although I can't quite remember why. I think it had something to do with "siesta," but I could be wrong. The three of us always get the exact same thing: two orders of the special *S* and one guacamole.

"Yess," Olivia says.

"I swear if you marry my brother, and we become related, I am getting you a speech therapist."

"Keep it up and I'm going to take Rose," Olivia shoots back.

Charlie puts her hands on her hips and looks at me. One of the unwritten rules of our friendship is that if the three of us are going somewhere together, then I always ride with Charlie.

"Maybe I'll just drive myself," I say.

Charlie rolls her eyes. "Maybe when pigs fly," she says. "Just get in."

Scene Six

We always take the corner booth near the windows and away from the fan. You get a good view of the parking lot and Cinema Screen next door, where people from our school sometimes rent movies. One time we saw Dan Jenkins leave with *Clueless*. Charlie laughed about it for a week.

The waitress comes over, and Charlie orders for us. Charlie always orders.

"And sparkling waters, please," she says when she's through.

"You mean club soda?" the waitress asks. The waitress always asks this, but Charlie just keeps ordering the same way.

"Sure," Charlie says, rolling her eyes. "Whatever."

"It's freezing in here." Olivia snuggles up to Charlie and starts nudging her nose into her shoulder. Olivia is always cold. We went skiing at Whistler last year, and she refused to even come outside. She sat in the lounge the entire four days drinking hot chocolate and flirting with the ski instructors who were on break.

"Oh my God. Did you guys see Darcy Sugarman today?" Charlie asks. "She was, like, practically dry-humping Jake after third." Charlie wiggles her shoulders to get Olivia to sit up.

"That's disgusting," Olivia says.

"She's a slut," Charlie says. Darcy Sugarman is the same girl who we think used to have a thing with Mr. Davis. Charlie says there's a difference between being a slut and being slutty. She thinks Olivia was slutty for hooking up with the Belgian, but she would never call her a slut. Her theory is that the distinction is the difference between how you act and who you are. Olivia's was an action, whereas Darcy's is a defining quality.

"Why does everyone want my boyfriend?" Charlie wails, putting her hands over her head like the ceiling is collapsing.

"So we're using the term 'boyfriend' now?" I ask.

"I told you this morning that things were good. And don't be jealous just because you guys have some catching up to do."

"You're gross," I say.

"Better hop on it, pretty lady. Rob may not be around forever."

Olivia is smiling with the corners of her mouth, and Charlie is gyrating her body like she's trying to hump the table. I figure now is as good a time as any to tell them about the start of summer and this morning, except when I open my mouth, the only thing that comes out is a kind of gurgle.

I don't know why I feel so hesitant about telling them. They are my best friends. They should know this. I mean, it *is* a big deal. Unless I completely dreamed up this morning. Maybe he thought my leg was the edge of the chair? Totally possible. He might not have even known we were touching. Or what if he tried to move away but I didn't move away and he didn't want to be rude? And that comment, about not seeing anyone this summer? I completely read into it. He tells me everything. Of course Rob would tell me if he dated anyone this summer. I was the first one he told that he kissed Tracy Constance during a round of spin the bottle. I remember him saying she tasted like newspaper.

"So are you going to tell us about sucking face with my brother or not?" Charlie says. She crosses her arms and raises her eyebrow at Olivia. Olivia bites her lower lip. She's nervous, it's obvious. She does ballet and gets this way before every dance recital. Charlie and I usually sneak backstage to see her, and she's always biting her nails and hopping around like she's had too much caffeine.

"I already told you this morning. What else do you want to know?" She takes a small sip of water.

"Don't be cute," Charlie says. "You still haven't said how this started."

Olivia looks up at the ceiling and then back down at her glass. "Do you really want to know?"

"Yes. And I'm still not over this. Since when can you keep a secret? *For two months?*"

Olivia sends me a nervous glance, looking for support. "We weren't sure it was going to be anything."

I know that Charlie can be scary, and intimidating, but honestly I think it just comes out of how much she cares. She's tough on Olivia, though. Especially because this couldn't have come as a total shock to her. I mean, I all but saw them make out multiple times this summer. It was clear they were getting closer. I don't really buy that Charlie missed it.

"I can't believe you make out with my brother," Charlie says.

"He's a good kisser."

Charlie's eyes go wide, and she holds up her hand, palm flat, like, *Stop.* "I lied. I have no interest in hearing about this." Olivia smirks and elbows her, but Charlie doesn't crack. "I'm still totally offended you lied to me, though."

Olivia makes a puppy-dog face, which means she isn't too concerned. I'm not either. In fact, I'm remembering something from sophomore-year prom. How Olivia went with Taylor and they got into this big fight when we were there because he wanted to smoke and she was pissed about it, and Charlie said—I remember this specifically—"My brother would never show up high."

"I have a date with Rob tonight," I say. Both of their heads spin to look at me. At once, like in one of those horror movies. "Umm, yeah," I say. "We're sorta going out."

"Like, *romantically?*" Olivia asks.

"Sure, maybe. I don't know." And then it all comes tumbling out. This spring and our good-bye and his letters. "I told you," Charlie says. "He really missed you." And then, our knees this morning. Olivia totally loses it.

"So he legitimately said go *out* to dinner?"

"Yes," I say. "He was very specific about that part."

"What time?"

"Oh. I guess he'll just come over?"

"He can't just show up," Charlie says. "If it's a date, he should pick you up. In a car. Not just crawl through the grass and come knocking on your window." She looks at me and raises her eyebrow, tapping her finger once on her nose. It's this thing we do when we're both thinking the same thing. Right now I know she's thinking about the time in the sixth grade when Rob hacked a hole through the wire fence separating our houses so we wouldn't have to go all the way up and down each other's driveways. It was Halloween, and he came dressed in this psycho mask. He showed up at the side of the house, and Charlie and I screamed our heads off. He legitimately looked dead.

Our food comes, and Olivia starts setting chips onto her

napkin. She always does this. Like she's afraid we're going to eat them all without her or something. In her defense, she does eat really slowly.

"Are we going to Malibu this weekend?" I ask, trying to change the subject. I'm not sure how to keep talking about this. It's not like discussing a date with a normal boy. It's Rob. Luckily, Charlie and Olivia are easily distracted today. I suspect they're both still thinking a little bit about Ben.

I wipe my fingertips on the corner of a napkin. The cooks make their chips in-house, and they are always deliciously greasy.

"Yes!" Olivia says. "Let's do it."

Olivia has a beach house in Malibu that her parents never use. It's about forty-five minutes away, but we always have parties there. Olivia's been bribing her housekeeper since we were fifteen and used to drive down illegally with just permits. There was a very complicated round-robin phone tree in place then to ensure our parents never found out we had left San Bellaro.

"We can't this weekend," Charlie says, slipping a *queso*-ed chip into her mouth.

"Why?" Olivia asks.

"Hello? Fall Back? Honestly, was anyone paying attention in there?" She puffs out her lip and looks up at the ceiling. She even closes her eyes briefly, for effect.

"What about the weekend after?" Olivia asks, ignoring her.

"Let's see."

"You have other plans?" I poke her, and she shrugs.

"Maybe." Charlie really likes being the one to suggest things. Last year we had a New Year's Eve party at Olivia's, and Charlie almost didn't come because she hadn't been consulted about it beforehand. Even though she was, technically, visiting relatives in Oregon until the thirtieth. But of course she'll come around. Charlie loves Malibu.

"Why don't we say yes and we'll see how it goes. The guys will come, won't they?" Olivia turns to me.

"I guess." I try to make it sound as casual as I possibly can. The truth is, the prospect of an entire weekend in Malibu with Rob has sent my spine tingling.

"Sure," Charlie says, "if Jake decides to behave for another week." She takes out her phone, looks at it, and then tosses it away in a huff.

"Are you okay?" I ask. "You seem super on edge."

"I'm fine." She sighs. "Just tired."

"It's only the first day," I say. "Things will even out."

"That is exactly what Ben said to me today," Olivia says. "I was superupset because we didn't get calc together, and . . ."

But I'm looking at Charlie, who has stopped listening and is pointing to a newspaper on the table next to ours. She makes a move to get up.

"Watch it," Olivia says. "These are new. *Hello.*" She points to her shoes. Burberry flats with the print on the underside. Charlie ignores her and grabs the newspaper. She sets it down on our table, knocking over Olivia's neatly stacked chips.

It's the local paper, and Charlie flicks her pointer finger over the words. SENATOR CAPLET RETURNS. And there, right below the headline, is a picture of my uncle, his wife, and a girl I haven't seen in ten years.

"Is that your family?" Charlie asks.

"Yes," I say, peering closer.

"'The senator and family return to San Bellaro after almost a decade away,'" Charlie reads. She has her elbows on the table and she's leaning over the paper, like a little kid at the library. "'The Caplets' move to Beverly Hills nine years ago caused much rumor and speculation. This will mark their first return to our town since their departure.'"

Charlie looks up. Olivia is looking at me too.

"Strange," I say, because I'm not sure what to say. Does my dad know? Is he upset about it? And where will she be going to school? With me?

"'The senator's only daughter,'" Charlie continues, "'is delighted about the move. "I can't wait to spend my senior year in a new place," she says. "I'm truly looking forward to making San Bellaro my home."'"

"What's her name?" Olivia asks.

"Juliet," I answer. Charlie squints at the paper and then back up at me. "Her name is Juliet."

What's in a name, Shakespeare? I'll tell you: everything.

Act Two

Scene One

"You can just show your cousin your sweater," my mother says. "You don't have to wear it now."

It's Christmas Eve, and I'm sitting in the backseat of our station wagon with my arms crossed, beads of sweat rolling down my seven-year-old forehead. I have on my new reindeer sweater, the one I insisted on purchasing for our trip down to Los Angeles. It's wool and itchy, but it has antlers and bells on it. Real bells. And because of this, I think it's spectacular.

"She has to see it *on*," I say for what's probably the tenth time.

My mom nods and turns back around in the front seat, glancing at my dad. He's gripping the wheel tightly, his jaw set. We've been in the car for a while, and tensions are running high.

I gaze out the window and watch the passing coast. It's a record ninety-five degrees today, the hottest ever in over a decade of Decembers. It doesn't bother me, though. I've only ridden to Los Angeles a few times in my short life, and I'm excited. Especially because we are going to spend Christmas Eve with my cousin, Juliet. She left our town about two months ago, and I can't wait to see her. We are best friends. Juliet, Rob, and I have played together in our backyards practically since we were born, and even though I like Rob, and I'm getting used to things, I really miss Juliet.

We pull up to Juliet's house, and my mom takes out a piece of paper with some numbers on it and hands it to my dad. He punches them into a keypad. Huge gates swing open, and we drive all the way up and around a road lined with rosebushes.

Their house is gigantic. Not at all like Juliet's house back at home. It looks more like the library my mom and I go to on Saturdays. The one with the big white columns and so many rooms that it's impossible not to get lost inside. The gardens all around are filled with roses, and there are cherry trees hanging over either side of the driveway. It's like stepping into a fairy tale, and I think how lucky I am that my cousin lives here. That because we're family, it's almost like it's my house too.

My mom makes a fuss of straightening out my clothes, which she usually never does. She asks me one more time if

I'll take off the sweater, but I just shake my head. I've made it to Juliet's front door. I'm keeping it on. I know Juliet will love it.

We ring the doorbell, and Lucinda answers. They call her a housekeeper, but she's really like a great big grandma. I throw my arms around her, and she hugs me around my middle. We call her Lucy, but not around Juliet's mom. My aunt doesn't like it.

Lucy leads us through what feels like an enormous maze of marble and glass until we get to a big living room. There are huge floor-to-sky windows on three walls of the room and a television that looks like a movie screen. Then I spot her. Juliet is sitting on the floor, playing with a gigantic collection of stuffed animals. They must be new. I'm never seen them before.

I run and throw my arms around her. I start babbling about the drive and our tree house and how much I've missed her. I pull back just long enough to shove my reindeer sweater under her nose.

"Look!" I declare loudly.

Juliet sweeps her short brown hair out of her face. She was always a little bit shorter than me, and now her hair is shorter than mine too. It doesn't matter, though. I bet we could still wear our matching dresses and look like twins.

Lucy leaves, and Juliet's mother stands up from the sofa. I didn't even see her there. Her dress looks like the same print as the couch. "I'm so glad you made it," she says.

Juliet's mom calls her over, but she doesn't go right away. She is looking me over, her eyes on the bells on my sweater. She doesn't seem impressed, though, and suddenly I wish I wasn't wearing it. Or that it was gigantic, so I could crawl inside and disappear.

Something is wrong.

"Juliet," her mother says, a little bit louder, "please say hello to your cousin."

Juliet makes a fuss of getting up, dragging a stuffed-animal horse by the mane. We're face-to-face, but she still doesn't move to hug me. She doesn't even smile.

"Hi," I say.

"Hi," she says.

"Can I play with you?" I ask.

"I'm finished."

How can Juliet be finished playing? We used to play for hours. Outside, inside. In my house, her house, Rob's house. In our driveways, in our living rooms.

"Jules," I try, "let's play." She turns her head and doesn't look at me. "Joo Joo?" Still nothing. Then I think of it: She's mad at me. The problem is, I don't know what I did wrong.

I'm starving by the time Juliet's father comes home, and my stomach is making loud growling noises when we all sit down to dinner. No one is really talking. I leave my sweater on because it's freezing in their house. As cold as it is in the ice cream section of the grocery store.

After dinner my dad says we should open one present tonight. It's a tradition at our house. One present Christmas Eve, the rest on Christmas.

My mom starts to say we shouldn't, because we're driving back tonight and we can do it at home, but my dad convinces her. "Come on," he says. "Just one."

Juliet gets to pick hers from under the tree. She chooses a gigantic one. A box so big it takes up the entire left side of the tree. Then my mom hands me my own, and from the way she's smiling I know she knew we were going to open it here all along. It's a small, long box, and the wrapping paper is sparkling in the white Christmas lights. I take it from my mom, gently, and turn it over.

Juliet is already tearing at her paper, ripping and yanking. Inside is a dollhouse. It's beautiful, like a tiny copy of the house we are in. Even the white columns are the same. I'm so enthralled with it, I almost forget to open my own gift. Juliet, however, doesn't seem remotely impressed. She takes one look at the dollhouse and puts her hands on her hips. "Where's my American Girl?" she wants to know.

"You already have all of them," I say.

"Not the newest one," she says. She looks at me like I smell weird.

"Your turn," my father whispers to me. I brush some hair out of my face and focus on the present in my hands. I fold down the corners the way my mom does, careful not to tear anything. She always saves the wrapping paper for later.

"Hurry up," Juliet whines. She still has her hands on her hips, and her eyebrows are knit together.

When I finally see what's inside, my mouth hangs open. It's exactly what I hoped it would be: Beach Barbie. The new version. The kind everyone at school has been talking about. The kind you can't just walk into any old toy store and pick up. The kind you have to order special.

I start screaming and rip open the box. My dad puts his arm around my mom.

Juliet does *not* look pleased. She's peering at the Barbie in my hands, leaning so far forward she's balancing on one foot.

"Let me see," she says firmly.

I'm cradling the doll in my arms, and I don't want to give her up, but I also want Juliet to like me again. I want her to take me up to her new room and show me all her things. I want us to play on her floor the way we used to. I want to be best friends, just like we were. And since the reindeer sweater didn't do the trick, Barbie might be my only option.

"Okay," I say. "Just be careful." It's what my mom always says when she hands me something she really cares about. Like the good dishes to set the table or the brush with the porcelain handle she keeps on her dresser.

Juliet takes the doll and looks her over. Then, with one swift motion, she snaps her head off. It happens so fast, I'm not even sure if I should be upset. She just takes the doll, looks at her, and cracks her in two.

Everyone starts to talk at once. My dad is yelling, and my mom is mumbling something, and Juliet's mother is talking over everyone, saying that she thinks it can be fixed. I don't say anything. I don't cry or try to snatch the doll away. I don't even look at Barbie, or what's left of her. Instead I look at Juliet. She's staring at me like she's just won a game of tag. Like she's beat me. Then she tosses the two halves down onto the ground and marches out of the room.

Juliet's father follows her out, but not before he turns to my dad and says a bunch of things, all of which end with a word I've never heard before—traitor.

We drive back to San Bellaro that night. I pretend to sleep in the car but I can't. All I can see is Juliet's face before she walked out of the room. Determined. Angry. Like I had taken something from her, not the other way around. I left the broken Barbie on the floor where Juliet threw her. My parents offer to get me another one, but I refuse. I don't want her anymore.

Scene Two

Rob might be here any minute to pick me up for dinner, and I'm feeling ill. I'm sure some of it has to do with the gobs of *queso* I inhaled after school, but mostly it's about the fact that at any minute my best friend is going to take me on a date. That might end in us kissing. Rob. Kissing. I need to sit down on the bed just to keep my head from exploding.

I wanted to ask my parents about Juliet. I even brought the newspaper home to show them, but they aren't here. My dad sometimes teaches night classes, and my mom's yoga schedule is impossible to keep up with, but it's fine. I have enough to think about with Rob.

Charlie and Olivia are over, and they're both lying on my bed, looking through last year's yearbook. It's a tradition we have to look at last year's book around the first day of school. Usually we do it before and decide who we think is going to have come back better-looking, worse, smarter, sexier, most changed, etc.

"I think Jake got cuter," Charlie says. Her feet are in the air and she's on her back, the yearbook straight up in her hands. She looks like a dead bug, the kind you find belly up on our back porch over the summer.

"Eh," Olivia says. "He has a nice body, I guess."

"Surfing." Charlie flips over and raises her eyebrows. I know that look. She's trying to tell me that Rob has the same body too.

I launch myself into my closet, blushing. "Where did you put the white one?" I call.

"On the bed," Charlie says. "Chill."

"You sound like your boyfriend," Olivia says, folding a magazine and hitting her over the head. "Chill, dude."

Charlie rolls her eyes. "Whatever." She tosses me the dress, and I slip it on. It's a halter dress, something Charlie bought me for my birthday last year after I complained about never having any sundresses. It was an ironic gift, given that my birthday is on January first. A white dress in the middle of winter. So Charlie.

Just the fact that Charlie and Olivia are always up to celebrating my birthday is a big deal. I mean, I was born on January first, which is basically, like, National Hangover Day. It's the official stop date of the holiday season, and everyone's usually burnt out and exhausted. Not that I mind. I've never been a huge fan of birthdays anyway, but still, something about it is always kind of disappointing.

"What do you think?" I sway my arms by my sides for effect, and the dress rocks slowly, like waves lapping at the shore. *Swoosh, swoosh.*

"Hot," Olivia says. Charlie gives me a thumbs-up.

"My face looks bloated." I puff out my cheeks in the mirror and run some blush over them, adding mascara to my lashes. I look at Olivia and Charlie perched on the bed, effortlessly attractive, and then back at the mirror. *He called you beautiful,* I remind myself. *You. No one else.*

"Take two Tylenol and some orange juice," Olivia says.

Charlie gives her a look like she's just suggested I wear argyle. There are few things in this world Charlie hates worse than plaid. One of them is definitely argyle.

"What?" Olivia says. "It works."

I find two Tylenol and swallow them with some water from the bathroom sink. That will have to do.

"You really look great," Charlie says. "Scout's honor."

"Agreed," Olivia says. She turns on her side and surveys me. "I'm just so proud."

A car honks. Charlie and I exchange a glance, and then we're all at the window, looking down at Rob's silver Volvo. I see the door open, and I spin myself around from the window before I can watch him get out. My insides feel like a racetrack: cars zipping hundreds of miles per hour all around my stomach and chest.

"He's here!" Olivia shrills.

Charlie motions me closer and puts on the serious face she uses in history class. "I'm really happy for you," she says. "This is totally a big deal, and Rob's the best, and I want you to have a really good time."

"Kodak moment." Olivia smiles and makes like she's snapping a camera.

"We're adorable," I deadpan, giving Charlie a hug. I hold on for a minute longer than I intend to. I guess I am sort of nervous.

"Okay, clingy." Charlie pulls back and holds me at arm's length. "Knock 'em dead."

"You'll be great," Olivia says. "Don't do anything I wouldn't do!"

"Except do," Charlie says. "It's way more fun."

I take the pillow from my desk chair and hurl it at her. "Good-bye, hooligans."

"Ciao," they say together. I can hear Charlie call jinx, and then Olivia starts whining.

I run down the stairs and then pause at the doorway, trying to catch my breath. *It's just Rob,* I remind myself. *Just a date. Just Rob.*

I open the door still attempting to settle my heartbeat. He's almost at my doorstep and stops when he sees me. Then he smiles, and it's like his face lights up my entire driveway. I just stand there, looking at him like an idiot.

"You look beautiful," he says, which makes my heart leap up and out of my chest. I can't believe it's the second time he's told me that. It's almost like he thinks it's true or something.

"So do you." He laughs, and I cringe. "You know what I mean."

"I do," he says. "Oh, these are for you." He pulls a bouquet of roses out from behind his back. "Your favorite," he says. "Roses for Rose."

I take a deep breath and then will my feet to move toward him. He hands me the flowers and then pulls me into a hug. It's brief, but the smell of him is overwhelming. Apples and soap, just like always.

"Sorry I'm late," he says.

"We didn't set a time," I say. "You can't be late."

"I guess I wanted to see you sooner."

I set the flowers inside and close the door, then walk with him over to the car. He opens the passenger door. It takes him a few tries to get the handle, and when he does, he laughs nervously. "Been meaning to fix that." Inside his car still smells like pine. It has smelled this way since we picked up a Christmas tree last winter. For some reason we decided it would be a good idea to shove it into the backseat instead of strap it to the top. There's this place by the water that sells them. The trees, I mean. I'm surprised the smell has clung on through the summer, even if we were still finding pine needles in May.

"So how was day one?"

"Pretty good," I say. "The usual. Except AP Bio, which is ridiculous." I make a move to hike my knees up onto the dashboard but stop myself. It feels wrong to be that casual tonight.

"Mrs. Barch?"

"Mhm."

"At least it will look good on that Stanford app." He takes his hand off the steering wheel and runs it over his forehead. Stanford is Rob's dream too. We've planned on it since we were kids.

"Even if I flunk?"

Rob takes his free hand and reaches over to tap my knee. "You never flunk. You're Rosie."

"Guess who's back?" I say, remembering I haven't told Rob about the newspaper article yet.

"Eminem?"

"Funny. No. Juliet."

Rob frowns. "Your cousin?"

"Exactly."

"Wow. How come they're back here?"

I shrug. "I dunno. I haven't asked my parents yet."

"Didn't your parents have a falling-out with them?"

I nod. "Yeah. I mean, I don't think I've seen Juliet in a decade."

"Me either."

"Well, obviously." I poke him with my elbow, and we both laugh. It makes me relax.

We drive in silence for a few minutes. I think about reaching over for his iPod, but I don't. I don't want this to be like any old Wednesday night. I don't want this to just be Rob and Rose, hanging out. This is a date. It has to be different. And just like I can't recline my legs up on the dashboard, I also can't be in charge of the music.

"You want to go to Bernatelli's?" he asks, breaking the silence. Bernatelli's is this Italian place by the water that our parents are really into. I'm surprised Rob wants to go. The only thing I've ever heard him say about it is that Domino's pizza is better. I don't bring this up, because it seems like a good date spot and tonight is about things being different.

"Sure," I say.

He doesn't say anything, and I'm suddenly acutely aware that we are alone together. We've been alone hundreds of times before. Thousands, even. But this is the first time I've ever noticed. I cave and fiddle with his iPod and put on some music. I don't even know what's playing. Not like it matters. My ears are still humming their own speedy rhythm in time with my racing pulse.

I open my mouth, but I'm not sure what to say. There doesn't seem to be anything remotely unimportant *to* say. It's like the second he put his knee on mine this morning, or even maybe before that, maybe when he put his hands on my face in May, he annihilated everything trivial. All the stupid stuff that used to make up our friendship, like whether Jason was a good kisser or whether Rob really looked as ridiculous as he felt in collared shirts, seems impossible to talk about now. We're not just two friends informing each other about our day anymore. Which is fine, and I'm happy. I want this. I just feel like I'm sitting next to a stranger.

"So Ben and Olivia," Rob says. "When did that happen?"

"I don't know!" I practically scream. I'm so grateful to him for talking that the words come out rushed and frantic. "This summer. The beach, maybe? I don't know. I don't know!"

He laughs. It makes me feel calmer. The knot in my stomach starts to loosen.

"I think she really likes him."

"Mutual," he says. "The guy's had a thing for her since we were freshmen."

"Really?" I screech. "Why did you never say anything?"

"Dude moral code." He lifts his eyes off the road and glances at me. "Plus, he never thought he actually had a chance."

*   *   *

The Ben and Olivia discussion carries us all the way to the restaurant. There is a little snag when Rob comes around to open my door and I've already done it myself, but things seem to be improving as we walk in.

"Remember when we used to hang out by that thing?" Rob says when we're inside.

He's pointing to the gigantic lobster tank by the hostess stand, where people can come and pick out which one they want for dinner. Rob and I were obsessed with it when we were younger. Rob's dad would always send us off to "pick the biggest one."

There is a little boy in front of it now, tapping on the glass. His mother is behind him, tugging on his T-shirt.

"Yeah," I say. "We were so into those things."

"I don't even like lobster." Rob gives me a lopsided smile. "It must have been all you."

We sit at a table in the back left corner. I never noticed before, but it's sort of romantic in here. There are candles, and the lighting is kind of dim.

Okay, truth? I've thought about what a date with Rob would be like. A lot. Probably since high school started, maybe even before then. It never really mattered because I didn't think it would actually happen, but I have the fantasies. They even come complete with little outfits, like we're tiny cutout paper dolls. Whenever I can't sleep and I'm just lying in bed, I imagine Rob and me on one of our fantasy dates. Alone, together. It helps, to think about him. It always has. Something about being close to him just makes me feel calm. He's the one thing in life I can really rely on.

So in no particular order, my three favorite dream dates with Rob:

1) Picnic at a Park
   Me: white dress, yellow cardigan
   Rob: jeans, white T-shirt
   Dialogue:
   Rob: It's always been you.
   Me: Why did it take you so long to realize?
   Rob: I was scared; we were young.
   (He takes my hand in his.)
   Rob: I want to be with you. Forever. As long as I can
      breathe, it will only be you.

2) Romantic Restaurant
   Me: black dress, red shawl
   Rob: dark jeans, blue button-down
   Dialogue:
   Rob: I'm so happy we ended up here.
   Me: I just don't know. I mean, we've been friends for
      so long. . . .

Rob: You don't have to know. *I* know. For now that's
        enough, and I will do everything in my power to
        convince you that this is right.
(He takes my face in his hands. Kisses me passionately.)
Me: I think it's working.

3) School Dance
    Me: silver dress, heels
    Rob: black suit
    Dialogue:
    Rob: I'm so crazy about you.
    Me: You are?
    Rob: I can't believe I'm here dancing with Rosaline Caplet.
        I'm so lucky.
    Me: Are you sure this is right?
    Rob: There is no one else on the planet for me. Only you.

The Rob in my fantasy dates is never nervous. He's always
self-assured. But the Rob sitting across from me looks kind of
freaked out. I thought we'd worked all this out in the car earlier,
but as soon as we sit down, it's like he remembers we're on a
date and immediately freezes up. I take a gulp of water and start
coughing. It startles Rob, and he looks at me with this mixture of
confusion and surprise. Great. I am so not what he bargained for.

I'll bet he's not even going to kiss me now. I'm going to graduate from high school with Jason Goddamn Grove still on my lips.

But then Rob reaches across the table and lays his fingertips right by my plate. He's looking at me and biting his lower lip, like he's not sure this was the right move. I sort of edge my fingers onto the table, to encourage him, and then caterpillar them closer. This is weird. This is weird, right? I mean, there are Rob's hands, right in front of me, and I'm trying to figure out where to put mine, how to hold his, if that's even what he wants. (Although, if it wasn't what he wanted, why would he be reaching way the hell over to my plate? Why would he have leaned his knee against mine in assembly this morning? Why would we even *be* here?) This feels ridiculous, this finger dance. In my fantasies he always just takes my hand firmly. There are no sweaty palms. There's no awkwardness. No uncertainty.

Finally he takes my thumb in his hand. Of all the fingers to grab, this would not have been the one I would have picked, but whatever. He sort of just holds it between his own thumb and index finger. Which is, truth be told, not very sexy. We should have gone about this all differently. I want to call a time-out and start over. First dates are important. I want us to get this one right.

"So, what are you going to order?" I ask. He's still holding my thumb, and my other hand is just kind of lying there, so I use it to pick up my water glass.

"Pasta," he says. He's studying my thumb now. He's staring at it. Running his index finger up the side.

"Cool."

"You're getting the Caprese pizza, right?"

"Dunno." My menu is underneath the thumb debacle, and even though I *usually* get the Caprese pizza, I'd still like to look. Everything else is different about tonight. No reason my order shouldn't be too.

He drops my thumb and picks up his water glass. He looks sorta proud of himself, which is disconcerting. Does he think that just went well? I bury myself in my menu and pretend to seriously consider another option besides the Caprese pizza. I find none.

"Have you two decided?" The waiter winks at me, and for a second I see Rob and me through his eyes: a young couple in love. Maybe a little bit awkward, but definitely not just friends. I'll take it.

"What would you like?" Rob asks.

"The Caprese."

Rob laughs and shakes his head. "Thanks for giving me a hard time, Caplet."

"He'll have the pasta Bolognese," I shoot back.

Rob opens his mouth to protest, but the bow tie waiter cuts in, "Your date has great taste."

Rob smiles and turns his hands up. "I can't argue with that."

When he's gone, Rob again puts his hands across the table, but this time he takes both of mine in his in one clean, swift movement. It doesn't feel awkward, just nice. I think maybe we're getting better at this. The interaction with the waiter seemed to give us some confidence.

"You still haven't told me about the summer." I try to keep my voice steady because it's distracting, his fingers on mine like this. But distracting in a good way. Like a really great song playing when you're trying to study for an English exam.

"It was good." He shrugs. "You know Kwebec, not much to report. It never changes. Larry is still there, and he's as crazy as ever."

Larry is the camp director. No one knows exactly how old he is. Sometimes he looks eighty, and sometimes he looks forty. It's the weirdest thing. He isn't married, so it's not like you can tell by his wife or anything, and as far as I know he has no children.

"Cool."

"It rained a lot." Rob pauses, considering it. "Yeah, it was sorta annoying, actually. There's only so long you can keep those kids indoors."

The waiter comes over with our bread, but Rob doesn't immediately drop my hands. Instead he turns them over in his and draws little circles on my palms. He traces the lines of my veins like he's a fortune-teller.

"What do you see?" I peer at his fingers.

"You will live a long life," he says in his best Dumbledore voice.

"That's it?"

"What else do you want?" He looks up at me, his voice Rob again.

"It's my *destiny*. Something good."

I break our hands apart and reach for a piece of bread. Rob starts talking about Jake and whether or not their before-school surfing routine is going to work through the fall.

"I think Jake is probably headed to CC next year," he says. CC is the community college here. It's different than the big university in town, where my dad teaches. CC isn't a great school, but Jake also isn't exactly a fantastic student. I think this really upsets Charlie. She wants to go to Middlebury in Vermont next year, and sometimes, in their better moments, she wants him to come with her.

"When are our applications due?"

"I think end of September," he says. "You're applying early, right?"

"You have to ask?"

He smiles, reaches across, and squeezes my hand. It's starting to feel normal now.

"You think this is going to work out, right?" I ask. "I mean, it's so supercompetitive these days."

Rob flips his hand to dismiss the comment. "We're fine.

Unless Lauren decides to forgo Harvard. Then we're screwed."

I laugh, but I can feel the bread turn over in my stomach. I hadn't even thought about anybody else applying. What's stopping Lauren or even Stacy Tempeski from edging in on our spots?

"Do you think they'll take both of us?"

Something flickers across his face for half a second. I barely register that it's doubt, before it's gone. "I don't think we have anything to worry about."

Our food arrives, and we segue out of Stanford talk. Rob wants to know about my parents and whether or not we are finally going to build that pool they've been talking about for years. "Honestly, I think they should invest in air-conditioning first." He takes my olives; I take his onions. By the time dinner is over, I'm not really nervous at all. It feels like I'm just out with Rob. My best friend Rob, who knows that I hate yellow peppers and that every time I lost a tooth I used to sleep over at his house the next night because I thought that I could trick the tooth fairy into coming twice.

We split a dessert—chocolate cake with vanilla ice cream—and when the check comes, Rob brushes me off. "No way," he says. "This is mine."

We walk to the car, and it's gotten a little cold out. I didn't bring a sweater, and I hug my arms around me. Rob tosses me the Stanford sweatshirt from the backseat. I pull it on, and when I poke my head out, he's smiling at me.

"What?"

He shakes his head. "Nothing. It just looks cute on you."

The comment makes my heart start racing and my hands feel numb. "I don't want to go home yet," he continues. He puts his hand softly on my kneecap. It's warm and dry, and he leaves it there. It feels very different than this morning. More definitive, because I don't have any more questions. I know now. Rob and I are going to kiss before this night is over.

"Okay."

"Should we go to the Cliffs?"

His hand is still on my knee, and I nod in agreement. We start driving back past Grandma's Coffeehouse and the school and up toward the water. The Cliffs are this area of San Bellaro above the ocean. Pretty self-explanatory except for the fact that there's a cemetery there. Which completely creeps Olivia and Charlie out. It's always been somewhere I've gone with Rob. Our place. It's quiet and peaceful, and all you can hear, besides the occasional passing car, is the sound of the waves crashing. I've spent my whole life living by the water, and while I don't surf and, yeah, my skin is whiter than a sheet of paper, there is something comforting about that sound. It's so eternal. Like Rob, one of those things I can just count on.

I keep my window down, and when I wet my lips, I can taste the salt air. Rob and I are quiet on the way over, but it's a good quiet now, a quiet we're used to. Watching movies, studying at my kitchen table. That kind of quiet.

It takes us about ten minutes to get there, and the entire time we're driving with the windows down, music playing and the salt air settling onto our skin, he has his hand on my knee. It's just resting there, like it fits. Like we're these two puzzle pieces that have finally been put together.

We pull into the parking lot, and Rob cuts the engine. It's quiet—so quiet I can actually hear the wind whistling through the grass outside. Rob takes his hand gently away and then gets out. This time I wait for him to come around, and when he does, he opens my door easily, on the first try.

I hug the Stanford sweatshirt closer around me.

"Come on," he says, taking my hand.

We walk through the grass to this place at the end of the cemetery where there are two big rocks that are so close to the edge of the cliffs, it feels like you're literally hanging over the water. I've always been afraid of heights. I was that kid who refused to go on the monkey bars and hated gymnastics. I still don't even like to fly. Being high up freaks me out. All of that space. All of that possibility for complete and total catastrophe. One wrong move, and everything changes.

"Nothing's going to happen to you," Rob says. It's the same thing he's been saying for years. Every time I get close to the rocks, I just sort of freeze up. I can't help it. It is a long way down into that water. If I knew anything about math or geography, I'd probably put it around way too many feet.

"I know. Just give me a minute."

"Okay." He stands on one of the rocks, arms spread out like he's flying. "Check it out, Rosie. No hands."

"Please stop." My heart is racing and my blood is pounding so hard, I can hear it in my ears. It feels like it's going to thump straight out of my body.

Then Rob trips and his arms flail out, and he's literally inches from the edge, his torso so far forward I swear he's going to topple over. In one tiny, terrified moment I start screaming.

Rob rights himself effortlessly. "Relax, Rosie. No problem."

He tries to take my hand, but I yank it away. "It's not funny." I know I sound petulant, like a little kid, but I can't help it. "I hate when you do that."

"Okay, okay," he says, softening. He brings one hand to my waist and puts the other underneath my chin, tilting my head up toward him. "I'm sorry," he says, and I can tell by the look in his eyes that he means it.

I grumble, "Okay," and let him lead me over to the rock just behind the one he was standing on, where we settle down next to each other.

He points to the sky. The stars are brilliant, so specific that it feels like if I tried, I could count them. And from our spot on the rock it looks like they are all around us. Even underneath us. Like we're in a universe composed entirely of stars.

"What's that?" I ask, pointing up at a circular constellation. Rob has moved just a tiny bit behind me so my back is resting half on his chest and half on his shoulder.

"I'm not sure. I was never too good at astronomy."

"Me neither."

He runs his hand down my arm and then secures it around me. My heart starts to speed up again, like a runner in the last mile of a marathon. Just when I didn't think it could go anymore, it takes off again.

"This is funny, huh?" he says. He clears his throat. "I just mean, you and I."

"Funny?"

"Well, no, not *funny*. Just different."

"Well, yeah. I mean, usually we're not sitting like this." I gesture to his arm that's still resting on my side.

"No, usually we're not." He doesn't remove his hand. Instead he presses me closer.

Something is bubbling up and out of me, and even though I want to keep it inside, rest my head on Rob's chest and just enjoy how nice it feels to be near him, I know I have to say it. I turn around to look at him.

"I'm worried," I say.

"About what?" He takes his other hand and brushes some hair out of my face the way he did at prom last year.

"You're my best friend," I whisper. "What if this doesn't work out?"

"You're already planning our demise?"

"Not demise." I exhale. "I'm just worried, is all."

He takes my hand in his and presses his thumb into my palm. His hands feel strong and soft. "I know," he says. And then, with his thumb still in my palm, he adds, "But I haven't even kissed you yet."

I drop my eyes down to the rock, but I know without looking at him that he's staring at me, and when he releases my hand, puts both of his on the sides of my face and lifts my head up, I see that I'm right.

He leans in slowly. So slowly it feels like we're in slow motion. And then his lips are on mine. They are so soft and warm, and it's not until he pulls back gently that I realize how much I've wanted him to kiss me. How it's really the only thing I've wanted.

"We'll figure it out, Rosie," he says, stroking my cheek. "I promise." And then he's kissing me again, and it feels so good to be close to him, his hands on my back, his lips on mine, that I can't believe there was a time before we were doing this at all.

Scene Three

When Rob drops me off, we're holding hands across the front seat, my palm lightly resting in his.

"Should I come in?" he asks.

I glance from our intertwined hands to my front door. "No," I say. "Why don't we shelve that conversation. Just for a little." There wouldn't be anything strange about Rob coming in— Rob and I have been out a million times, and he always comes over after—but I'm not sure how much my parents know, and how much I'm ready to tell them.

He smiles and cuts the engine, releasing my hand and leaning over in his seat. He plants a kiss on my temple, one above the bridge of my nose, and then one gently on my lips.

"Okay," he says. "Sleep sweet, Rosie." It's the same good night he's been giving me since we were kids, but this time it makes my heart rattle in my chest.

"Sleep sweet," I whisper. I stumble out of the car and into my house, dizzy from his lips.

Our front door opens into our kitchen. My parents are always hanging out in there, drinking tea and reading the paper in their bathrobes until midnight. I swear if it wasn't for the fact that it's dark out, you'd think it was morning.

Tonight when I come inside, they're not there, though. Instead they are in the living room with Rob's parents. They're talking so loudly, they don't hear me enter.

"I don't know what to say," Rob's mother says. She's sitting on the arm of Rob's father's chair. He has his elbows on his knees and his head in his hands. My mom is standing, holding a glass, and so is my father, which is strange, because neither of them ever drinks. They don't even like wine with dinner.

"Have you spoken to them?" Rob's father asks.

My father shakes his head. "I left a message with his office, but no one has gotten back to me." He looks at my mom. "I don't even have their home number."

"Why call?" Rob's mother asks. "Isn't it best to leave things as they are?"

"This is a small town, Jackie. You know that. We'll run into them sooner or later," my dad says.

"This is a nightmare," Rob's father says. He looks angry, which is new for him. He's got four boys, and he rarely ever even raises his voice.

My mom takes a sip of her drink. "Why come back now?" she says.

"Isn't it obvious?" Rob's mom says. They all look at her intently, their backs erect. "They want revenge."

The floorboards choose that moment to creak under my feet, and all four heads swivel to look at me standing in the doorway.

"Rosie," my mom says. She turns around and must send my dad some kind of look, because in the next instant he sets his glass down and comes over to me.

"Sorry for all the ruckus," he says.

"Hi." I wave to Rob's folks.

Rob's mom smiles weakly, and his dad chirps up, "Hey, kiddo. How was dinner?"

My cheeks flush pink. "Good," I say. "We had Italian." Everyone nods.

"Sounds delicious," Rob's dad says.

"Everything okay?" I ask. Asking your parents if everything is okay is a little like asking your math teacher is she's really going to give that pop quiz. You already know the answer.

"Oh, yeah," my mom says. "Just politics."

My dad smiles to second what she said.

"Well, I'm gonna hit the hay," I say. "AP Bio in the a.m." I give them a look like, *You know,* although no one seems to.

"Good night, cookie," my dad says. The living room erupts into a chorus of good nights, and I turn from them, perplexed, and climb the stairs. But I don't want to think about Juliet's family or guess how Rob's parents are involved in whatever went wrong. Tonight is about me and Rob. I just want to fall asleep remembering his kisses.

Scene Four

"I'm *coming,*" I yell. Charlie is laying on the horn outside, and I'm frantically running around the kitchen, grabbing toast and saying good-bye to my parents. They both look a little worn this morning, and they're hunched over their mugs, sipping slowly.

"Have a good day." My mother yawns. I consider asking them about Juliet, but I don't have time. Later.

I run outside, toast in my teeth.

"Hey, hot stuff," Charlie says. "Have fun last night?"

I roll my eyes and climb inside. Olivia is in the back, which is different. The three of us haven't carpooled since Olivia got OLIVE16.

"What's going on?" I ask.

"I wanted to hear about your date," Olivia says. "Also, Ben has my car." Charlie makes a huffing sound, but Olivia doesn't seem to notice. She hooks her elbows around both of our seats and leans so far forward, I can smell the strawberry on her. Olivia has been wearing the same perfume since I've known her. One time we were all shopping and she went to buy more. It turns out, it's a house spray. Like the kind of stuff you spritz on your couch to cover up the smell of wet dog. We pointed this out to her and found it hilarious, but Olivia refused to change.

"That's like using Clorox as hand soap," Charlie said.

"I don't care," Olivia said. "I like it, and I'm sticking to it." That's one of the things I really love about Olivia. If she's happy, she doesn't really care what other people think. She still wears these pajamas she had in the fifth grade. They are way too short and way too big in the waist and have horses on them, but she says they're soft and help her sleep. I bet if Ben slept over, she'd even wear them around him.

"So what happened?" Olivia says. "Details."

"We went to dinner." I glance back at Rob's house as we screech out of the driveway, but we're moving too fast for me to catch a good view.

"Bo-ring." Charlie taps her hand on the steering wheel like she's counting. "Get to the good stuff."

"I mean, we kissed."

Olivia starts wailing, and Charlie starts honking. She makes like she's just lost control of the car and swerves right. I cover my ears and sink lower in my seat.

"Can you guys please calm down? I'm going to go deaf here."

Olivia keeps repeating, "Oh my God, oh my God," until Charlie sends her a look in the rearview and she shuts up.

"Was it good?" Charlie asks.

"Sure." I'm blushing, and I turn away. When I used to tell them about kissing Jason, it was always just sort of situational. "We were at this party" or "He tried to suck my neck." (True, by the way. It was awful.) We've never talked about whether I liked it or not. Or how it felt.

"'Sure'?" Charlie slides her sunglasses up on her head and gives me a look like she's never been so disappointed in her life.

"It's *Rob*," I say.

"We know," Olivia says. "But that doesn't really answer the question."

"It was good, okay?" I hike my knees up against the dashboard and keep my eyes fixed ahead. "It was amazing."

"I knew it!" Olivia squeals.

"Well, obviously," Charlie says. "I mean, it's Rob. Clearly it would be."

"I am *so* into this," Olivia says.

"Yeah," I say. "I know, but I'm just kind of worried." About a million things. Like does this mean we are together? Should I ask him? Is he going to kiss me this morning? Has he told his friends?

"Clearly he likes you," Olivia says. "What is there to be concerned about?"

"He's my best friend." It comes out harsher than I mean it to, and immediately I feel Olivia sit back and Charlie glare at me. "You know what I mean," I say. "My best *guy* friend. My oldest friend."

"The best romances totally develop out of friendship," Olivia says.

"Okay, Hallmark."

"It's true," Charlie says. "I mean, look at Jake and me. We can't stand each other, and we're definitely not friends. God, Jake." She pummels the back of her hand against the steering wheel.

"Things not good this a.m.?" I ask.

"No," she says, "he just doesn't care." She nods and her sunglasses flip back down onto her face.

"What happened?" Olivia asks. She leans her elbows on the center console and gives me a wide smile. There's a piece of blueberry in her third tooth, and I point to it.

"I don't know," Charlie says as Olivia pulls out a compact and starts attacking her mouth with her pinkie finger. "He's so hot and cold sometimes."

"Trust me, I know," Olivia says. I turn around and give her a pointed look. The last thing Charlie wants to hear is some boyfriend-bashing on her brother.

"Sorry," she mouths, her finger still in her mouth.

"I have an idea," Charlie says, glancing out the window and making a right.

"Hmm?" I mumble.

"Why don't we go to Fall Back together, just the three of us?"

"What do you mean?" Olivia asks. There is a tiny bit of drool down her face, and she flicks the back of her hand across her mouth.

"I mean, why don't we go without the guys?" Charlie swings into upper and lays on the horn. Some freshmen scatter. It's completely illegal to honk on school premises. Not that this has ever stopped her.

"I kind of wanted to go with Ben," Olivia says. She sticks out her lower lip, but Charlie doesn't turn around. "Rose, don't you want to go with Rob?"

"Yeah, sure, but it's not like he won't be there. Plus, we're gonna have to go early to set up."

"What?" Olivia asks. She sounds totally appalled.

"SAC? Hello?" Charlie says. She pulls into a spot and kills the engine, but not one of us moves. Charlie unclips her seat belt and turns way around. "All I'm saying is, we have to stick together.

Because it's a total free-for-all out there, and men are completely crazy."

"Did you read this in the book?" Olivia asks. She looks doubtful.

Charlie bought us all *Why Men Love Bitches* for Christmas last year. She says it's how she got Jake, although (1) I'm not sure that's such an achievement, and (2) frankly, if she's following the advice, it isn't really working.

"No," Charlie snaps, "I'm serious. We're friends, right?"

Olivia shrugs.

"I think it's a great plan," I say. I'm trying to end the conversation because I've just spotted Rob. He's standing in upper with Ben. Olivia's car is parked next to them with surfboards stacked on top, and Ben is pulling a T-shirt over his head. It looks like he joined Rob and Jake surfing. There's something about the familiar way they're standing that makes me feel inexplicably safe. Like we all really belong together.

I am about to suggest we talk about this later, when Olivia bolts from the car and goes and attacks Ben. He scoops her up into a gigantic hug, lifting her off the pavement. They look like that poster of the couple kissing in Paris. I used to have it on my wall, but Charlie said it was going to scare boys away and I had to take it down. Not that any boy besides Rob is ever in my room. And he saw it, like, a million times and never seemed to mind.

"Appalling," Charlie says as we walk toward them. She puts her arm around my shoulder. "Go say hi. Rob won't bite. Unless you're lucky." She wiggles her hips like she has a Hula-hoop around them, and I roll my eyes.

"Are you serious with that?"

"Dead." She blows me a kiss. "See you in Spanish."

"Hey, Kessler," Rob says. He gives Charlie a lopsided smile as he slides one arm around my waist.

I can't believe he's touching me like this. In public.

"'Hey' yourself. I'm getting out of here before my brother sucks her face off." Charlie looks at Rob's hand on my waist and then at me. I'm silently saying a thank-you that she's wearing her sunglasses, because Charlie's facial expressions tend to give away everything she's thinking.

"Smart woman." Rob pulls me a little closer as Charlie disappears down toward Cooper House.

"Hey," he says. His face is inches from mine, and images from last night come back to me like firecrackers. His warm sweatshirt and my head on his chest. His hands on my face. His lips on mine.

He looks so cute today in his khaki shorts and blue T-shirt. His hair is still a little wet from surfing, and there are a few water droplets on the back of his shirt. "How did you sleep?" he asks.

I move a little closer to him and mutter, "Good. You?"

"Yeah, same." He takes his hand and cups my elbow, bringing our torsos together. His face is right above mine and he's moving it down, lower, so that our lips are just a whisper away. I close my eyes, ready for him to kiss me, but just then Olivia sashays over.

Rob immediately drops his hand from my waist, and I must look disappointed, because Olivia gets sheepish. "Sorry to interrupt," she says, "but Ben needs you."

"Your boyfriend's impossible," Rob says, but he's smiling. That's one of the things I love about him. Nothing really annoys him for too long.

"He is not!" Olivia squeals, but I can tell she's pleased. She's never called someone her boyfriend before, and she doesn't correct Rob now.

"You guys are adorable," she says when he's gone. "Seriously, perfect."

I don't say anything, but secretly I'm pleased too. Things feel right. Like we're all finally where we should be. Being with Rob is the one thing that's been missing, the thing that makes my life just, I don't know, *make sense*.

"Who's that?" Olivia asks.

"Who?"

"That." She's pointing to a white Mercedes SUV that has just pulled in next to Charlie's car. Too close. Everyone knows Charlie totally freaks if someone comes within four feet of Big Red. And

that Mercedes definitely doesn't belong to any senior at this school. Olivia has the nicest car on campus.

"Probably a parent." I shrug, but Olivia shakes her head. There is a girl climbing out.

The first thing I notice is that she has blond hair. The kind of blond Charlie calls "prescription strength," meaning you need serious chemical help to achieve it. The second is that both her bag and her sunglasses seem way larger than she is.

Olivia and I look at each other. Olivia steps closer to me. "LA transplant," she says. "Definitely." She crosses her arms, and her strap slides down to her elbow so that her MIAMI book bag is dangling dangerously close to the ground. She doesn't seem happy. This new girl, whoever she is, is definitely competition.

"Were we getting new students?" I ask. But before I even have time to consider my own question, I know who she is. The girl from the newspaper. My cousin. Juliet.

"What are you doing?" Olivia spits, but she follows me over to the car where Juliet is busying herself with unloading books.

"Hey." I'm not usually the welcoming committee—usually that's Charlie's role. Well, maybe more like making new people feel afraid—Charlie isn't exactly the "come join our circle" kind of girl. But Juliet *is* my cousin. Just because we haven't been friends in a decade doesn't mean we couldn't start now. She's the only family I have, besides my parents.

"Hey," she says back. Even with her sunglasses on I can tell she's looking me up and down. It's slow, too, like she's not trying to hide it.

I go ahead and blurt it out: "Do you know who I am?" I shake my head. "Not like that. I just mean, we're cousins? Rosaline Caplet?" I tap myself on the chest like I have a name tag.

She flips her hair off her shoulders. "Yeah, I know."

I'm relieved, until I realize she's not following that up with anything. "This is Olivia," I say, to say something.

"Hey," Olivia says. She has one eye on me and the other on Juliet. I try to see what she sees. Juliet's pretty. Not Charlie-gorgeous but definitely attractive. She always was.

"I don't think I've seen you since we were, like, seven." I run my foot back and forth across the pavement. I suddenly don't want to look at her. I wonder if she remembers the doll incident.

"Does Rob still live here?"

"What?" Olivia answers for me.

Juliet looks at me. "Rob Monteg? I'm sure you remember. You guys were best friends."

"Right, yeah. He still lives here." I can feel Olivia's eyes on me, but I don't offer anything more. I'm not sure what to say, anyway. That Rob's my boyfriend now? Is that even true?

"It's been a long time," she says, but it's unclear whether she's talking to me or remembering to herself.

"So you guys just moved?" I ask, steering the conversation away from Rob.

She nods. "Your parents tell you?"

I shake my head. "Actually, no. I saw it in the paper."

She smiles slightly and clicks the lock on her car. "Makes sense."

"This is kind of weird," I say. "It's been forever."

"Yeah," she says, but again, that's all.

When I was little, I used to think about this moment over and over. If she ever came back, if I ever got to see her again, what I would say. How I would forgive her or apologize or throw my arms around her neck and beg her to play dolls with me. But we're seventeen now, not seven, and I'm not sure how to act. Rob's better at this. He can talk to anyone, about anything. One time we went to Colonial Williamsburg on a trip with our parents, and he talked to the shoemaker for an hour about their mutual love of the Lakers. I didn't even know colonial people watched television, but Rob got it out of him. His smile just kind of melts people. They end up spilling.

"So where are you guys living?" Olivia asks.

"Some house by the beach," she says. "It's fine."

"Cool." Olivia looks at me like, *Good luck with that,* and turns to go back over toward Ben. "Nice to meet you!" she calls over her shoulder.

Juliet smiles, but it's stiff. And she doesn't wave. It's a smile far better suited to the girl who beheaded my favorite Barbie than the one who was my best friend in kindergarten.

"Do you need help finding classes or anything? Thursdays we don't have assembly, so we just go straight to first period."

"I need to find . . ." She rummages in her gigantic bag and extracts a piece of paper. "Mr. Johnson," she says.

"He's probably in his office at Cooper House," I say. "Come on. I'll show you."

We start walking. Rob, Ben, and Olivia are descending toward Cooper House below us, but I decide not to call down to them.

"So how come you're starting today?"

"We were in Italy yesterday," she says. "My dad couldn't get back." Italy. Right. I remember when we used to make pizzas at Rob's together. I guess life is pretty different now.

"Sounds exciting."

"I guess," she says flatly.

Okay, then. "So, what brings you guys back?"

"My mom wanted a change. LA gets tiring after a while." She readjusts her book bag. It's Tod's. White leather. The kind Olivia wanted to get this year.

"Mhm, I'll bet."

"Have you ever lived there?"

"Oh, no," I say. "But, you know, I get it." Of course I've never lived there. I would have called her. We would have been friends, wouldn't we?

She gives me a look that I take to mean I definitely do *not* get it. Luckily, we're at Mr. Johnson's office. So for now, my time with Juliet is coming to a close.

"Here's your stop. He should be in there." I point to the left, past the entryway.

"Thanks."

"We usually have lunch in the courtyard, if you want to join us. And I guess our families will get together, so I'll see you." The silhouette of Rob's and my parents in our living room last night comes back to me. Something tells me that they're not quite as interested in rekindling a friendship as I am. And I am. Seeing her again makes me think about how close we were, and how I miss her, even after all these years. Maybe once she settles in, she'll let her guard down.

"Sure," Juliet says. She smiles, and it seems genuine, or at least as close to it as I've come so far. I glance down at my watch, and I'm already a minute late for Spanish. Charlie is going to kill me. I open my mouth to say good-bye, but I'm met with the back of her head. She has already moved on.

Scene Five

"So I'm telling Jake this is ridiculous," Charlie is saying. "I mean, who would possibly camp out outside an IHOP? It's not like it's the opening of *Star Wars*, or whatever. It's a twenty-four-hour diner."

"That's why I love Ben," Olivia says. "He's totally unexpected."

"Love?" Charlie guffaws, and some of her sandwich goes flying across the table.

"No, not *love*," Olivia says, blushing. "You know what I mean."

"I just don't understand." Charlie sighs. "I ask Jake to plan a fun weekend activity, and this is what he comes up with?"

"He wants you to camp out at an IHOP?" I ask. I'm draped over the table sipping on a Coke. I've forgone sparkling water today. I need the caffeine.

"Yes," Charlie says. "Obviously my life is a joke."

Olivia nods in agreement, and Charlie shoves her. "I'm just trying to be supportive," Olivia mumbles. "Anyway, I thought we were going to Malibu?"

"We cannot go to Malibu. We have a school dance. A dance we are *planning*." Charlie looks at me, and I'm surprised to see her eyes are welling up. "I'm just so sick of doing everything all by myself."

"You can't let him get to you like this," I say. I can't believe she's this upset about Jake. I mean, it's Jake. He still thinks fart jokes are funny and refers to his parents by their first names.

But then I realize I have it all wrong, and I could practically kick myself for being so stupid. She's not thinking about Jake. She's thinking about her mom. She presses her fingertips against her temples, and it's all I can do not to go over and lean my head on her shoulder and wrap my arms around her. She wouldn't let me, though. Lunchtime in the courtyard is not the place she wants to be talking about her mom dying. Not that she likes to talk about her at all, actually. I think we've had exactly two conversations about it since her mom passed away in the seventh grade. The first was when we started high school. My mom took us shopping for back-to-school clothes, and Charlie started crying in the dressing room, saying how she wasn't sure if she should buy this black sweater because her mom always said she looked so much prettier in color.

The second time was when she decided to sleep with Matt. She knew her mother wouldn't approve, and she started asking me all these crazy questions about whether I believed in God and what if religion had it right and we were going to hell. Because really, she said, how would we know?

Charlie's comment has silenced the three of us, and I'm not sure Olivia understands why, but she's not saying anything either way.

When Charlie's mom first got sick, Charlie slept over at my house for a week. She refused to go home. She wouldn't even talk to her mom on the phone. I remember being terrified. I think I was more scared of her reaction than I was when her mom actually died. There is something about Charlie that is so hard sometimes. So set and determined. It was like she couldn't figure out a theory on death, and until she did, she wasn't going home.

"If you had to rank who is cutest in our class, who would you list as the top five?" Olivia asks, looking thoughtful.

"Do they have to be in order?" Charlie asks. She looks grateful for the subject change.

"Yes. But it has to be objective. Like, you can't put Jake first."

"Well, what if I think Jake is the cutest?"

Olivia considers this. "That's fine, I guess. So we'd have Jake, Ben, obviously, Rob. Definitely Matt—" Charlie looks revolted at the mention of her ex, but Olivia continues. "Char, come on. It's true."

"Who would you put down?" Charlie asks me.

"Rob, I guess."

Olivia nods, writing. She looks up, kind of sheepish. "You know who else I'd put?"

"Hmmm?" Charlie hums, pulling apart her sandwich.

"Len." Olivia bites her lip and looks at Charlie.

"Len?" Charlie balks.

"You're kidding," I echo.

Olivia squints at the entrance to the cafeteria. Len is standing there talking to Dorothy Spellor. I wonder if they're dating, but I doubt it. Somehow he doesn't exactly seem like the boyfriend type.

"That's nauseating," Charlie says.

"I just don't see it," I say. "His hair is greasy."

"Exactly," Olivia says, eyebrows raised. "It's sexy."

"Are you attracted to the drive-through guy at McDonald's too?" I ask.

"Funny." Olivia looks back down at her list. "There's just something interesting about him, you know? Like there's more to him than meets the eye. Stuff we don't know about him."

"He's an idiot," Charlie says. "That's really all I need to know."

I glance back at Len. He's juggling two apples, then tossing one to Dorothy. She smiles.

"Hey."

I turn around, and Juliet is standing there. She has changed outfits since I last saw her, or maybe it's just that she now has a bright pink cardigan over her white dress. She's balancing a tray with a sandwich and an apple. I'm happy she decided to join us. Maybe it's a first step.

"Here, sit." I gesture next to me, and Olivia reluctantly moves over.

Charlie gives me a sideways glance with her eyebrow arched—*Who is this girl?* The only people who ever eat with us are Jake and Ben and Rob, and maybe Lauren, but generally only if SAC's afternoon meeting has been canceled or we have business to discuss. Charlie would say inviting a stranger to sit with us without checking with the others first is not appropriate courtyard behavior. But Juliet's not a stranger. She's my cousin.

"Hey," Olivia says. She lifts her hand off the table and gives a small wave. "How's your first day going?" Her words are a little slurred. She has her lunchtime apple stuck in her mouth.

Charlie clears her throat, and I interrupt. "Sorry. This is my cousin, Juliet. Juliet, this is Charlie." I flip a casual hand in Olivia's direction. "You guys met this morning."

Charlie smiles coolly. "You're from LA, right?"

"Yeah," Juliet says. She doesn't question where Charlie got her information, but why would she? Her move was announced on the front page of the paper. I'm sure she's used to strangers knowing her life story.

She plays with the edges of her napkin, and everyone goes back, more or less, to eating.

"So what's the deal with the guys at this school?" Juliet asks.

"Do you have a boyfriend at home?" Olivia says.

"Not really. My parents think I do. Some intern from my dad's office." She waves her free hand around like even the idea is ridiculous. "His name is Paris. Can you imagine?"

Olivia smiles. "I once dated a guy named Belgium."

"That wasn't his real name," Charlie interrupts. "Anyway, the boys here are okay. We *tolerate* them. Well, besides Rose."

Charlie winks at me, and I can feel my face get hot. *Please don't say his name. Please don't say his name.*

"What's up with you?" Juliet asks me.

"Nothing," I say. I glare at Charlie and search for her leg under the table.

"She's dating the best guy in school," Charlie says, unfazed. "It's totally unfair. He's, like, the only good one."

"Hey!" Olivia interjects.

"Oh, please." Charlie rolls her eyes. "Ben is my brother. It's well within my rights to call him an ass."

"So far I've only seen one who I think is pretty hot," Juliet says.

"Yeah?" Charlie says, leaning over me. "Len?" She looks at Olivia and winks.

Juliet shrugs. "Dunno his name. We didn't meet. Cute,

though. Blue T-shirt, khaki shorts. Great body. Totally my type."

I swallow. Hard.

Rob has on a blue T-shirt today. Rob is also wearing khaki shorts. Is it possible she wouldn't recognize him after all these years?

Charlie clearly hasn't caught on, because she mumbles something about pointing him out. "You're pretty," she says, looking Juliet over, "and boys at this school are idiots. You'll do just fine."

Charlie has a rule about new friends. It's really simple: She doesn't make them. Not good ones, anyway. She says loyalty is hard to come by, and once you find it, you hold on to it. She doesn't trust new people. It took her almost a year to get to the point where she really let Olivia in. I know Charlie isn't being incredibly welcoming to Juliet, but I'm impressed she's being this nice.

"Are you coming to the dance tomorrow?" Olivia asks.

Juliet looks up from her sandwich. "I didn't know there was one."

Olivia nods enthusiastically. "Fall Back. We plan it. We're on the social committee."

"We *are* the social committee," Charlie corrects. I can tell she's wishing Olivia would stop talking. We can both see where this is going.

"We've decided not to bring dates, though," Olivia says.

"Why?" Juliet looks put off, but it's hard to tell if that's just her permanent face. Everything seems like it mildly offends her.

"We're spending some girl time?" Olivia looks at Charlie to clarify. Charlie just rolls her eyes. "Anyway," Olivia says, "you're welcome to come with us."

"Thanks." Juliet glances at Taylor Simsburg as he passes. Olivia notices and opens her mouth to object, or something, but Charlie pipes up first.

"Here come the Three Musketeers now," she says.

Ben, Jake, and Rob are headed our way. Jake is wearing a baseball cap, so I know immediately he will be fighting with Charlie. They're illegal on school grounds, and Charlie is constantly saying things like "Why don't you get in trouble for something worthwhile?"

Rob, as I thought, is wearing a blue T-shirt and khaki shorts, and the second he comes into view, Juliet squeals, "That's him!" It's the most animated I've seen her get about anything all day. Italy included.

"Who?" Charlie says. She's already accusing. There is no good option out of the three.

"Blue T-shirt," Juliet says, clearly not catching on to Charlie's tone. She pulls a tube of lip gloss out of her Tod's purse. I put my sandwich down. All of a sudden I feel like I'm going to lose my lunch.

Charlie opens her mouth wide and looks at me, but by the

time she is ready to say something, the boys are already at the table. Juliet is delicately blotting the edges of her mouth with a napkin. I wonder what her power move is. Whatever it is, I have a feeling I'm about to see it.

Thankfully, Rob comes over and stands directly behind me, placing his hands on my shoulders. I lean my head back on his stomach and close my eyes, briefly. It's the most forward I've been with him in public, but I want to do something to show Juliet that he's taken. That he's mine.

"This is Juliet," Olivia says to Ben, who has scooted himself in next to her and is picking off her plate.

"You have no manners," Charlie announces.

"Tell Dad," Ben says, winking.

Rob takes one of his hands off my shoulders and extends it to Juliet.

"It's been forever," he says. "It's good to see you again."

"Oh my God. Rob?"

Rob laughs. "Yep, that's me." His voice is soft, and he lets his hand brush the back of my arm.

She nods and bites her lower lip. I study her, closely. That might be it. The power move, I mean. It's hard to tell. A lot about her seems, well, *structured*. Like she's got a plan. One thing she doesn't seem is surprised. Not shocked that Rob is clearly with me. Not even remorseful of calling him hot.

"How's your first day back?" he asks.

"Okay, I guess," she says, not taking her eyes off him. "Better now." She glances quickly at me and Charlie to show she doesn't just mean Rob. "Hey, are you going to the dance tomorrow?"

For a second I'm not sure who she's addressing, but then Rob lifts his hand off my hair, and I see Juliet is staring at him.

"Think so," he says.

"Be my date."

I can't possibly have heard her right. She did not just invite Rob, my Rob, to be her date to the school dance. His hand is on my shoulder. We're *touching*.

"Oh, come on, Rose," Juliet says. "You girls are going together. Lend him out. I don't know anyone else. And it would be good to catch up." Her tone of voice has changed. She's talking to me like we actually *are* cousins. Like we've known each other for forever and she's asking to borrow my gray sweater. Not Rob.

I look at Charlie. I'm desperate to have her say something, anything, but she has ripped the baseball hat off of Jake's head and is waving it around. She might as well be in the math cubicles, she's so far away now. Olivia is whispering something to Ben and giggling. I'm alone here.

Rob will turn her down. Any second now he will say "Sorry, I don't think so" or "You should go with the girls." But he doesn't say any of those things. I arch around, and he's staring at her. His expression has changed. He looks confused. Like he doesn't know the answer. *How could he possibly not know the answer?*

"Come on," Juliet says slowly. "It's just a dance." She bites her lip again.

"You should really come with us," I interject. "It'll be fun, and we're getting ready at Olivia's. Her house is, like, the size of Texas." I'm pulling out all the stops, but Juliet's house is probably better stocked than Olivia's. I doubt this is even tempting her.

"I want to go with Rob," Juliet says.

Here's the thing about me: I've never liked confrontation. Ever since I was little, I've been terrified of upsetting people. I'd much rather just keep the peace. Which is fine, usually, but it also means I have absolutely no idea what to do now. Charlie is the one who can tell people off, the one who has no trouble standing up for herself. And me? Well, I'm used to standing behind her.

I'm still wrestling with how to handle this when I hear Rob speak behind me. One word: Sure.

Sure? As in *yes*? I can't have heard him right. I need some kind of clarification. Someone to tell me that, no, Rob did not just agree to escort my cousin, Juliet, to Fall Back. My cousin, Juliet, who thinks he has a hot body. My cousin, Juliet, who couldn't care less about me, or the fact that Rob and I are kinda, sorta together.

"Great," Juliet says. "Then it's all settled. I gotta run." She picks up her tray. She hasn't touched a thing on it. "Ciao," she says to the table. I have a feeling that's her standard departure. And we're going to be hearing it a lot.

Charlie gives her a backhanded wave. She's still yelling at Jake.

"See you later," Juliet says to me. And then, a little lower, "I'm glad I'm back. I think it's going to be a great year."

Charlie said the same thing yesterday, and it already feels like forever ago. Even though I have Rob and should be psyched, I can't help but fear that they both might be wrong.

Scene Six

"I seriously cannot believe you're okay with this," Charlie is saying.

We're all at Olivia's house getting ready for Fall Back. We're in her room, clothes strewn everywhere, and torn-out pages of *InStyle* and *Glamour* on the floor, from which we are trying to get ideas. It's a mess, but it doesn't matter. Ten minutes after we leave, everything will have been cleaned up.

Olivia's is more like a hotel than a house. She has her own suite complete with marble bathroom, walk-in closet, and lounge. You could seriously spend a year in her house and never have to leave. We tried to do that for the weekend, once, but Matt Lester ended up having a party Saturday night, so we didn't make it all the way through.

The lounge off her bedroom is always stocked with our favorite snacks (Twizzlers, lollipops, and Swedish Fish), and she has every single channel on On Demand so you can get any movie you want anytime you want. We don't have that at our house. We don't even have HBO. My parents have never been into TV. It took them until I was fifteen to even get cable.

Tonight there isn't time to indulge in Twizzlers, though. We're late. We were supposed to be there to set up a half hour ago, and I'm experiencing some serious guilt about abandoning Lauren. I can imagine her standing in the courtyard holding up lights to string, looking around for some help. Charlie's never-be-late rule doesn't apply to functions, but tonight I really wish it did. It's upsetting me, and, ignoring Charlie's comment, I ask, again, if anyone has texted her.

"I thought you did?" Olivia says. She's at her vanity, blotting her lips and looking in the mirror. Her blond hair is curled, the product of about seventy-five minutes of serious quality time with her curling iron. Charlie is standing next to her, trying to hip bump her out of the way. Charlie's hair is up, and a few perfect spiral strands loop gracefully down onto her face. Stuck into the edges of the mirror are pictures of us since freshman year. There is one of us making a human pyramid in Charlie's backyard the time we tried to get San Bellaro to start a cheerleading squad. We ditched the idea after about a week, though, when

Charlie refused to accept any new members. There are a few pictures from Malibu, and one of Olivia and Ben eating Popsicles. It must be new. I wonder who took it.

I take my phone and send an apologetic text to Lauren: *We r so late. Sry. B there asap.*

I toss the phone down and then immediately pick it up to see if she's responded. She hasn't.

"It's true, though," Olivia says. "You're handling this really well."

I shrug and tell them the same thing Rob told me yesterday. "She's my cousin. He's just doing me a favor."

"Some favor," Charlie says, shimmying into her red dress.

"They used to be friends too. Plus, she didn't know," I say.

"Whatever," Charlie says. "It's not cool."

"He's not even picking her up," I argue. "And besides, he's not my boyfriend." I want to add *Not yet, anyway,* but I don't.

"I sort of thought tonight might be the night," Charlie says.

"What night?"

"That you and Rob, you know."

"Ooooo," Olivia says. "Really?"

"No," I say. "Come on. We've just kissed." The memory of Rob's lips on mine makes me blush. He was supposed to come over last night, but he got caught up helping his dad repair a car. His dad is obsessed with old cars, and he and Rob have been

when you were mine   *137*

fixing them up together since Rob was a kid. It's kind of sweet, this thing they do together, just the two of them. His dad sells them afterward. Sometimes we'll see someone driving one around town, and Rob will say, "There's another Monteg." Anyway, by the time they finished, it was already nine and he had homework to do. I know this doesn't necessarily mean anything. Rob never ditches out on plans with his dad. It's something I really respect about him. But I would like to know a little more of what to expect tonight. Especially because we're not going to this dance together and we've still just had those few kisses by the Cliffs.

Even so, I can't help but think about what Charlie's saying. So maybe it won't be tonight, but what if Rob and I are headed for a real relationship? Sex would be involved, I guess. Sometimes I picture Rob and me lying in bed together, but he's usually just holding me, his hand in my hair.

"Do you think Ben would like the blue or the yellow?" Olivia asks. She's moved to the full-length mirror and is holding up two dresses, alternating them in front of her body.

"Blue," Charlie says. "He has a thing for blue. Have you seen his bedroom? Even his sheets are . . ."

She stops talking and turns back to the mirror. Olivia looks away, and I can see she's blushing.

"I like the blue," I volunteer.

"What are you wearing?" Charlie asks.

I gesture to Olivia's bed, where I've put my dress. It's silver, something I picked out with my mom this summer at one of those shops by the water that always smell like potpourri.

"You need to own this," my mother had said, grabbing it off the display and thrusting it at me.

My mom is always picking things out for me that are, well, a little trampy. It's not that she wants me to dress slutty, I don't think. She just always says things like "You're only young once" or "That sweater looks way too old for you." Charlie says I'm lucky. She used to have to change her outfits at school, in the bathrooms. But that was before her mom got sick. Now she can wear whatever she wants.

"I dunno," I'd told my mom. "It's kind of . . . flashy."

"Exactly," she had said, and pushed me into the dressing room.

I knew we would buy it even before I put it on. It's a halter top that's completely backless. It's short but not too short and a very sparkly shade of silver. I felt out of place in it—silly, even— but the more the saleslady and my mother oohed and aahed, the more I felt like maybe I didn't look completely ridiculous. After I took it home that night, I tried it on with a pair of light blue heels, and I felt, I don't know, *pretty*. Like I was someone else. Someone in a movie, or a magazine. Even Charlie or Olivia. When I put it on, I felt like the kind of person who belongs in a dress like that. I'm secretly hoping it has the same effect tonight. And that Rob notices.

I slide it on, and Charlie starts hooting.

"You look totally hot!" Olivia squeals. "Rob is going to lose his mind." I roll my eyes, but inside I'm buzzing. I feel full of possibility. Tonight stretches out before me like an ocean. It feels expansive, limitless. Like I could float in it forever.

"We gotta go," I say. I glance at my watch. We're already forty-five minutes late, which means by the time we get there, the dance will have already begun.

"We know, we know," Olivia says. She's running around her room with a tiny clutch, tossing things inside. Charlie is just standing there, smiling at me.

"What?" I say. "What are you looking at?"

"Nothing," she says, mock choking up. "I'm just so proud."

"Done," Olivia calls, snapping her bag closed. "Let's rock."

We leave her room and file out into the hallway. Olivia's staircase is gigantic with an enormous crystal chandelier hanging from the ceiling right smack in the middle of the foyer. It's the kind of staircase you imagine descending from on your wedding day. Charlie makes a fuss of gliding down, and then we follow Olivia into the kitchen, our heels clicking on the marble floors.

"I hear the troops," her stepdad calls. He and Olivia's mom are chasing Olivia's two little brothers around the table. Her mom looks up to give us a frazzled smile. One of Olivia's little brothers, Josh, charges her.

"If you touch me, I will murder you!" Olivia yells, but she's already bending down to hug him back. "Just keep your hands where I can see them," she says, tousling his hair.

"You girls look amazing," Olivia's mother says. "Gabe, where did you put the camera?" Olivia's stepdad grabs it off the kitchen counter and waves for us to follow him out of the kitchen.

Olivia's mom positions us at the front door. "One, two, three," she says. "Smile!" She's holding her leg out to prevent Drew from storming us, and her other arm is positioned on Olivia's stepdad's shoulder. It's an impressive balancing act.

Charlie locks her hand on her hip and juts her arm out, Olivia wiggles her shoulders, and I, per usual, stand in the middle of them, not sure exactly what to do. Unlike them, I don't have a signature picture pose.

"If you put your hand on your hip, it takes off five pounds," Olivia says through her teeth.

I barely have time to register what she's saying before Charlie is dragging me out the door and we're all piling into Big Red, Olivia's mom calling, "Have fun! Be safe!" behind us.

Everyone is already in the courtyard by the time we get to campus. Lauren didn't respond to my text, but she waves at us, looking unconcerned. She's dressed in a periwinkle slip dress that shows off her slim shoulders. Her sandy-blond hair is pulled up in a knot.

"I'm so sorry," I say. "What can we do?"

She waves me off with her hand. "Nothing," she says. "Seriously, no biggie. We're all set."

She's done a great job. The courtyard is strung with twinkle lights and paper lanterns. The trees are sprinkled with silver and gold tinsel, and flower garlands hang down from the breezeway. It reminds me of *A Midsummer Night's Dream*, a play I saw once with my mom in LA. I was ten then, and I didn't really understand much of it, but I remember the set looked like a kind of fairyland. Like magic.

Students are milling around sipping apple cider out of champagne flutes. It doesn't feel like just another school dance. It feels enchanted, important, like maybe something special is happening here tonight.

I spot Jake, Ben, and Rob by the punch table with Charlie and Olivia. Rob is wearing a suit jacket, which he never does. He keeps tugging down the sleeves. It's sort of adorable, actually, how uncomfortable he looks. I can't see Juliet anywhere. She must not be here yet.

In the time it's taken me to talk to Lauren, Charlie and Jake have already started arguing and Ben and Olivia are on the cusp of making out. She's giving him her power move—chest out, stretching—and he's got his arms around her back.

I look at Rob again. He's so cute in his suit jacket and gray pants. He has on a pink-and-white-checkered shirt underneath. It's one of my favorites, and he never wears it.

I want to go over and put my arms around him, but then I remember that, technically, he isn't even here with me. I haven't really let myself think too much about it. I just keep hoping she just won't show up.

As I cross the courtyard, "Kokomo" by the Beach Boys starts playing.

"You know, I think I've been to all of the places in this song," Olivia says. She's holding out her fingers and counting along with the lyrics. "Yep, all seven."

"You are such a snob," Charlie says. Ben seems to have found this comment endearing, though, because he takes Olivia's hand in his and kisses the back of it. She giggles.

I can feel Rob's eyes on me, and I will myself not to look at him. Not yet. I know as soon as I open my mouth, I'll just be Rosie, and I'm enjoying having the dress speak for me, just for a moment.

"Wow," he says. He comes up next to me and runs a hand down my arm. "You're stunning."

"You like it?" I drop my hands by my sides and play with some of the material. I'm feeling just a little bit tipsy from Rob's hand on my arm. Like I've had a drink or something, even though I'm dead sober.

"You look great," he says.

"So where's Juliet?" I ask it casually, but I can see him grimace.

"I dunno," he says. "Haven't spoken to her."

"Oh."

"Rosie, I told you it's no big deal. I'm just doing this for you." He draws me close to him the way he did by the Cliffs. It feels nice, safe. It makes me start to relax. "We're okay, right?"

"Yeah," I say, angling closer to him.

"Good, because regardless of who my technical date tonight is, I want to dance with you."

"Corny," I say, "but I'll take it."

He stabs himself in the chest with his hand. "Only for you."

"Okay, Romeo," Charlie says. "Are we dancing, or what?"

The song changes, and "Walking on Sunshine" starts playing. Charlie thought old songs would be appropriate for the Fall Back theme. "Like throwback," she said. I've always loved this song. It reminds me of summer and being young, and when Rob grabs my hand and starts twirling me on the dance floor, all thoughts of Juliet fly right away.

It's dark out, and as Rob spins me around, the paper lanterns zigzag beams of light across the courtyard. I feel like I do on the swings ride at Six Flags, like the world is going a million miles a minute and yet I'm completely lost in one moment. Things moving by so quickly, they look like they're completely standing still. The best kind of paradox.

Charlie and Jake are getting along for the moment, and Olivia is stuck to Ben, dancing way too slow for this song. I find myself smiling so hard I start to laugh. It's perfect, this moment. So completely wonderful I want to stay here forever.

The song ends, and Rob twirls me one last time. "Nice moves, Rosie," he says. We're both a bit breathless.

My dress has shifted dangerously low, and my hair is wet, some of it matted to the back of my neck. I already feel like a drowned rat, and we practically just got here. I need to freshen up.

"I'm going to go to the bathroom," I say to Rob.

"I'll be waiting for you," he says as he pulls me to him and kisses me once softly on the cheek. He's a little bit sweaty, and the kiss is damp, but I still walk away with my hand over the spot where his lips have just been. It's perfect. This entire night is turning out better than I ever could have imagined.

A few freshman girls are in the bathroom, and they take one look at me and scramble to leave. It's funny to remember feeling that way—small and insecure. Between this dress and Rob's kiss, it seems like such a long time ago.

I'm alone in the bathroom, in front of the mirrors. I feel dizzy, like I need to sit down, except I'm too excited to even stand still. *You're beautiful,* Rob said, and being here now, for the first time since he said it, I think it might be true. I look at this girl in the silver backless dress and *feel* beautiful. I was so silly to think that things might not work out for us, or to even give two seconds to this Juliet thing. It's Rob. And me. And when he kissed me, it felt right. I was so comfortable being close to him.

I mean, Rob was the one who rode behind me the day I took the training wheels off my bike. He was the one who, when I got stung by that wasps' nest while pulling up tomato plants in my mom's garden, bought me sunglasses to cover how swollen my eyes were. He was the one who trained with me every day in the pool at summer camp our fifth-grade year so that I could finally make it to the color orange group. He was there when our dog, Sally, died. He was the one who insisted we have a funeral and even wrote a poem: "Sally did not dillydally. She died today. It's sad to say." He was the one who held me when Charlie and I got in a gigantic fight last year, when I thought that maybe we wouldn't be friends anymore. He was the one who knew it would all be okay.

He knows that Twizzlers are my favorite candy and that up until the fifth grade I thought my middle name was spelled a different way. He's Rob. And the fact that I've known him forever and that he knows me, really knows me, is proof that it was always supposed to be us. That he's the one. And what makes it really remarkable is that he's out there right now, waiting for me.

My body is buzzing with this quiet excitement. I can feel it in my toes and through my fingers. Maybe this is our night. I can't think of anyone else I'd want it to happen with, and standing here now I can picture a lot more than Rob's hands in my hair. Charlie's right. This is going to be the best year ever. And next year Rob and I will both be at Stanford. Suddenly I can see the rest of my life laid out in front of me like a red carpet. All I have to do is step onto it.

I apply some more lip gloss with a shaky finger, smooth out my dress, and walk down the breezeway. I feel invincible. Like Beyoncé in a music video. Like I have my own personal wind machine in front of me.

I can hear the notes of a slow song playing. It's that one from the movie *Ghost*. The one that goes, "Oh, my love, my darling." Usually slow songs make me uncomfortable, but I'm already anticipating being in Rob's arms, having his hands around my back, resting my head on his shoulder. I'm walking so briskly, I don't even notice that I've walked right into someone. "Sorry," I say, not looking up.

"Hang on." Len puts his hand on my arm, stopping me.

"Umm, hey," I say, shaking him off.

"I was actually looking for you," he says.

"Has hell frozen over?"

He cocks his head to the side. "Yeah, it has," he says. "But it's kind of a nice change from this sauna of a summer."

"Is there something you need?" I ask, impatient. I want to get back to Rob. To tell him, absolutely and definitively, I want to be with him.

Len shrugs. "Need? Nah. I just wanted to ask what's up with your man."

"My man?"

"Cut the act. I've seen the groping."

We have not been groping, have we? "There hasn't been any groping."

"You know, you're right. It was nothing compared to what's going on up there." He gestures above the courtyard.

"Up there?"

"Look, don't say I didn't warn you."

He gives me a little salute with two fingers and then stuffs his hands into his pockets, walking backward and away.

"What are you talking about?"

"He's a jackass," Len says, turning. "You heard it from me first."

"Who?" I mutter stupidly, but he's off the breezeway already, and if he's heard me, he doesn't answer.

*　　*　　*

I glance around the courtyard. Charlie and Jake are swaying together, although it looks a little like Charlie is leading. Ben and Olivia are completely tangled up in the corner. It's impossible to see whose limbs are whose. I can't seem to spot Rob, but I still feel dizzy. It's making it hard to focus.

I weave in and out of people on the dance floor. Couples, swaying. Matt and Lauren are locked in an embrace, and I wonder, briefly, if they're together. Stranger things have happened, I guess.

I'm standing in the middle of the dance floor when instinctively I look up. And as soon as I do, I understand what Len meant.

There's this little balcony over the breezeway that was part of the old mansion and that the school kept, even though it serves no practical function. It's small, probably seven feet by four or something, and it's covered in ivy.

Rob's up there. His brown hair is falling slightly into his eyes, and the collar of his shirt has come undone. He's swaying to the music, just like I imagined. He looks handsome and strong and charming all at once, and I want more than I ever have to be in his arms. The problem, though, is that somebody else already is.

He's holding her. His arms are around her back and her head is on his shoulder, and they're swaying slowly, so slowly they look like they're not even moving. The girl in his arms should be me, but it's not, not even close. The girl he's swaying with is none other than Juliet.

There's something in the way that he's holding her that makes me stop in my tracks. It's not friendly and it's not platonic. He's holding her like she's a leaf, like she might just at any moment blow away in the wind. She looks like a ballerina in his arms, so small and delicate and fragile. And then I see him lean over and smell her hair, and it's like someone has just knocked the wind out of me. I just stand there, gaping. They're so close together, you couldn't even fit a feather between them.

I blink, but they're still there. She doesn't pick her head up off his shoulder. He doesn't move his hands from her back. They could be a statue, that's how still they are standing together.

Is anyone else seeing this? Olivia and Ben are still smothering each other, but I don't see Charlie. I suddenly desperately don't want her to know. I don't want anyone to know. I want to take back the last forty-eight hours, to avoid this humiliation. I want to run as far away as I possibly can from here and never look back. I want to reverse time. I want to do a million things rather than stand here, watching them.

I finally look away from them, and Len's face comes into view. He's looking at me, and I expect him to smirk, to roll his eyes, but he doesn't do anything. He just looks away.

Then Charlie is there. Her red hair has fallen out of its bun, and it's hanging around her face like braches on a weeping willow tree. She's seen them too, and she's looking at me, her expression mirroring mine. She crosses over to me in two paces, and I feel her take my hand in hers. She squeezes it twice, the way she did on our first day of high school in the car when I was nervous. The way she always does when things get to be just a little bit too much. It's her way of saying, "I'm here."

And then, still holding my hand, she leads me away. Off the dance floor, through the breezeway, past Cooper House, and out to upper, where she opens the door and helps me inside Big Red. It's only once we're pulling out of the parking lot that I start to cry.

Act Three

Scene One

I wake up before my alarm. All night, all weekend, I'm actually not sure I have been sleeping at all. I've been in and out of consciousness, hoping for something to change but knowing it won't. My chest hurts, or is it my heart? It's hard to tell. People are always throwing around the term "broken heart," but this *is* physically painful. So much so that as I lie in bed, waiting for the buzzer to sound, I press my hands over my heart, like if I apply enough pressure, I can keep the pieces from drifting apart.

"Charlie's here," my mom calls.

Obnoxiously early, again. Except when I glance at my clock, I see that it's 7:10. We're already late. I have no idea if my alarm went off. Maybe I never even set it.

"I'll be right there." I leap out of bed and throw on yesterday's jeans. I pull on a white tank top and a blue cardigan that's dangling over my desk chair.

I've been avoiding Charlie's calls and texts. Olivia's, too. I don't really know what to say to them, and I don't feel like hearing how sorry they are for me. Especially since I haven't heard it from Rob. He hasn't called me or come over. Which makes me feel like he isn't going to apologize, because whatever happened Friday night is just the beginning of something else.

The worst part is, I'm not even sure he was home once this weekend. I stayed up Friday night, almost until morning, just to see if he got in. He never did. No tires on the gravel. No bedroom light. Nothing.

"Everything okay?" Mom asks when I come drudging into the kitchen. I know I probably look like a mess. I haven't washed my hair since Friday, and I didn't even bother trying to find my makeup bag this morning.

"Yeah," I say.

"You sure? You've been really quiet." She puts her hands on her hips and peers at me, the way she does when she knows I'm not telling the whole truth. I'm surprised she even noticed. She and my dad have been locked in his study whispering for most of the weekend.

I perk my voice up and give her a quick kiss on the cheek. "Don't worry."

"What am I, chopped liver?" My dad is sitting at the kitchen counter, and he taps his cheek with his index finger. I go over to him, and he pulls me into a hug. "Knock 'em dead, cookie," he whispers to me. There's no reason for him to say that today, but I'm not surprised. He has always known when something's not right, and how to make it better. And today, more than anything, I wish I could go back to being a little kid, when my dad calling me cookie could turn back time and erase anything that was wrong. Instead I put on a smile, steal a sip of my dad's coffee, and head out to Charlie's honking car.

Olivia is in the back, her arms looped around the front seat. Twice in a week. We've definitely hit a new record.

"Hey," I say. "Sorry I'm late." I slip in and click my seat belt into place. Maybe if I act normal, the world will play along.

"How are you?" Charlie asks. She's turned to me wearing this grave expression, her features all set in a row. I expected her to be pissy about my being nonresponsive all weekend, or at least about my being late this morning, but if she is, she's not acting like it.

"Um, fine. Are we going?"

Charlie glances back at Olivia.

"He's an asshole," Olivia says.

"She's a bitch," Charlie says.

I shrug. "It's fine."

"It is not fine," Charlie says. She has that tone she uses with Jake when they're about to get into a fight. I suddenly have the intense desire to bolt from this car. To run back into my house, curl up under my covers, and just never come out.

"It's not like he was my boyfriend or anything," I say.

"What?" Olivia interjects. "That's so unfair."

"It's true," I say. "We weren't *together* together. And she was his date and all. . . ." My voice trails off, and I look out the window. We're rolling out of my driveway. In the rearview mirror I can see my parents in our doorway. My dad is reaching up to the light fixture on the porch, and my mom has a hand on his back, holding him up for balance. I purposefully keep my eyes trained on my house as we pull away. I don't look to the left, to Rob's.

"I mean, I thought she was a bitch for asking to go with him," Olivia says, "but this is too much. *Kissing* him? She's your cousin."

They kissed?

"We're aware," Charlie says. I can feel her glance at me, but I keep my eye trained on the passing trees. Of course they kissed. They were practically glued together when we left. But the thought of his lips on hers makes me feel like someone is trying to suck my stomach out through my belly button and shove the whole thing back down my throat.

"It's fine," I force myself to say. "Honestly."

None of us says much more after that. We drive in silence, aside from the music that creeps steadily from the stereo. Something low and dull that I don't recognize.

When Charlie broke up with Matt, her sophomore-year boyfriend and the first guy she slept with, it was bad. She listened to crappy R&B love songs on repeat for, like, a week. And she didn't even love him, I don't think. Once, she said she liked that he wanted to be a doctor, but that was the only time she talked about anything besides the way he looked in a sweater.

The truth is that I feel humiliated and betrayed. How could Rob have been standing there, holding her, when just a few nights ago he was holding me? The entire school saw them together, dancing and kissing, and now I'm what? Yesterday's hookup? The idiot who believed her best friend wanted to be her boyfriend? And who trusted that her cousin wanted to be a friend, rather than a backstabber?

When we get to upper, I try hard not to look for Rob's car. I don't want to see him. I'm afraid that if I do, I'll either fall apart, beg him to change his mind, or say something that will cut him out of my life forever. I want him gone, but I also want him here. That's the worst part. The fact that I want him to make this better. That I *need* him to make this better. He's the only one who can fix it. Whenever there's a problem, Rob's the one that handles it. I need him to handle this, too. For him to call himself a jerk, maybe even punch himself in the face, and then bring himself back to me.

Olivia makes a move to head over to Ben, who has driven her car and is now waiting for her, but Charlie grabs her by her MIAMI book bag, and the three of us make our way down to assembly with Ben trailing behind.

But we're late, of course, because of me, which means assembly has already started and there is no way for us to get to senior seats. We actually have to stand in the Trenches. We've never stood here, not once, and all of the things that are wrong with this day sort of congeal into the fact that I don't have a seat. That I've been kicked out of my whole life.

I see Rob in his usual spot on the far side, and my stomach flips so badly, I think I'm going to be sick. I hate myself for still thinking he looks perfect. Jeans and a green T-shirt, the one with the tree on it that I love, and for a second I think maybe he wore it for me, that when he was picking out his clothes this morning he saw it and thought of me. That he wanted to be wearing it when he tells me Friday night was a mistake, that he was only humoring Juliet, and where did I disappear to after we danced.

But then I know that is never going to happen, because sitting next to him, in a black skirt and pink candy–colored tank top, is Juliet.

Charlie puts her arm over my shoulder. Olivia stands on the other side, arms crossed, Ben behind her. They're flanking me, like human pieces of armor.

Rob can't see me from this angle, which is worse than if he could, because it means I can stare as hard and as long as I like. He whispers something to her, and she laughs, then brings her finger to her lips to tell him to be quiet. But it's in that cute way certain girls have that lets everyone know they don't really mean it. That she wants him to go on bothering her forever. Even while turning him down she's inviting him. Forget the lip biting. This is definitely her power move.

He's leaning so close to her that it takes everything in me not to run right over and tear them apart. And part of me wants to. Part of me wants to fight. To tell him to pick me. To beg him to stop what he's doing, erase the last three days, and just come back. But I'm already fading into the background, like a house in the rearview mirror. I can feel myself getting smaller and smaller, shrinking, so that when Mr. Johnson says, "Have a great day, everyone!" I think I might have just disappeared.

And then assembly is over and students grab their bags and descend from the bleachers. We start getting trampled, jostled to the side. Olivia yells, "Owww!" pushing back against the crowd, but I let it shuffle me outside.

I feel like a pebble in the river—small, smooth, and sinking.

I don't even have enough weight to settle, though. I'm just kicked forward by gravity.

Someone's hand is on my shoulder, and I turn around. It's Charlie, and she buries her chin into my hair and whispers, "She is so going down. Don't worry." I wish there really was something we could do to fix this. That ostracizing Juliet would in some way keep them apart. More than that, though, I just wish this wasn't happening. That she'd never invited him. That he'd never said yes. And that it hadn't taken me so long to realize he was the one I wanted to be with.

"It's fine," I say.

"It is not fine," Charlie says again.

"Listen, I'm going to be late for calc." I wiggle myself out of her grip. "I'll catch up with you at lunch?"

"Okay," Charlie says, but she's squinting at me, trying to read something off of my face. "Hey, Rosie," she says. The sound of my nickname startles me. Rob is the only one who usually calls me that.

"Yeah?"

"It's going to be okay." She says it firmly, like she's trying to convince herself as much as me.

"I know," I say, but it's not true. For the first time it feels like nothing is going to be okay. Like something went very, very wrong. That the course of things, the natural order, has been tampered with. As I trudge up to the math cubicles, I can't help but keep thinking, *This isn't how it was supposed to go.*

The day moves absurdly slowly, like it's dragging its heels. Everything seems to be happening in slow motion, like I'm falling backward, except I never hit the ground. I wonder if this is how it's going to be from now on. If I'm going to be stuck in high school forever.

AP Bio is even worse than last week. Mrs. Barch gives us a pop quiz at the beginning of the period that I haven't done the reading for because I've been moping around my room all weekend like somebody died.

I literally do not know the answer to a single one of these questions. I'm sandwiched between Lauren, who is bent down intently, methodically working through the problems, and Len, who is scribbling animatedly, like he's trying to piss me off. I feel beyond pathetic. Even the class joker is managing to ace this thing.

The worst part is that after we're finished, Mrs. Barch makes us grade each other's quizzes while she runs an errand. Since it's an AP class, we're supposed to "use our sense of merit" while she's gone. Of course, since Len's my lab partner, we're meant to swap quizzes.

He gives me that lopsided smirk and rubs his hands together. "Hand it over, Rosaline."

He tosses his to me freely, like he's Charlie passing me a spar-kling water at lunch. I look it over. I'm surprised to see his hand-writing is actually neat and his problems look fairly organized.

"Since when have you shown any initiative?" I ask, holding it up.

He shrugs. "I was in the mood to study this weekend."

"Right. Sure. You just felt like it."

He smirks. "Why so blue?"

"Mrs. Barch is ruining my life," I mutter.

"She's not so bad," he says, knocking me on the back. "You know she runs drama?"

"How is that relevant?"

He makes a face like, *Yikes,* and holds his hands up. "You get extra credit if you help out with one of her plays."

"For bio?"

Len nods. "So are you going to show me that thing?" He ges-tures to the quiz that's still tucked neatly under my elbow.

"I didn't . . . ," I start, but I'm not sure what to say, so I give up and hand it to him.

He whistles. "I didn't think you had it in you."

"Are you kidding me?" I hiss. "I couldn't answer a single ques-tion."

"I know," he says. "Ballsy."

"Not ballsy. Incompetent."

"Relax," he says. "It's a quiz, not the goddamn SATs."

"Relax?" I say, my face getting hot from frustration. "Do you know quizzes are twenty percent of our grade? If I get an F on this one, that means that even if I pull As on all the rest, the odds of still getting a B in this class even if I work and study constantly for the rest of the semester is very likely. And a B is a 3.0. Do you know what Stanford's admission average is? It's like a 4.3."

"Breathe."

I exhale and fold my head down onto my desk, knocking my forehead on the wood. When I look up, Len is smiling.

"You're so dramatic," he says. "The way I see it, it's not that big of a deal. But if it really means that much to you, fine."

He takes his quiz out from under my hand and erases his name, putting mine in its place. Then he takes my quiz and erases mine, writing his own.

"Could you cool it with the hysteria now?" he says. "'Cause that panic attack was really getting in the way of my Monday."

My mouth hangs open as he puts a one hundred on one quiz and a zero on the other and hands both of them to Lauren to pass up to the front.

"What did you do?"

He puts his hand on my shoulder. "Helped a fellow classmate out. Revolutionary, I know."

"You just *cheated*."

He looks behind him. "I cannot catch a break around here."

"You're going to get an F now."

"So?"

"Don't you care?"

"Not really."

"*That's* your problem," I say, anger boiling up to my throat.

"My problem?"

"You don't care about anything."

"Correction: I don't care about anything unimportant."

"But I just explained to you—"

Len holds up his hand. "I get you're anxious about Stanford, or whatever. All I'm saying is that there's more to life than obsessing over quizzes."

"I get it. I'm lame. Just some totally type A spaz you have to work with. I just can't believe you'd go so far to prove it."

Len laughs. "You must have had a really rough weekend. Because you sound insane."

I sniff. "I did."

"Look, that guy's an ass," Len says.

"Rob?"

"No, Spartacus. Of course Rob."

I blink. I'm not sure what to say. Thankfully, the bell rings before I'm forced to answer.

"Don't sweat the quiz," Len says, stuffing his notebook into his seemingly empty backpack. "See you tomorrow."

I'm blowing my nose, leaving bio, when Rob grabs my elbow.

"I need to talk to you."

Len is in front of me, and for one brief moment I see him glance at Rob's hand on my arm. But then he's walking off toward the math cubicles.

I'm so defeated by the quiz debacle and surprised by Rob's presence that I let him lead me away, over to behind Cooper House. It isn't until we're facing each other, alone, that I pull away.

"Look," he says a few times, and then sighs, starting over. "Here's the thing," he says. "I didn't expect this to happen."

"What?" I ask. We both know *what*, but it feels important that he clarify.

"Her," he says. "You know, Juliet."

"It doesn't matter," I say. I don't want him to see that I'm upset. I bite my bottom lip and will my voice steady.

"It does matter. The thing is, I didn't expect to fall for her. But there's just something about her. It feels right."

I don't say anything, because the fact that he used "fall for" instead of "meet" has sent my heart throbbing. It feels like someone's just jabbed the sharp end of a pencil right into the center.

"It's like fate, or destiny or something," he continues.

"You don't believe in fate."

Rob inhales and looks at me. "I care about you, Rosie. You know I do. We're friends. Best friends." The sound of the word makes me lose it. *Friends.* That's what I've been telling myself for years, what I've been trying to talk myself into for months. He was the one who told me I was beautiful, who asked me out, who kissed me. He was the one who set this thing in motion, and now that I'm here, actually wanting to be with him, he wants to take it all back.

"We are? That's news to me." He looks taken aback. Hurt, even. Good, let him. "As far as I'm concerned, we're not friends anymore."

"But—" He swings his arms around and grabs on to his elbows. "Rosie?"

"I'm serious," I say. I'm fighting back tears now. I know I need to leave before I lose my cool. "You made your choice. Live with it."

Then I turn and walk away. And I walk until I start running. And I run until I'm sprinting. Past Cooper House and the math cubicles and all the way down to the lower soccer field. I don't stop until I'm at the edge of campus. And then I sit down and for what seems like the millionth time in a handful of hours, I let myself cry.

Scene Two

"So we're going to Malibu this weekend," Charlie says. She has Lauren's three-ring binder, the one she uses for SAC, and she's flipping through it.

We're in Olivia's room on her bed, a gigantic box of Twizzlers between us. After I pulled myself together post-bio and told them what happened, Charlie suggested we cut sixth and seventh periods and leave early. Usually I wouldn't be into this, given the Stanford plan, but today it seems to make sense.

Olivia, per usual, was not difficult to convince. She's not so worried about college next year, mostly because her stepdad has already made some deal with USC wherein he donates a building and she gets to go. It's not that Olivia is a bad student, it's just that school isn't really her priority. It doesn't have to be.

Olivia is standing in front of her mirror modeling a top she got over the weekend. It's purple with white stripes and accentuates her boobs.

"Cute," I say.

"Charlie?" Olivia asks. She turns sideways and sends the mirror a seductive stare.

"Mhm," Charlie says, not looking up. "Guys, seriously, I think we need to go."

"I'll tell Ben," Olivia says. She lifts her shirt up and over her head and stands there in her bra. It's pink and brown with a bow in the middle. I'm pretty sure her underwear matches. Olivia always buys sets. It's her thing. Like a seven, except only Charlie and I know about it. And maybe a few girls in gym class. Ben?

Charlie tosses her binder down and glares at Olivia. "I don't think you get what's going on here."

"What?" Olivia asks. Her hands are on her naked hips.

"Ben is going to want to bring *Rob*," Charlie says.

Olivia wiggles her nose and sighs. "We'll just tell him not to."

"No," I say. "I don't want him to think this is a problem. I don't want him to think anything."

Olivia shakes her head. Charlie nods.

"It's okay," Charlie says. She's talking slowly now. "You're allowed to feel totally screwed over."

"Look, we don't need to talk about this anymore. Like I said, he was never my boyfriend. We had one date, that's all."

"Okay," Charlie says, but I can tell she's not convinced. Charlie has an impeccable BS detector. One time she busted Olivia for ditching our plans to see *Pretty in Pink* at this indie theater downtown. Olivia said she had a dentist appointment, but Charlie caught her making out with the Belgian at her house. She actually made us drive over, just to prove it.

Realistically speaking, everyone is going to show up in Malibu anyway. Everyone always finds out about Olivia's parties. Inevitably Jake tells John and Matt, who tell Darcy, who tells everyone. I think there were something like seventy-one juniors at her house at the end of last year. I don't think this party will be quite like that one, but Rob will find out anyway. The question is just whether he'll actually show or not.

"Do you think he'd bring her?" Olivia asks.

"I don't know," Charlie says. "Are they together?"

"Yeah," I say, "I guess so." Rob used the word "destiny." I'm pretty sure that means they're at least considering making things official. I slide a Twizzler out of the wrapper and snap off the end with my teeth.

"We need new swimsuits," Olivia says, like this is our real problem.

Last year Olivia's parents took the three of us to Acapulco with their family for spring break. She had gone shopping before our trip and went armed with five new Lilly Pulitzer swimsuits. The sensory overload kind with the neon pink. When we got home, she was wailing about how she didn't make out with anyone the entire time even though there were tons of cute boys at the hotel.

"Maybe that's because you had electric-green elephants all over your body," Charlie said. Olivia pretended to be offended, but I hardly think that was the reason, anyway. I think she already had a thing for Ben.

"Fine," Charlie says, "but I think we should focus on the real issue here."

"I need a new black bikini." Olivia's rifling through her drawers now, things flying everywhere.

"Which is?" I ask.

"What we're going to do about Juliet," Charlie finishes.

"We could toilet paper her house," Olivia says. She's on her hands and knees, fishing a purple bikini top out of the bottom of her dresser.

"We're not twelve," Charlie says. She rolls her eyes at me and runs a Twizzler between her palms. "We need to get her out of here."

"Like make her quit school?" Olivia asks.

"Like make her move back to LA. If she wasn't here, this definitely would not be a problem."

"Maybe she'll sleep with Mr. Davis," Olivia offers.

"They'd just fire him," I say. I don't want to keep having this conversation, because getting back at Juliet won't help. It won't fix anything.

"True," Charlie says. "But seriously, Rose, snap out of it. This is not okay. *You're* not okay." She tosses a Twizzler in my direction, then perks up. "Do you remember when Fester first started school?"

"Brittany?" Olivia asks. She hops onto the bed, and Charlie sends her an annoyed look.

"Yes. She transferred in halfway through sophomore year and immediately tried out for drama," Charlie says.

"Mrs. Barch runs drama now," I say. Charlie looks at me like she has no idea why I know this, or why I've volunteered it.

"Anyway," she says, "she fell in love with Matt, remember? He was doing that Julia Roberts play." She waves her hand around like she can't quite remember.

"*My Fair Lady*?" I ask.

"Right."

"That's not Julia Roberts," Olivia says.

"Seriously?" Charlie asks. Olivia nudges her, and Charlie shrugs her off.

"Anyway, he wasn't into her, clearly. We were dating." She looks at each of us to confirm this information. We nod. "She completely fell apart and almost quit school," she says, like the point is almost irrelevant now. "I'm just saying."

"But Rob *likes* Juliet." Olivia bites her lip and looks at me. "It's not the same thing, is it?"

"So? You think Rob has any idea what he's doing? He's blinded by her hair or something," Charlie spits out.

I instinctively pull my ponytail over my shoulder and run my hand through it. I don't want Juliet to fall apart, but I also don't want Rob to be with her. I just don't want any of this.

"You know what I mean," Charlie says quietly.

"So we just need to get Rob to break up with her?" Olivia's eyebrows are furrowed, and she's looking at Charlie with a mixture of confusion and something else. Sadness, maybe, but it's hard to tell.

Scene Three

By Friday I'm somehow in the wings of the auditorium with Len, adjusting lightbulbs. On Wednesday, Mrs. Barch hit us with another pop quiz, and this time I didn't let Len switch our papers. I got a sixty-eight, so I currently need all the extra credit points I can get.

They're doing *Macbeth*. And so much for hiding out here with all the theater geeks. Turns out, in addition to being Rob's new girlfriend, my cousin is also a talented actress. She landed the role of Lady Macbeth. The news spread fast at school that she used to be an actress in LA. Nothing big, just some pilots and commercials, but enough to warrant some serious Internet presence.

Charlie is convinced that Juliet is the paper towel girl. "The one who does the commercials with the dog," she says. Olivia and I just shake our heads. "God, do you guys never watch TV?"

We look it up. Charlie is right. Not only is Juliet the paper towel girl, but she's also the Super Soaker girl and the allergy girl.

By some stroke of luck, my thespian cousin and I share no classes together, so at least I only see her between classes and at lunch. And it seems like she and Rob eat off campus most of the time, so even that hasn't been much of a problem. There's something about watching her onstage that feels comforting. Like I'm keeping tabs on her. Like at least I know she's not with Rob.

The Belgian is here too. He's playing Macbeth, which makes sense, because Mrs. Barch is obsessed with the Belgian. I think it's because he's basically the closest thing to British she's ever going to get. From my place in the wings I can see her fussing over him, asking him if he needs some water and making Lucy Stern, her sophomore assistant, fetch it for him.

Right now Juliet and the Belgian are wandering around the stage, taking directions from Mrs. Barch, who keeps looking at her clipboard and yelling things like "Stage right!" I don't know much about Mrs. Barch outside science, but I'm pretty sure she has no actual theater background. Which is probably why this entire thing feels more like a parody of a play than an actual play.

"Hey, a little help here?" Len is next to me, rifling through a box of big metal clamps.

"Sorry. What's up?"

He hands me a clamp and instructs me to keep the light still. "Right there. Good."

He tightens it in place and then nods for me to let go. It's dark up in the wings and kind of chilly despite the fact that it's eighty degrees outside and barely even September. I hug my arms to my chest and watch as Len works, brow furrowed.

"Why are you here, anyway?" I ask.

He answers without looking at me. "Because thanks to that quiz of yours, I'm currently pulling a D in bio. I need the points too."

"Yeah, but I thought you didn't care about grades."

He straightens up. "Why don't you tell me why I'm here. I'm sure your answer is better."

I glance down at the stage. "Just show me what to do."

"I've been at this awhile," he says. "I got it."

I plunk down in a plastic chair and look at him. "So when you're not taking bullets in bio or playing piano, you're stage crew?"

"Playing piano?"

Thank God it's dark, because my face instantly goes red. I can feel the heat creep up my neck like water rising in a bathtub.

"Um, yeah. Didn't you used to take lessons or something?"

Len crosses his arms. It's dark, but I can see the edges of a smirk. "Keeping tabs on me, Rosaline?"

"You wish."

"Don't worry. I remember," he says, handing me a red slide. "Here, take this."

"You do?"

"I may be—what do you call me? Vile?—but I'm not an idiot." I see something flit across his face. Like the sunset of a smile.

"I didn't— I mean, I didn't say that."

Len looks amused. "No? Must have been one of your minions." He picks up a metal clamp and then sets it back down. "So what happened?" he asks.

"I don't know. I just stopped playing. I got busy with school, and it was hard to find the time to practice."

Len shakes his head. "No. Not with piano, with him."

"Oh." I fiddle with the red slide. I put my hand underneath. It looks sort of distorted, like it's under one of those gigantic microscopes I used to have when I was little, to look at bugs. "I dunno."

"Here." He takes the slide out of my hands and slips it onto a light. Then he turns the light on. Immediately a spot on the stage is illuminated. It startles Juliet, and she curses, looking up.

"It's kind of like playing God," I say.

"Exactly." He hands me a green slide and helps me set it in place. Juliet jumps again.

"I like this," I say.

"I can tell. You have it out for Lady Macbeth, huh?"

I shrug. "She's my cousin."

He flips on a blinding yellow spotlight, and Juliet throws her hands up in the air. "Doesn't really answer my question."

Len stays perfectly still, looking at me. He looks different when he isn't busy smirking at me. He reminds me of one of those marble sculptures we're always reading about in history class. Even his curly hair looks kind of like the *David*'s. Who would have guessed that Len is actually kind of handsome?

I hunch my shoulders and blow some air out through my lips, biding time. "She's fine," I say.

"Convincing," Len says, but he doesn't move.

Down below, the Belgian looks bored and he's bouncing slightly, like he's listening to music. Actually, he is. I see the small snake of white wire that runs up to his ears. His iPod buds are in, and every time Mrs. Barch shouts something at them, he looks at Juliet. Which is actually a good bet, because she seems to be taking this incredibly seriously.

"This doesn't feel authentic," Juliet says, her hands on her hips.

"I agree," Mrs. Barch says. "I'm needing more from you."

"From me?"

"Yes," Mrs. Barch says, nodding. "You're not feeling it."

"I am feeling it," Juliet snaps. "I've already played this role. Twice."

"Well, our productions are really closer to community theater than a high school performance."

"Community theater isn't even good," Juliet says, "and this *is* a high school performance. I've done *commercials*."

Mrs. Barch has a look on her face that I've seen before. It's the worst kind of déjà vu. In chem sophomore year whenever students were late to class, she'd lock the doors. The lab classrooms have glass sliding doors, so she'd just stand there, on the other side, staring at the students who were late. It was so terrifying that the few times I knew I wouldn't be on time, I just ditched altogether.

Juliet, however, is staring right back at her. They look like they're sending death beams through their eyes. I honestly think they might start cat fighting right here in the auditorium, but then Juliet blinks and looks away. Rob has just come in.

She runs to him and throws her arms around his neck. Mrs. Barch seems flustered and goes over to the Belgian, who keeps nodding and smiling at whatever it is that she's saying in low, hushed tones. She doesn't seem concerned by his response, though. Maybe she thinks there's a language barrier. Olivia was convinced he couldn't speak English for the first two weeks they were dating. When Charlie asked her how she could possibly not know, she just shrugged and said, "We don't really talk that much. But I'm so into his hair."

I glance over at Rob and Juliet. He's holding her just like he was at Fall Back on Friday. Delicately, but firmly. Like she's something that might break or run away.

"Okay, Banquo. You ready?" Mrs. Barch asks.

"Yep," Rob says, releasing Juliet.

"Banquo?" I whisper to Len, who's still just standing there. "Who's Banquo?"

He picks up a script off the floor and flips through it. Then he hands it to me, pointing at a name.

Great, so he's in the play too? Just what I need, to watch the two of them onstage for two months.

Mrs. Barch has directed them into position, but Rob isn't paying attention. He's just looking at Juliet. He looks incredulous, assuming I got the word right on the SATs. Like he can't quite believe she's there. With him.

When Rob and I were in the third grade, we used to play "one, two, three, four, I declare a thumb war" in the car. His hands were bigger than mine, and eventually he'd win, but we used to argue about whether it was against the rules to "hide" or not. Meaning, was I allowed to drop my thumb down by my fingers so he couldn't catch me? Debates on the subject were usually settled with Rob's mom buying us ice cream. But right now, above him, hidden in the wings, I can't help but feel a little like my thumb. Like I'm hiding because I know the second I reveal myself, I will lose. And I'm just not ready for that.

"Hey," Len says, "you still with me here? I could use a hand."

I blink and look at him. The lights are coming up, and it's easier to see now, which lucky for me makes him fully aware of the tears that are sliding down my cheeks.

"Yeah," I say, swiping the back of my hand across my face. Len looks away and down at the stage, like he's giving me some privacy.

"What happened?" he asks after a minute. He doesn't take his eyes off Rob and Juliet, but something about his question makes me feel like he's staring right into me. Like I can't lie to him because he's already seen the truth.

"We had a thing for a minute," I whisper. "It didn't work out." I expect the confession to make me feel worse, but it doesn't. It actually makes me feel a tiny bit better. Like a small weight has been lifted.

"Then he wasn't your guy," Len says. I glance at him. His jaw is set, and he looks stern. Even a little angry. It's unnerving.

"I guess," I say.

Len shakes his head. "You don't get it," he says. "If he walked away from you, to her, then he wasn't yours."

"How do you know?" I say. "What if he was and everything got screwed up?"

Len smirks. "It doesn't work that way."

"Oh, really?" I say. "How does it work, then? Enlighten me."

Len sighs, like he's already frustrated. "Look, I don't really know how else to put this. You don't need to worry about some dumb guy falling in love with you. You're *you*."

"Exactly," I say. I'm me. Rose Caplet. Plain brown hair and brown eyes and the daughter of a history professor, not a senator. I'm not on magazine covers, and I don't do allergy commercials. I don't even *drive*.

Len turns to me, and he's looking at me so intensely, I think he might have just sucked the air out of my lungs. All of a sudden I feel like I can't breathe. "Sometimes," he starts, "the hardest part about letting someone go is realizing you were never meant to have them."

His words hang in the air as Mrs. Barch dismisses the actors below. She cautions them to get their acts together before the next rehearsal. Juliet looks annoyed. The Belgian just shrugs. Rob doesn't seem to hear anything; he's just staring at Juliet.

I'm thinking about what Len just said, how he has it all wrong. Rob and I were meant to be together. This isn't about letting go of him; it's about balancing things back out. About righting whatever went completely wrong when Juliet stepped onto this campus.

Then, like it's no big deal, Len stretches. "Looks like our

work here is done." He glances down to where Rob and Juliet are walking out of the auditorium, arm in arm. "Any fun weekend plans?" he asks me.

"No," I lie. We're going to Malibu. In fact, our stuff is already packed and we're leaving right after I'm finished with this rehearsal, but I can't tell Len. Charlie would kill me if I invited him. Not that I think he'd want to go. Besides Dorothy and Brittany, I'm not really sure who he hangs out with, but something tells me spending the weekend with Charlie, me, and Olivia isn't high on his list.

"You should make some." He grabs his backpack up by the handle. "Don't let some guy stand in the way."

Some guy. Right. I think about explaining this to Len. That Rob is not *some guy*. That I'm not the kind of girl that cries over boys. That this is different. That he was the one. But that sounds ridiculous, even in my head, so I know how it would sound coming out of my mouth. To Len.

"See ya," he says, and then he's hoisting his backpack onto his shoulder and heading down the stairs before I even have a chance to say good-bye.

"Where have you beeeen?" Olivia asks when I get to upper. She's leaning against her car, and Charlie is inside, in the front seat. Charlie has her sunglasses on even though it's completely cloudy out. The telltale sign that she's pissed or upset about something.

Probably the fact that I'm late. I went and dropped my books off at my locker after rehearsal, but it didn't take more than five minutes, and I told them that we would probably run over.

"Sorry," I say. "Rehearsal. You knew this."

Olivia huffs, and I climb into the backseat. "Hey," I say to Charlie, poking her in the shoulder.

"Jake is taking Big Red," she says. "They're meeting us there after surfing." She turns around and slides her glasses up. Her face is blotchy. "I saw Rob get in with them."

Olivia apparently has not heard this before now, because she spins around and puts her hand on my knee, right where Rob touched me after dinner the other night. It makes me jump.

"I'm sorry," Charlie says. "I'm so fucking pissed at him."

Charlie rarely curses. One of her theories is that people respect you less if you curse. Plus, she reasons, this way, when you really need a curse word, you pull it out and bam, it works like a shotgun. *Everyone* listens. Charlie is very into everyone listening to her.

"At least Juliet won't be there," I squeak out.

"My feelings exactly," Charlie says. The red is fading from her neck, and she looks at Olivia and lets out a long breath. "We could totally call Jake and cancel, but maybe Rob just needs some time away with us to realize he's a moron. And we can enact Project Get Rid of Juliet."

"Guys are stupid," Olivia says, like she's contributing something revelatory.

"Rob misses you. I'm sure he does. Maybe this Juliet thing was just a phase. Like the time Jake decided he was into flannel," Charlie says.

Olivia wrinkles her nose and starts the car.

"Should we pick up bagels on the way?" Charlie asks.

"One step ahead of you." Olivia reaches behind her and pulls up a bag from Grandma's. She wags it in front of Charlie's face.

"Olivia Diamond, I adore you," Charlie says, snatching it out of her hands.

I slump back in my seat as we pull out of the parking lot. What if Charlie is right? I mean, it's a long shot, and I know that. But what if some time away might make him realize his mistake? We have serious history. You can't just throw all of that away on a whim. And he must be missing me. I know he is. I keep opening my phone to text him or pulling up my email when something funny happens. It feels like the entire world is composed of our inside jokes. Everything reminds me of him. Even just seeing the mailbox this morning made me think of the time in the sixth grade when we snuck out in the middle of the night to switch our mailboxes. We thought it would be a funny April Fools' joke on our parents. We ended up breaking both of them, though, and had to use four months of our allowances to replace them.

Grilled cheese makes me think of the time we tried to make some with my hair straightener. Math class makes me think of last spring, when Rob swore he had helped Mr. Stetzler pick out Converse at Foot Locker. My room reminds me of watching DVDs together. Even my parents are reminders of Rob. Like the entire world is reflecting him back to me in every single surface. He must be seeing me, too. . . . How could he not?

"Music, please," Charlie says, holding her palm up like she's asking me to slap her high five.

I spot Olivia's iPod on the seat next to me and hand it to her. She puts on "Stop! In the Name of Love," and we all start singing along. When we were younger, Juliet and I would put on performances for our parents in my living room. We would dress up in my mom's cocktail dresses, the old ones from her brief Hollywood days, and make everyone gather around. Inevitably I would get shy right before, though, and Juliet would have to sing the entire thing herself.

Thinking about that now, it feels like thinking about a different person. The Juliet I knew isn't here now. She'd never do this.

"Can I talk to you guys about something?" Olivia asks. She turns down the music, and Charlie makes a sound like she's choking in disbelief.

"Be still my heart," Charlie says. "She has silenced the Supremes."

Olivia frowns, and Charlie holds up her hands. "Okay, okay," she says apologetically. "What's the what?"

"I really like Ben." She glances nervously at Charlie, who rolls her eyes.

"We know, we know," Charlie says. "You're crazy about my hugely lame brother. So what?"

"So could you pretend he's not your brother for a second?"

"How do you think I make it through the day?"

Olivia looks at me like she's not sure if Charlie's kidding.

"It's fine," I say. "Spit it out."

"I think I'm ready," Olivia says. "Not this weekend or anything. But I want to do it with him."

Charlie balks in the front seat next to her, yanking her glasses up onto her head. "Are you serious?"

"Yeah," Olivia says. She looks a little proud of herself. "I know I said that stuff about college, and whatever."

"Forget college," Charlie says, waving a dismissing hand. "I'm just saying, Ben is a virgin for a reason." Charlie arches around to look at me. "The man has read the entirety of *Moby-Dick*, like, four times."

"It's so weird," Olivia says. "I never thought it would be him." She sounds dreamy and distant, like she's not really talking to us in particular.

I can't believe how ridiculous it is that just a week ago

I thought I was ready, that Rob was the one. It seems almost impossible, how much has changed.

"Okay," Charlie says, raising her eyebrows. "Look, you like him. I love you. Therefore, I'm cool with this. But I'm not giving you pointers. That's just creepy."

"But you have to!" Olivia says. She snaps out of her state and slaps Charlie across the seat. "Who else am I going to ask?"

She's right, of course, but something about the way she says it makes me sit back. I'm not jealous exactly. I don't want to be with Ben, and I know Olivia's been waiting for the right person, and all of that. I'm happy for her. She's my friend and I love her. Of course I'm happy for her. But it's another thing Charlie and Olivia will have that I don't. They are already ridiculous beautiful, and they have boyfriends who don't run off with other girls. Is it too much to ask that they don't leave me in the dust on this, too? It feels like I'm standing on the opposite side of everyone else, and the longer time ticks on, the wider the split gets between us, like we're icebergs drifting apart at the north pole. I just keep thinking of that superdepressing *Planet Earth* episode with the polar bears. Where the ice splits and that one lone bear just drifts out to sea. It's enough to make me want to start weeping in the back of Olivia's SUV.

"You remember those Choose Your Own Adventure books?" Olivia says.

"Don't go getting all metaphoric on us now, O. It's just sex. Use your words," Charlie says.

"Noooo," Olivia drags. "That's not where I'm going with this."

"Whatever," Charlie says. "Can we please turn the music back on?" She reaches forward, and her seat belt snaps her back.

"Karma sucks," Olivia says, smiling at her.

"I read those," I say. I lean forward. "But I'd always skip to the end."

"Everyone skipped to the end," Charlie says. She's wrestling with her strap, her arms flailing.

"I didn't," Olivia says. "It used to make me so upset when I'd finish one, because then there were no more surprises."

"Weird child," Charlie says. She finally frees herself. "But I cannot listen to the oldies anymore."

Olivia flips her hand to say, *Whatever,* and Charlie puts her own iPod on.

"Anyway, I was thinking about those books because I was reading one to Drew. Like, it's sort of how life is, you know? One decision leading to an entirely different chapter?"

"This is way deep," Charlie says.

"Shut up," Olivia says, tapping her fist on the steering wheel. "I'm serious."

"I get it," I say. "It's definitely true. One moment can change everything."

Charlie gives me a pained smile and wiggles her nose.

"If you could know your entire life now—like, if you could flip to the end—would you?" Olivia looks at Charlie and then at me.

"Definitely not," Charlie says. "It would just bum me out that Jake is never going to get his act together. Also, what if I didn't get into Middlebury? I'd rather wait it out."

"I think I'd choose to know," I say. "I'd like to be prepared."

Olivia nods, and the song flips.

I would want to know. I *do* want to know. If I knew, maybe I could figure it out sooner. If I had any idea what was going through Rob's head and how this would eventually play out, I could act accordingly. I could move on or hang on. I wouldn't be caught in this in-between, feeling so completely useless.

The rest of the drive is uneventful. Charlie talks about whether or not we want to stay for Saturday night too, but we don't reach any kind of consensus. Olivia's house is right on the water. It's part of the Malibu Colony, this überexclusive community that's full of movie stars. Her neighbors used to be Zac and Vanessa, before they split.

There is a pool in the back, on the deck, and then steps down to the beach. The entire place is decorated in a million different shades of white and beige, and there are black-and-white photographs of Olivia and her little brothers covering the walls, and big glass bowls of shells sitting on coffee tables. Her house looks like the "after" on one of those home improvement shows.

We're the first ones there. The boys will probably stop at In-N-Out Burger on their way, after surfing. I'm relieved they won't be here for a little while. Just the thought of seeing Rob out of school is making my stomach knot. I don't know what it will be like when it actually happens.

It's cool when we step inside, the house full of ocean breeze—crisp and salty, the kind you can taste. Charlie and I toss off our shoes and race out to the sand. Olivia's stretch of beach is a long one, and some of my favorite memories of the last four years are of waking up, still slightly drowsy, and walking in sweaters with steaming mugs of coffee down the shoreline.

"Wait for me!" Olivia calls. She's already put on her swimsuit, a black bikini with multicolored polo horses.

The three of us drop down into the sand. The haze has lifted, and it's sunny out. I close my eyes, lying down on my back. The warmth feels good, and for the first time since last Friday, I think maybe things will be okay. The familiar surroundings and the promise of us all spending time together reassure me. Rob will come to his senses. We'll figure it out. That has to be the way the story ends.

Scene Four

Charlie is drunk. We've been taking vodka shots by Olivia's pool for the last hour, chasing them down with warm Diet Coke with lime. I'd put Charlie's and Olivia's count somewhere around five. I've been too nervous to have more than two shots, one and a half if you count the fact that I tipped most of the second one onto the deck when no one was watching. I know alcohol technically relaxes you, but I don't want to be silly by the time Rob gets here. If we have to have a serious conversation, I want to be able to have it. Coherently.

Charlie is wearing a white halter top and a denim skirt and gold, dangly earrings she borrowed from Olivia's mom's bathroom. Olivia's family keeps full wardrobes here even though Olivia says she can't remember the last time her parents came down. Olivia is still in her bikini, but she has a see-through purple cover-up thrown over it. I have on a sundress I've had since the seventh grade. It's one of those cotton ones from American Eagle Outfitters that Charlie hates. She didn't say anything tonight when I put it on, though. She just complimented my hair.

Olivia is wandering around with the vodka, haphazardly pouring it into red party cups.

"Who are those *for*?" Charlie asks, and cracks up laughing. She's trying to fish a swimming noodle out of the pool and is teetering in her platform wedges, her drink sloshing over the side of her cup.

"You are an inch from catastrophe," I say, but she doesn't hear me.

Olivia comes over and tips the vodka bottle toward me, pouring me a full cup. "You need to drink more," she informs me, and then taps her watch. "Any minute."

Her cell phone blares. She answers it quickly.

"I told yooou," she says into the phone, and then repeats some numbers, probably the gate code, and hangs up.

"They're pulling in," she says. Charlie nods, but her head doesn't quite make it all the way back up.

My heart is racing, and I take a few tiny sips of my vodka. It burns, and I wince. My hands feel numb, and I clench and release one fist and then the other, switching the cup as the three of us head back inside. I can hear cars parking and doors slamming. I see John Susquich and Jake first. Then they are in the pantry, pulling out Doritos. Charlie plods her way over to them.

"Yo, babe," Jake says, stuffing a chip into his mouth and attempting to kiss her at the same time.

"I missed you," she slurs.

John takes off with the bag, and Jake positions Charlie's arms around him.

"You smell like a burger," I hear her say, before they start making out.

Ben is here too, and he's accepting a drink from Olivia, his hand on the back of her neck.

Where is Rob?

"Hey, Caplet."

I spin around, but it's just Matt Lester and Lauren. They probably drove down with John. Lauren's always invited, but I think she's come once in the last four years. And that was when her family was in LA for the weekend and they dropped her off at two and picked her up at five.

"Hi," I say, giving her a wave. She seems to be wrapped up in something Matt is saying.

"What, did they, like, caravan down?" Charlie is behind me, breathing into my ear.

I shrug. "I guess."

"Are they *together*?"

"Matt and Lauren? Doubt it." Except I don't. As soon as she says it, I realize that's exactly what's going on. Matt has the same look he used to give Charlie, and his hand is dangerously close to Lauren's back. She's pretty in a soft, natural way. They actually make a cute couple.

"Whatever," Charlie says. "Who cares."

She stumbles off, presumably in search of Jake, and I crane my neck to check Olivia's entryway.

"Where's Rob?" Olivia asks, suddenly and to no one in particular.

Jake and Ben glance at each other, and Ben talks first. "He's parking."

Olivia seems to accept this, but something about it doesn't feel right to me. It only takes me another half second to realize why. I don't even have to turn around and see him to confirm my suspicion. He has brought Juliet.

She's wearing her signature sunglasses and carrying her gigantic bag. Everything about her is the same as it has been for the last week, except for one glaring difference. Instead of her halter dresses and skintight tank tops, she is wearing a sweatshirt. One that swallows up her small frame so you can barely see the denim shorts poking out from underneath. And blazoned across the front of the worn gray cotton is the word STANFORD.

Charlie raises her eyebrows at me, but she's too drunk to sustain the expression and instead decides to take her irritation at Juliet's arrival out on Jake.

Olivia hesitates and then goes to greet them, being a good hostess and passing them two drinks. Juliet keeps her sunglasses on, and they're so tinted, it's impossible to see her eyes underneath, or what expression she's wearing. She takes the cup from Olivia, smiles, and exclaims, "Thank you!" but keeps herself glued to Rob, her arm through his. Rob looks awkward, but just slightly. If you didn't know him, you'd think he was just settling into the party, shaking off the drive. But I know Rob better than that. He's nervous. He looks the same way he did on our date— or dinner, whatever you want to call it—last week.

He doesn't look at me but goes over to Jake, who looks confused as to what to do. Charlie stomps off in a huff, and Jake kind of stares after her. The only one who doesn't seem remotely concerned by this scene is Juliet. She's smiling and cheerful and looks completely at home in Olivia's house. And in Rob's sweatshirt.

"Rose," she calls. "Hey!"

She crosses the room in three long strides and gives me an air hug. It's the most physical contact I've had with her since she snapped my doll's head off a decade ago.

"Hey," I say. I'm not sure what to do. If I was Charlie, I would probably throw a drink in her face or blow her off, but there isn't enough time to figure out how. It's not until she releases me that I realize she's just won. By being nice to me, she's completely obliterated her chances of being perceived as in the wrong.

"It's sooo beautiful here," she says, sliding her sunglasses up on top of her head. "Have you been out back?"

What does she mean, "Have I been out back?" This is my best friend's house. I've been coming here since I was thirteen. Of course I've been "out back."

"Babe," she calls, and Rob looks up. That one motion is like a knife in my side.

"My parents used to have a house at the Colony," she says as he comes over, "but they sold it when things just got too busy. Now we have to come down and use the Pitts'."

Rob stops a few paces from us and makes like he's looking at the photograph hanging over Olivia's couch. It's a picture of Olivia's little brother Drew in a tin bucket, so I know he can't be that interested. Juliet is blabbing about Brad's involvement in her dad's charity when she stops, looks at me, and says, "Your parents don't have a house down here, do they?"

"No." Considering that the average home in the Colony is about fifteen million, I'd say pretty definitively that they never will, either. "The beach isn't really their thing."

"What is, then?" Juliet looks amused. She eyes me up and down, slowly, like she's taking inventory.

"Umm, hiking?"

She half laughs and then drops her voice low, so only I can hear. "Really? I thought you guys were just into backstabbing."

"I'm sorry, what?" I tilt my head forward, convinced I heard her wrong.

Juliet crosses her arms and looks me straight in the eye. "You heard me."

"What are you talking about?" My voice goes up at the end, and Rob shifts uncomfortably by the framed bucket baby.

"Oh, poor, little, delicate Rosie. Kept from all of life's trage-dies by her loving family."

"Have you lost your mind?" I whisper.

"Maybe," she says, squaring her shoulders. "I am in love, you know. I heard it makes you crazy." Her eyes twitch slightly, and I recognize something in them, something primal. And it's terrifying.

Juliet smiles, shakes her mane down her back, and turns, going over to Rob. She draws him into a long kiss, snaking her arms around his neck and up into his hair. I think I'm going to be sick.

I wander outside and try to suck in some fresh air. So, on top of stealing Rob, she's now attacking my family. I mean, I know our parents had a falling-out a long time ago, but my mom and dad aren't traitors. And where does she get off calling anyone a backstabber? Look whose face she's sucking.

But there's something nagging at me, something else. Rob's mom sitting in our living room and what she said about Juliet's family. That they wanted revenge. For what? Is this Juliet's revenge?

The only other people outside are Lauren and Matt, and they're in a corner, talking quietly. I sit down on one of the gigantic striped lounge chairs and look up at the sky. It's getting dark now. Soon Olivia will propose that everyone go skinny-dipping, except she'll conveniently leave her bathing suit on. The same thing happened last time we were here about a month ago. Rob was still at camp, but Jake and Ben came. Olivia had heated the pool by accident, so it felt like a hot tub, and we kept jumping in and out, lying on the lawn chairs and cooling off. I remember thinking about Rob. Wishing he was here. Wondering if when he got back we would be snuggling together, sharing a towel, our feet dangling in the water.

I see Olivia and Charlie inside. They are standing around with Ben and Jake, and Rob and Juliet are right there. The six of them. All at once I see the entire year stretched out before me like a movie reel, and it doesn't involve getting back at Juliet at all. Here's what will happen: Charlie and Olivia will call her a slut for a while, hold a grudge against her because she "stole" Rob. Then they will start to spend more time with her, and it will become increasingly difficult to keep up that bitchy front. She'll wear them down. They will start to forget why they hate her so much. She's Rob's girlfriend, after all. Then the six of them will be at a movie together. Juliet will comment on how much she likes Olivia's headband, and Olivia will tell her where she got it. Juliet will suggest a shopping trip, maybe even in her dad's limo. Olivia will glance nervously at Charlie before accepting. They'll invite me. It's been months, they'll reason; we should all be moving on. We'll go. Juliet will talk about Rob, but not a lot. She'll reference Jake and Rob's surfing trips. Charlie will roll her eyes knowingly. They share something now. Afterward we'll go to Grandma's and get bagels, and the boys will meet us there. Everyone will pair off. Everyone, that is, but me.

"It's cran *apple*, not cran *grape*," Olivia says, wandering outside. She's holding the nozzle of a juice container in one hand and a towel in another. Charlie trails behind her, staring into her red cup like she's looking for something.

"There you are," Olivia says. She sets the juice down and sits on the edge of my chair, throwing her towel down onto my legs. She pulls her cover-up off and tosses it onto the ground.

I shake my head. "No," Charlie says, voicing my thought, "I don't want to go skinny-dipping." She holds her hand up to stop

Olivia from saying anything and crawls into my chair, stretching her body out next to mine and resting her head on my collarbone. "I can't believe she even showed up," Charlie says. Her breath smells like vodka, and I turn away, looking out at the ocean. The moon is fairly full, and the water looks silver underneath it. I remember once hearing that the only reason the ocean is blue is because it reflects the sky. If you could see the water at night, maybe it would just look clear. Maybe you could see all the way down to the bottom.

"Do you want me to kick her out?" Olivia asks.

I don't answer, and Charlie mumbles something against my chest. Whatever it is, it isn't adamant. Partly because she's drunk, of course, but partly because they are already getting over this. Whether they know it or not, their protestations have rounded edges now. The sting of this betrayal is wearing off, and their comments are beginning to sound repetitive and dull. How many times can they tell me I'm prettier than her or that Rob is an ass? It's wearing on them, and it's obvious. So obvious, in fact, that when Olivia announces, "She's a slut," Charlie barely nods her head in agreement.

There are so many competing thoughts floating around in my head right now. My anger at Juliet, my confusion about her backstabbing comment, my feelings for Rob. And that's the problem, that I still care about him. I still want him back. I can't believe I can turn my head and look at him and at the same time not be able to speak to him. I would settle for just his friendship now, but that's over too. I wish we had never shared that kiss, that we had never said those things to each other. Maybe then we could still go back. Maybe then I wouldn't miss him when he's standing right here.

"Who's up for the water?"

I tilt my head and open my mouth to turn Olivia down again, but it's not Olivia who's doing the suggesting. It's Juliet, and she's standing over us, a light pink bikini pulled tightly over her chest. She's smiling, her pearly whites beaming. Gone are the grizzly teeth she bared inside. Of course, there are other people around.

Olivia stands up and bounces slightly on her heels. "I was going to go anyway," she says to Charlie and me.

Charlie waves her off with a hand and keeps nuzzling my chest. Olivia hesitates but then grabs her towel. She and Juliet descend the stairs to the ocean, their blond hair indistinguishable in the moonlight, so that after a few feet it's impossible to tell who is who.

"Love it here," Charlie murmurs, and even though she's pressed up against me, I feel farther away from her than I ever have before.

Act Four

Scene One

It's true California doesn't have East Coast seasons, but there's something about the fall in San Bellaro that I love. No, the trees don't change and our campus doesn't look like a postcard of yellow, red, and orange, but the air is crisp and cool, and there's this sense of newness. Like maybe change is possible, even if you can't see it.

And things have changed.

"I think Mrs. Barch has it out for me," I say. We're sitting in the courtyard, finishing lunch. By the time you make it to October at San Bellaro, some kids have decided to park themselves in the cafeteria until spring. Not us. "We're troupers," as Charlie likes to say. We wear sweaters, and we stay outside.

"Hmm?" Charlie murmurs. She's watching Jake where he's

standing on the breezeway. They broke up last week over what Charlie deemed "weekend abandonment." Jake decided to go to a concert with John Susquich and left her alone Saturday night. She hasn't yet recovered, and they're still not speaking.

"I still can't believe you're not in physics with us," Olivia says. "Yesterday Mr. Dunfy brought in cupcakes. We just ate them all period." She looks at Ben for confirmation, and he nods.

"It's true," he says. "All period."

The truth is that this bio thing actually is a problem. I applied early to Stanford but they're going to want to see my first semester grades, and right now I'm barely pulling a B minus.

"Who's your bio partner?" Olivia asks.

"Len."

"Stephens?"

Charlie picks her head up and looks at us. "What are we talking about?"

"How I'm failing bio."

"Should have taken physics," Charlie says. "Do you know we had—"

"Cupcakes, all period. I know."

Olivia picks up her apple. She takes an unenthusiastic bite and sets it down.

A look I know well by this point dances across Charlie's face, and I glance up to see Rob and Juliet walking by, hand in hand.

Juliet looks over at our table and at the same moment reaches up to tousle Rob's hair. She nuzzles her head closer to him and keeps one eye on me as she loops his arm around her back.

It's been over a month, but every time I see them together, it catches me by surprise. Like I still expect Rob to come up behind me, lay his hands over my eyes, and ask me to guess who. Charlie says it's normal to mourn someone for a while, that when her mom died, she still expected to see her every day for a year. Rob isn't dead, though. He's right here.

"He might as well be dead," Charlie says, reading my mind. "You don't even say hello to him."

Olivia has English with Juliet and Rob and has informed me that they do nothing except talk to each other. She also says that Rob has basically stopped hanging out with Ben. "He doesn't even go surfing anymore," Charlie adds. "And I heard he's fighting with his family."

"No way," I say. "Rob and his parents are really tight."

"Way," Olivia confirms. "Josh told me."

"Josh is six."

"Yeah, and Mathew's best friend." Mathew is Rob's brother, the youngest of the four boys.

"Why are they fighting?"

Olivia shrugs. "I don't know. But I wouldn't be surprised if it had something to do with her."

Me either.

"Look, right now bio is the more important issue. I'm screwed," I say, resting my forehead on the table.

"Maybe it wouldn't be the worst thing if you didn't end up at Stanford," Charlie says. "What the hell do you want another four years with that guy for?" She gestures over her shoulder to where Rob and Juliet are disappearing into the cafeteria.

"I don't even know if he applied early," I say.

"But wasn't that the plan?" Olivia asks.

"A lot of things were the plan," I say.

I drag my bio book off the table and stand up to go to lab. Charlie whines, "Where are you going?" but she doesn't take her eyes off Jake. I still have ten minutes until class, but I need to reread the latest chapter. Every time I look at the textbook, it feels like the words morph into another language. Like I bought the Arabic version by accident or something.

Len is already there. He's sitting at a computer in the back, wearing that purple lightning shirt. One long curl rests on his forehead, and I have the sudden, intense urge to pull it and watch it bounce back.

"You're early," I say.

"Class is canceled," he says without looking up.

"Yeah?"

He gestures over his shoulder to the board. I read the words

"Mrs. Barch Out. Assignment to complete with partner is on my desk."

"She's out," I say.

Len nods. "Yep. It was probably the play. I mean, all that bad acting was starting to make me sick to my stomach too."

He turns around and smiles. "What's up, Rosaline?"

"Should we start the assignment?"

He waves a dismissing hand. "Later. Pull up a chair." He grabs a plastic one and slides it next to his, patting the seat.

I drop my bag and sit down, craning to see his computer screen.

"A little privacy?"

"Please. Like you care."

Len snorts and angles the screen between us. Immediately I see a picture of Juliet's family.

"What is this?" I ask.

"The news? Contrary to popular belief, I do, in fact, know how to read. Hey," Len says as I turn the screen and scan the article. It's something about education reform and Senator Caplet's commitment to family.

"His policies suck," Len says.

"You follow his career?"

Len blows some air out through his lips. "I'm an informed citizen," he says.

He reaches over me to grab the mouse, but I slap his hand away. I have an idea. My fingers are already on the keyboard. I type "Richard Caplet" into the search page of the *San Bellaro News*, and a thousand articles come up.

"Obsess much?" Len asks, amused.

I methodically click through, moving backward in time. Two years, three years, four, five, scanning the headlines for what I'm looking for. When I get to the last section, there it is, in big, bold font, dated over ten years ago. But the headline is something I never expected. I read the words once, twice, and then look at Len to see if he's reading the same. I click open the article.

There is a picture of my dad and Juliet's father, and typed above the photo are the words BETRAYED BY HIS OWN BROTHER.

Scene Two

Richard Caplet's campaign had a surprise disruption Tuesday night. On the heels of Steve Monteg's announcement that he would be running as Mr. Caplet's opponent in the upcoming mayoral election, Mr. Caplet received word that his brother and former campaign manager, Paul Caplet, would be supporting Mr. Monteg's candidacy. The two brothers have been close up until this point, and it's unclear what made Paul Caplet flip. Paul Caplet is a professor at the local college whom many anticipate has his own political aspirations. When asked about his endorsement, the professor replied, "Steve Monteg is the right man for our town and our state. I put my full trust and faith in his powers of leadership."

Len finishes reading and sits back in his chair. Students are starting to file into the lab, picking up their assignments and taking their seats. Neither one of us moves.

"I don't get it," I say.

"People do strange things for power," Len says.

"Not my dad. You don't know him. He's a teacher."

Len nods. "I understand," he says. "But this all happened a long time ago."

"This is why Juliet called my family backstabbers." I sit back and hit my chair with a *thunk*. "She was right."

"He must have had his reasons," Len says gently. So softly, in fact, that I turn to look at him, just to make sure that he's the one talking. He is.

"It doesn't matter," I say. "My parents still turned their backs on their family."

"Did they?"

I throw my arms up and gesture toward the screen. "You just read it!"

Len takes a deep breath and speaks slowly, like he's explaining arithmetic to me. "I just think there are many different definitions of 'family,' that's all. Maybe the Montegs were your parents'."

"It just doesn't make any sense. I know my parents. They'd rather be Switzerland than choose a side."

"Being Switzerland has its own faults," Len says. "Bad weather, for example."

"And why have they never told me about this? That this was the reason Juliet's family left town?"

Len is quiet.

"He won, you know," I say. "Rob's father was the mayor for four years when we were kids."

"I know. I remember." Len looks at me. "So Juliet's family took off with their tails between their legs, huh?"

"Honestly," I say, "I don't really remember. I was barely seven."

"Looks like a lot has changed."

"All I know is that we were like sisters, and then they moved and she turned on me. But I'm sure her family hated us. Juliet must have felt it."

I look at my father's face on the screen—fresh, young, and excited. He's standing with his arm around his brother, and they're both smiling. They look almost like twins in their blazers and button-downs, clipped haircuts, and matching dimples.

"I'm sorry," I say. "This is so not your problem."

Len laughs. "Are you always this neurotic?"

I squeeze one eye shut and look at him. "Probably."

"Look." Len arches around and glances at the clock. "We only have, like, fifteen minutes left of class, and since I know you're going to make me do this assignment anyway, do you maybe just want to do it after school?"

Len volunteering to spend time with me in a nonacademic environment? Shocking. "Um, sure. Any chance you could come over, though? It's been a long day, and I kind of just want to get out of here." I loop my finger in the air to display crazy.

"No problem."

I hike my bag onto the table next to the computer and pull out a pen. "Here. Let me give you directions."

I tear off a piece of notebook paper and am touching the pen down when Len covers my hand with his. His touch startles me. "It's cool," he says. "I remember."

"You've never been over before," I say. I don't have parties, and the only people who ever really hang out at my house are the six of us. Sometimes Lauren or John, but I could count the number of times on one hand.

"Yeah, I have." A look flashes across his face for a split second, but it's gone before I have a chance to register what it is. "My mom forgot to pick me up from Famke's one time. Your mom let me wait at your house. It's not a big deal."

"Oh."

He looks down at his textbook. "You were always outside when my lesson finished." He looks up and smiles. "Sorry about that, by the way. I was probably terrible back then."

I shake my head. "You were great. Listening to you play was my favorite part of lessons." I can feel my cheeks turning red. I have no idea why I just said that. Beyond the fact that it's sorta true.

He doesn't seem thrown off by it, though. He just looks at me and says clearly, "Thanks."

The moment stretches, and it's long enough for me to realize that neither one of us is speaking. "Should we get out of here?"

"I thought you'd never ask." He flicks the screen off, and my dad's face disappears.

We gather up our stuff and duck out the double lab doors. Len starts doing an impression of Mrs. Barch directing the Belgian. It's hilarious. He's actually pretty funny, and I would never admit this to Charlie, but I'm starting to see what Olivia meant. About him being cute, I mean. Not just striking but kind of adorable. Yeah, his hair is sorta long and he's kind of a slacker, but he's got this confidence. Like he just doesn't care what anyone else thinks.

"I need to talk to you."

I hiccup back a laugh and see Rob there. He looks frazzled, haphazard, like he's not sure what he's doing himself. Ben is there too, and he looks apologetic.

I just stare at Rob.

These are the first words he's spoken to me in weeks.

"Hey," Len says to me, "I'm gonna head to English. See you after school?"

Rob frowns and looks at Len. "What are you guys doing?"

That familiar smirk creeps back onto Len's face, and he shakes his head slowly and mumbles something under his breath.

"I said I need to talk to you," Rob says to me. His jaw twitches slightly.

"Hey," Ben says. He puts a hand on Rob's shoulder. "We're gonna be late." Rob shakes him off, and Ben looks at me. It's the same look I see him give Olivia when she's detailing a shopping failure. Like he really cares, but he just isn't sure how to help. The truth is, neither am I. This is foreign territory. In all our years of friendship I've never seen Rob really, truly angry. The Rob I knew was sweet and kind and totally nonconfrontational. That's not who's standing here. I guess Juliet has turned him against me too.

"Look," Len says, "maybe you should go." He offers the suggestion casually, like he's asking Rob if he wants a soda.

"Don't tell me what to do," Rob says. He turns on Len and grabs his backpack. Ben again reaches for Rob's shoulder, but Rob knocks him back.

"Are you crazy?" I say, trying to move between them. "Let go."

"You're going to fight for him now?" Rob bares his teeth like he's some kind of wild animal. His eyes look burnt, cold. Like he's been frozen out of his own body.

"I'm not fighting for anyone," I say. "I'm not *fighting* at all."

"It's cool, man," Len says. "Just relax."

I can see Mr. Davis walking toward us. "Just stop it," I plead. "Seriously. Stop." But Rob's not listening to me. And he won't let Ben get close. He's moved on from Len's backpack and is now holding the collar of his shirt.

"Don't tell me to relax," he spits at Len. "You don't know a thing about me. Or her." Then in one clean sweep Rob uses his free hand to send a punch clear across Len's face. Len stumbles back, and Rob just stares after him. He looks at his hand and then at Len and then at me. "I'm—" he starts, but it's too late. Mr. Davis has seen everything, and he's on Rob before Rob can get a second word out.

"What is going on here?" Mr. Davis demands.

Ben tries to step in and say something, but Mr. Davis dismisses him, rounding on Rob and Len. "Mr. Johnson's office. Both of you. Now."

He turns Rob around and starts marching him by the shoulders.

"Are you okay?" I whisper to Len. "I'm so sorry."

"Yeah," he says. "It's no big deal." He smiles like he's reassuring me. "Grab the homework, okay? We forgot to get copies."

"Sure," I say. "But are you sure you're all right?"

"I'll live." He smiles, gives me a little salute, and follows

Mr. Davis, who is already halfway to Cooper House, his hands still on Rob's sunken shoulders.

"I can't stand that girl," Olivia says. "She's been trouble. Day one."

We're in calc, our last period of the day, and I've just told Olivia about the fight. Mostly on the corner of my notebook, because Mr. Stetzler is sort of a stickler about talking.

"Well, this one I'd pin on Rob," I whisper.

"Whatever. It all goes back to her. Rob was totally sane until she came around. Now he's picking fights, ditching his friends, and not talking to his parents?" Olivia is keeping one eye on Mr. Stetzler and the other on the Belgian, who is sitting to the far left of us. He doesn't usually show up to class, but when he does, it's enough to send Olivia into a tailspin. Matt has the same effect on Charlie. Maybe you never really get over the people you once dated, or cared about.

"He probably wants out at this point," Olivia continues. "I'm sure he's realized she's completely psycho and high maintenance. But it's not like there's anything he can do now."

"They're not married," I say. "He's not under contract." I'm drawing lazily in my notebook, doodling around our conversation. It's always hot in the math cubicles, regardless of the time of year, which makes it incredibly difficult to focus. Mr. Stetzler also has this superdeep, intense voice, like a movie voice-over, and it's kind of hypnotizing. Not in a way that makes me want to flirt with him like Olivia does. Just in a way that makes me want to fall asleep facedown on my proofs.

"Yeah, but would he want that guilt on himself?"

"What guilt?"

Olivia tucks her hair back behind her ears. "She threatened to kill herself."

I make a sound somewhere between a cough and a sneeze, and Mr. Stetzler looks over, frowning.

"That's a rumor," I say. The senior class has been buzzing today about Juliet overdosing on pills or something. But since no one can pin down an actual time or reason, I'm finding it hard to believe. "What reason does she have to kill herself? Her life is perfect."

"Her boyfriend is still in love with his ex?" Olivia raises her eyebrows at me and puckers up her lips. I jam her with my elbow and bend back down over our assignment. I wish I could believe that were at all true.

"You know what else?" Olivia whispers. "She stole my flats. The new Tory Burch ones. She went and got them on preorder."

"Juliet?"

Olivia is giving me a look like, *Please get there faster.* "Obviously," she says. "Who else would be able to do that at this school?" She looks at me and bites her lip. "You know what I mean."

"I do," I say.

Mr. Stetzler throws a pointed look in our direction, and we both make like we're incredibly busy with a problem in our notebooks. When he goes back to lecturing, Olivia leans over. "I know I'm not supposed to be talking about her with you. Charlie made me swear—" The Belgian lets out a burp, and everyone starts laughing. Olivia scrunches up her nose and looks at me.

"Charlie made you promise *what*?"

"We just didn't want to upset you," Olivia says gently. "We just love you. And want you to be okay."

"I am okay," I say. "I've been okay for weeks."

Olivia fiddles with the end of her pencil. It's chewed down the same way her nails are. She likes to gnaw on things when she's nervous.

"It's still hard to lose a friend," she says. She looks at me with her big blue eyes.

"You were telling me about Juliet," I say, glancing away, because all of a sudden I think she's talking about losing me. About the fact that I haven't been around lately. Not really, anyway.

"Yeah," she says, inhaling sharply. "I think she's kind of sneaky. I mean, who goes to Barneys, looks up what I preordered, and then cuts in front of me on the list? Is that even legal?"

I've never really understood Olivia's obsession with shopping. I mean, I like clothes, I guess, but I've just never been the type of girl who wants to spend all day at the mall. For Olivia shopping is a profession. She's incredibly talented at it, so I can see how someone beating her at her own game would really piss her off.

"It's like she's trying to take everything away from us," Olivia says. "Stealing Rob from you just isn't enough anymore."

Mr. Stetzler is handing around the homework assignment, and when he gets to me, I don't recognize a single problem on the list. We always work through half in class so we have "some models" to go off of, but today I took no notes.

"I didn't hear a word of this class," I say.

"Whatever," Olivia says, taking a handout. "*Queso* at Cal Block?"

"I can't." Everyone is filing out the back, and Olivia and I follow. "I have a study session."

"For what?"

"Bio," I say. "Len's coming over to help me out. Unless Mr. Johnson has him in detention or something."

"Len, huh?" Olivia raises her eyebrows and shimmies her shoulders. "You two have been spending a lot of time together."

My cheeks flush pink. "We're *lab* partners," I say, glancing away. "If I fail, it makes him look pretty crappy too."

"Since when has he cared about grades? And the play—" The Belgian walks by, and Olivia arches her back so you can see a small stretch of stomach. I don't think it's lost on him. He glances back, but Olivia is immersed in our conversation. Or at least she appears that way.

"I think thou doth protest too much," Olivia says, giggling.

"You're crazy."

"I told you," Olivia says as we make our way down the stairs. "I've always thought he was pretty cute."

"He's so sarcastic."

"So?" Olivia says. "It's kind of sexy. He's like a rebel."

"Well, you're welcome to him."

Olivia rolls her eyes. "I like Ben." She bites her lip and stops walking. "Actually, I love him."

I stop too. I figured as much, but I hadn't actually expected Olivia to cop to it. But now she's looking at me like there's more.

"What's up?" I ask, shifting my book bag.

"We sorta—" She exhales and kicks some dirt with her shoe. "We had sex."

"Does Charlie know?" I'm not sure why that's my first question, but it seems important.

"Yeah," she says. "I told her this morning."

"Well, how do you feel?" I'm not sure what to say. I figured when the time came, I'd know more about the whole sex issue. Wrong again.

Olivia shrugs. "Not much different, I guess."

"Yeah."

"You know what, though?" she says, her voice bulking up a little. "I really liked it."

"Well, that's good, right? That's sorta the point?"

"No, not *that*. That's not what I mean." She frowns and crosses her arms. "I mean I really liked being that close to someone. I really liked being that close to *him*."

I know we give Olivia a hard time about being silly and careless, but I think deep down she has some fears too. That she takes some things seriously. I know she wanted this, and in a way, I think, I'm kind of proud of her for going for it. And making the decision on her own.

"Anyway," she says, "back to Len. I'm just saying I support it. That's all."

"Well, I appreciate your vote," I say. "Thanks."

Charlie is waiting in upper for us, leaning against Big Red. She's got her sunglasses on, and her hair is picking up the sunlight so it looks like an impossible color of orange. Translucent, somehow. Like a butterfly's wings. "We need to talk," she says when she sees us. "Cal Block?"

"Actually," Olivia says, "I think I'm gonna go have a hot date with your brother." She winks at me and climbs into her car.

"I knew they were doing it," Charlie says, staring after her. "She's been unnaturally happy."

We climb inside. "How about you?" she asks. "Ben told me a little bit about the fight, but I need more details. And you heard about the suicide story?"

"I have a study session with Len," I say. "Assuming he shows, I have to be home."

Charlie eyes me as we pull out of the parking lot and onto the highway. "What's going on there, anyway?"

"Where?"

"Come on. Don't play coy with me. Two guys break into a fistfight at school, and you want to tell me Rob wasn't jealous?"

"Jealous? Even if Len and I were dating, which we're not, Rob has no reason to care. Need I remind you, he has a *girlfriend*?"

"Something's up," Charlie says, clicking her tongue against the roof of her mouth. "Things just feel weird."

"That's because things *are* weird. Rob's turned all green hornet, and Juliet's suicidal, apparently, and I've just found out we're some scandal of a political family."

"Explain, please," Charlie says, sliding her sunglasses down her nose.

I tell Charlie about my discovery today, with Len.

"Well, it sort of makes sense," she says. "Why she has it out for you."

"I guess. I still can't understand really why she would hate me like that. And I just can't believe my dad would hurt his brother for no reason, you know? It's so out of character."

Charlie shrugs. "Maybe Rob's dad really was the better candidate. I mean, your parents were always close with Rob's parents. Maybe it was just politics, not personal."

Charlie pulls into my driveway, and Rob's mom's car is parked next to my mom's. Usually she just walks over, but I guess she was coming from somewhere. She has the SAN BELLARO SOCIAL CHAIR bumper sticker on the back window that Rob and I had made for her birthday two years ago.

I heave my book bag out of the car.

"Good luck with . . ." Charlie waves her hand around in the air like she's looking for a word.

"Len," I say.

"Right, *bio*." She flips her sunglasses down and dots the air with a kiss. "Call me tomorrow. I think we may have to stalk Jake this weekend."

"I completely forgot it was Friday."

"Yeah. Sorta makes this study session seem like a date, huh?" She winks at me and swings out of the driveway, calling, "Ciao, bella," on her way out.

I wave and head into the house. Rob's mom and mine are in the kitchen at the counter, talking. It reminds me of the millions of times I've come home and seen the same thing. Of baking Christmas cookies together in our kitchen. Of summer dinners on the patio. Of the one time Rob's mom and mine let us share a glass of wine with them at the counter. It makes me miss Rob like crazy.

"Hey," I say, making my way into the kitchen. "Secret convention?"

Rob's mom smiles. She's got the same liquid chocolate eyes as Rob, and for a second I have to stifle something kind of hot in my throat. She motions me over with her hand. "Hey, cutie," she says. "How are you?"

"Good," I say.

"School going well?"

I nod. "Bio is killing me." The urge to ask her about Rob is suddenly overwhelming. The impulse is so strong, I have to bite down on my tongue to keep from talking.

I don't need to, though, because in the next breath my mom says, "Jackie was just telling me about Rob. You know he got suspended today?"

"Yeah," I mumble. "I mean, I didn't know he got suspended, but I figured something was up."

Rob's mom shakes her head. "It's that girl. Juliet. I'm sorry," she says, looking at my mom, "but he's not the same person since she's been around. All of a sudden he's getting in fights and

228   rebecca serle

applying to USC. His father thinks we should forbid him from seeing her, but . . ."

"He didn't apply early to Stanford?" My voice cracks, and my mom and Rob's exchange a glance.

"I'm sorry, honey," Rob's mom says, but it's quiet. "I don't know what happened."

We all know what happened. USC is the perfect school for Juliet. She'll return to LA and major in drama and get to pursue acting at the same time. Rob wants to be with her, so he's agreed to follow her there. He's taking on her dream now. Stanford is already outdated.

"I have a friend coming over to study," I say. "I'm going to head upstairs."

"The girls?" Rob's mom asks. She loves referring to Charlie and Olivia as "the girls." When we were younger, she once took Charlie and me down to LA for the day on a "girls' shopping trip." Thinking about that and standing here with her, I realize how much I miss them all. Rob's family, I mean.

"No, this guy Len," I say.

"Len Stephens?" my mom asks. She perks her head up from her coffee cup.

"Isn't that the guy who Rob—?" Rob's mom taps the table.

"Yeah." I swallow. "It was no one's fault, really. Things just got out of hand."

"Rob punched Len Stephens?" my mom says, her eyes wide. "He was such a sweet kid. He used to have lessons right before you at Famke's, remember? He was so talented."

"He still is," I say. I don't even know if that's true, but I feel like I need to say something in his defense. And it's easier to stand up for his talent than his sweetness.

Rob's mom squints and runs her pointer finger back and forth across her forehead. "Rob admitted it was his fault, you know," she says, her eyes closed. "He didn't even try to argue."

"He's a good kid," my mom says gently, putting a hand on her shoulder.

"I think he misses you," she says, looking at me. "And that Juliet . . ." Her voice trails off, and she brushes her eyes and straightens up. "I'm sorry," she says. "I know this isn't easy on you. You all used to be so close."

The doorbell rings, and I use it as an exit strategy. "It was good to see you," I say. "Mom, we'll just work in my room."

"Do you guys want some apples?"

"It's not a playdate."

"I know," she says, standing up and coming over to me. "Just let me take care of you while I still can."

I roll my eyes and glance at the door. "Try to restrain yourself," I say, giving her a quick hug. "We'll be upstairs."

Len is standing at the door, his hand against the side panel.

He's got a deep purple bruise all around his right eye.

"Jeez," I say. "You look like a mess."

"Thanks," he says. "You're not so bad yourself."

"Do you want some ice?"

"I'll be fine."

"I know, but that thing looks pretty bad."

"Could I just come in?"

"Sure," I say, stepping to the side. "Sorry. My room's upstairs."

"You run a tight ship," he says. "No guided tour?"

"Later," I say. "Right now we have to work."

He's holding a bag of Twizzlers in his hand, and his backpack is missing.

"Where is your study stuff?"

He holds up the bag.

"That's *candy*."

"Your favorite kind, no less."

I stop. "How do you know that?"

"Chop, chop," he says, pushing past me and starting up the stairs. "Don't make me eat these all by myself."

"But we have to study," I say, trudging up behind him.

"Let's just chill for a second," he says. "The doctor said I really should be resting."

He halts at the top of the stairs and places a hand daintily on his cheek.

"You're lying," I say. "But fine."

"Which is yours?" he says, stretching a hand out in either direction.

"On the left."

We settle on my bedroom floor, the Twizzlers between us. He opens the bag and offers me one. I take it.

"So what happened?" I ask.

Len sighs and rolls a Twizzler between his palms. "Nothing, really. Rob took the blame. They let me go, but I heard he got suspended." He looks to see my reaction.

"Mhm, me too. You must be relieved."

Len shrugs.

"Oh, right. I forgot. Suspension is like a paid vacation for those uninterested in school."

He squints and looks at me, leaning his elbows casually on his knees. "Is that what you think?"

"Yeah," I say. My voice gets quiet. All of a sudden he's making me nervous. "I mean, you never do homework and you're always giving teachers a hard time. Are you even applying to college?"

I pull another Twizzler out of the bag and busy myself with tearing it down like string cheese.

"Didn't know you paid so much attention to me, Rosaline." He tilts his head to the side and gives me a lopsided smile.

I open my mouth to talk, but he holds up his finger.

"For the record, I do the homework. I'm here, aren't I? And I don't give all teachers a hard time, just the ones that could use it. And as for college?" He raises his eyebrows. "I already got in."

"But early admission decisions don't come until next month, at the earliest."

"I got in last year," he says. He flops his knees down to the ground and grabs the candy bag.

"We were juniors."

"Mhm," he says, chewing. "Good point."

"You can't even apply to college junior year."

"Yep," he says. "All true."

"What is it, then? Continuing education courses? Having to repeat high school doesn't count as college."

"Thanks for your concern," he says. "But actually, no. Juilliard."

My jaw drops so far, I think I might have to manually pick it up off the floor. When I finally start speaking, it comes out like word vomit: "What? Are you kidding me? Why?"

Len laughs. "The surprise I can take, but 'why' feels a little harsh."

"I'm sorry, but are you being serious?"

"You want to see the acceptance letter?"

I eye him closely. It's impossible, but I also don't know why he'd lie about it. It seems like the sort of thing he'd like to keep quiet, actually. But Juilliard?

"Isn't that the school for prodigies?"

"Prodigy," he says, tapping his chest. "Right here."

"In what?"

"Okay." He folds his arms across his chest. "Piano."

It makes perfect sense now. Why he's so smart but doesn't care about school. "You kept playing," I say.

I stand and extend my hand to him. He gives me a curious look but lets me help him up. I march him, in much the same way Mr. Davis did Rob this afternoon, down the stairs and into the den. My mom and Rob's mom have disappeared from the kitchen, probably outside. When he sees the piano, he starts laughing.

"You kept it," he says.

"Yeah, my parents always thought maybe I'd come back to it." I sit down on the bench and face him. "Will you play something for me?"

He interlaces his fingers and spins his thumbs, like he's considering it. "Yes," he says, "but only if you'll play something for me first."

"I'm not the one who just got into Juilliard."

"Actually," he says, "I got in last year. So it's been a while."

"Funny."

"Come on," he says. "I think you'll find you remember more than you think."

I take a deep breath and lift up the fallboard. Then I place my hands on the keys. I try to remember a piece I used to love, *Fleur de Lis*. The first few notes and measures sound rusty—like the spokes on an ungreased wheel. But as I go, I start to loosen up a bit. It's harder than I remember, and I get out of breath in just a few seconds, but it also feels wonderful. Like finally moving my legs after a really long airplane ride.

I stop after about a minute, and I realize I'm nearly panting.

"Not bad," Len says. "You need to start playing again."

I do. I'd forgotten how alive piano used to make me feel. The music sends my cells spinning, like the adrenaline high you get after a long run.

Len slides in next to me and runs his hands over the keys, and I notice it again—that birthmark on his thumb. It's red, a deep burgundy, and when I follow it, I see it runs up the length of his arm, or at least up to where he has his shirt sleeves rolled up. It looks like a map, the way it spans and dips and runs like continents and countries and rivers across his skin. It's actually beautiful, not gross at all, and now that I see it, I can't believe I missed it all these years.

Len's breathing slows next to me and his eyes slip closed, and I realize I'm holding my breath too, that the whole room is. It feels like the moment before a rainstorm, the sky heavy and dense, the moisture so thick you can already feel it. And then the first droplets fall, cool and precise and quiet. They build slowly until the moment when the heavens open up and it pours.

I recognize the tune immediately. It's by Frédéric Chopin and it's called, if you'd believe it, *Raindrops*. Famke used to play it for me. Sometimes if I was being stubborn or tired or just off, she would sit me down at the edge of the bench and let me listen to her for a change. If it's possible, Len plays it even better than she did. His fingers glide over the keys like the wind dancing on the beach. Pulling up the sand, twirling it, asking it to play. I tear my eyes away from his hands and look up at his face. His eyes are no longer closed, but they're still, calm, focused. Like the counterpart to the motion of his fingers: steadfast and unmoving.

He stops, and the room falls silent. But the silence is pulled tight, stretched, as if the room itself—the sofa and chairs and even the curtains on the windows—is restraining itself from breaking into applause.

Len lifts his fingers off the keys, slowly, and returns them to his lap. Then he looks at me, and it's kind of like I've never seen him before. Because this person next to me isn't the guy from school who gives teachers lip. He's not sarcastic, but funny; and he's not rude, but witty; and his hair isn't messy, it's, well, kind of sexy.

He runs a hand through it and smiles down at the keys. Then he reaches to close the fallboard and so do I, and for a moment our fingers touch, midair. Immediately something shocks me, and I pull back.

"Static electricity," Len says, pointing to his T-shirt.

I shake my head to say no big deal, but there's something besides the electric shock lingering in my fingertips. And it makes me look away, because I'm pretty sure my cheeks are starting to speak for me.

Instead I focus on that mark on his thumb.

"It's called a port-wine stain," he says. He's not looking at his hand, but at me.

"Oh," I say. "Sorry. I didn't mean to stare."

"It's not a big deal," he says, holding up his arm. "I've had it since I was born." He pushes up his sleeves farther, and I see that the birthmark runs all the way up to his shoulder, even farther than I thought before. Instinctively I reach out and touch it, tracing the outline, and when I do, he smiles. His skin is warm and soft.

"It's beautiful," I say before I even realize I'm speaking. "I've never noticed how cool it is before."

"It's always been there; you just weren't looking," he says, letting me turn over his arm.

"Is that why you always wear long-sleeved shirts?"

He laughs, and I internally kick myself. "I'm sorry. That's none of my business."

"It's okay," he says. "I don't mind." He takes his arm away and pulls down his sleeve. "In the beginning, when I was a kid, I guess, yeah, I was a little self-conscious about it. But not anymore. Now I kind of like it. It's different." He shrugs. "I guess that's the thing about getting older. You realize your differences can be good things. Not just bad ones. But the long sleeves kind of stuck around."

The room is still humming in the wake of his music.

"So if you got into Juilliard last year, why didn't you go already?" I ask.

I look up at him, and he's staring at me with a mixture of calm and confusion. Like he's trying to figure out what to say but is not too concerned about how long it's going to take him to get there.

"I guess I just wasn't finished here yet," he says.

"With San Bellaro?"

He keeps looking at me. It feels like it did in the wings of the auditorium. Like he can see right through me.

"High school isn't as bad as you think," he says.

"I guess, but it doesn't really seem like your scene. Plus, it's Juilliard." I let my fingers wander to the keys. They're cool, light, so soft. When I press one down, it barely makes a sound.

"Juilliard will be there next year," he says. "Some things are worth waiting for." I can feel his gaze on me, and it's hot, somehow, strong, like the microscope lens that can light a piece of paper on fire just by focusing on it.

Len stands and runs his hand over the family pictures that are propped up in frames on the ledge of the piano. One photo of my parents and me on the beach on Maui during winter break of freshman year. I have a pink flower in my hair, and we're standing behind a waterfall. I remember getting so many bug bites that day that I had to bathe in a thin layer of calamine lotion when we got back to the hotel.

Len picks up the next photo. It's Rob's and my prom picture from last year. It's the only one I haven't been able to bring myself to take down, mostly because my parents would realize it was missing. In it he's dipping me like we're dancing, and I have one leg extended up toward the ceiling. I'm gazing up at him with this look of adoration. The same way my mom is looking at me in all those pictures of me as a baby. He's looking at the camera with this goofy grin on his face.

I reach up and grab the picture. "That shouldn't even be out," I say.

Len nods. "Sometimes old habits are hard to break." He gestures toward his T-shirt.

He takes the photo out of my hands and sets it down. His fingertips brush mine, and even without the static electricity I still feel a charge between us. He's looking at me, and that little curl has fallen down onto his forehead. I want to touch it, brush it away. Not pull it, just sweep it to the side.

"Tell me something," he says softly. He's leaning so close to me, I can smell his cologne. It's intoxicating. The electricity isn't just in my fingertips now but in my entire body. It zips up from my toes through my spine and into my head, where it lingers, making me dizzy.

"Okay," I say, trying to keep my voice steady. "What do you want to know?"

"Would you ever want to hang out without the excuse of a study session?" He looks at me, point-blank, and my stomach turns over so fast, I swear I hear it thud. My hands feel numb and my heart is racing. He's making me totally nervous. And he's still so close, our foreheads are almost touching.

"Like a date?" I whisper.

"Something like that," he says, pulling back just a bit.

He's looking at me again with that same intense expression that makes me feel terrified but alive all at the same time. Like he's seeing something in me that maybe wasn't there before. And all at once I want to say yes. The prospect of spending an entire night alone with Len is intriguing. I want to be close to him, for him to keep leaning toward me in the same way he is now, and for him to brush my fingertips and maybe even—

But I don't say anything. I just run my big toe back and forth across the carpet underneath the piano, because all of a sudden all I can think about is Rob's mother outside. It feels like a betrayal somehow, being here with Len, agreeing to this.

"No go?" he says. "Did I botch the landing?"

"It's not you," I say.

"So what is it?" he says. He sits down again but this time straddles the bench, facing me.

I take a deep breath. "I don't know."

"Which part?"

"What?"

"Which part don't you know?"

I shake my head slowly. "I just don't."

I'm nervous about explaining this to him, but I also want to. I *need* to. There's something about Len that makes me feel understood. Like he really sees me. Not just as Rosie the girl next door but as something else, too. Something more. It feels like whatever I would say he'd be able to handle. Sitting next to him right now, I feel like I could say anything and he wouldn't judge me. He wouldn't even blink.

"It's just been a complicated semester, is all. And I'm not sure I'd be the best date right now."

"I understand," Len says. "You guys were friends for a long time." He nods to the photo of Rob and me.

"It's not only that," I say. I want to explain to him that I've never really thought about being with someone else, that it never occurred to me there could *be* anyone else. I want to tell him that when I'm close to him, I feel things that I never did with Rob and that it scares me. That it feels like I'm somehow betraying the course of my life just by being here with him. I want to, but I'm just not ready to say those things out loud.

"I think I just need a little bit more time," I say.

He looks amused and raises his eyebrows. "That's it?"

"What were you expecting?"

"It's just that, you know, patience is one of my best qualities. This one is a breeze for me." He interlaces his fingers and pushes them out in front of him. He yawns too, although I suspect it's just for effect.

"You seem to have a lot of good qualities," I say, gesturing to the piano.

"Funny," he says, smiling at me, "I was just thinking the same thing about you." I can feel my cheeks start to turn pink again. It's so frustrating to be someone who blushes easily. It's like everything I'm thinking and feeling gets projected right onto my face. No privacy.

"Study time." I clap my hands together.

"Already?" he says. "Fine, but I need my Twizzlers." He smiles that lopsided smile of his.

"I thought they were for me."

"These?" he says. He pulls one out of his pocket, dangling it out like he's baiting me. "No way." Then he leans close to me, so close I can feel his breath on my ear. "I forgot to tell you," he whispers, his words dancing on my neck. "They're my favorite too."

Scene Three

After I walk Len out, I find my mom in the kitchen, sipping tea out of a red mug with CURIOSITY KILLED THE CUP written on it. The logo has never made much sense to me, but she loves it. She bought it in Portland on a trip we took the summer before I started high school. Whenever she's not feeling well, my dad will make her a cup of hot chocolate in what he calls her "curiosity cup." It always makes her smile.

"How did it go?" she says when she sees me. She sets down her mug, and I flop my elbows onto the counter.

"Good," I say. As soon as the word is out, my mouth turns up into a smile. This ridiculous grin that I'm sure makes me look like I'm psychotic or something.

My mom, however, is smiling right along with me.

"What?" I say, trying hard to turn the corners of my mouth back down.

"Nothing," she says, taking a sip but keeping her eyes on me. "You just sounded pretty good playing that thing, that's all."

"Oh, yeah." I straighten up and run a hand through my hair. "I'm glad we kept it."

"Me too."

I have to ask her about the article, and I'm trying to figure out the best way to do it, but I just don't think there's ever a good time to ask your mom if your dad's a traitor, so here goes. "Hey, can I ask you something?"

"Of course." Her eyebrows knit together.

"I read something at school today." I wiggle my lips side to side, trying to figure out the best way to move forward. "And I need to know the real story."

"Okay," she says. "Want to ask me?"

I take a deep breath and place my hands on the countertop. "What happened with Uncle Richard? With their family, I mean. Why did Dad choose the Montegs?"

My mom sighs and folds her hands around her mug. "I knew this would all get stirred up once they got back. I told your father—"

"Mom?"

She nods her head like, *I know.* "How did you find out?"

"The Internet," I say. I don't mean for it to come out in such a sarcastic tone, but it does.

"Things were complicated," she says. "Your father and Rob's dad have always been close."

"That's not it," I say. "It doesn't add up. It doesn't explain why Juliet's family would hate us or why they had to leave town."

My mom looks at me, and for the first time in my entire life, I realize that she looks older. That she hasn't always looked like this. That sometime not too long ago her skin didn't have a single wrinkle. That a million things have happened to her that I don't remember, that I wasn't even around for. And maybe it's because of this that when she says what she does next, I believe her.

"They had an affair," she says. "Rob's mom and your uncle Richard. It was a huge mess, and your father and I somehow got caught in the middle. Your father chose his best friend. He thought he had to." She stands up from the counter and comes over to me. She tucks an arm around my waist and holds me so I'm facing her. "Sweetheart, people make mistakes. We all did with this one. Sometimes you can recover, and sometimes you can't. Rob's mom and dad mended things. They have four beautiful children together. Unfortunately, your father couldn't fix the falling-out he had with his brother."

I nod, taking it in. "Do you think he ever will?"

My mom sighs. "I don't know, but I hope so. I wish for it every day."

"Did Rob's mom—" I swallow, not sure how to ask this. "Did she love him?"

My mom looks thoughtful for a minute. She takes a piece of my hair and tucks it behind my ear, the way she used to do when I was little. "Yes," she says. "But she loved her husband more."

Six months ago I would have said it was impossible to love two people at once. Romantically, I mean. And I think part of me will always love Rob. But it doesn't really stop me from having feelings about other people. It didn't stop me from grinning like an idiot on that piano bench with Len. For the first time I'm glad Rob and I aren't speaking. I don't want to have to keep this from him. Or be the one to tell him.

"Honey," my mom says, "can I ask you something now?"

"Shoot."

"Why didn't you tell us about Rob?"

I run my fingers over the cool granite of the countertop, playing with the grooves. "What's to tell?" I shrug. "He got a girlfriend. He's just not around as much."

My mom nods, but it's the nod she gives when she knows I'm not telling her the whole truth. The nod that says, *I won't push it, but I'm onto you.*

"I gotta go finish up bio," I say. "Thanks for being honest with me."

She smiles and plants a kiss on the top of my head. "Do me a favor, will you?"

I nod. "Sure."

"Don't follow in your father's footsteps. Don't hold on to something for so long it hardens." And with that she releases me, picks up her mug, and marches out of the room.

Scene Four

One of my mom's secret talents is that she can anticipate things. When I was little, she always knew when to pack an extra sandwich at school, what day I'd want to wear my green shirt, and one time, on a camping trip, she even managed to swing an impromptu visit from the tooth fairy. In other words, it doesn't really come as a huge shock to me that she's invited Juliet's family over for dinner on Sunday.

I know my mom is just trying to smooth things over, but dinner feels like a pretty intense way to start. Might as well invite Rob's family over too! Except when I suggest that, she just looks at me sternly and asks me to continue setting the table.

I'm all for letting the past be the past, but this feels like a bit of a stretch. I can't believe they even agreed to come. There's no use explaining to my mom how painful this will be, spending a whole night with the girl who stole Rob right out of my arms. I try to fake a project with Charlie, but somehow all six of us wind up seated around our dining room table, serving ourselves pasta primavera.

Juliet's mom brought roses, and my mom keeps commenting on how lovely they are. I think she's said it four times in the last five minutes, but no one is saying much of anything else, and, well, it's getting awkward.

"So, Juliet," my father says, "how is school going?"

"Great," Juliet chirps. "I mean, classes are good. I got the lead in the school play. And I have a boyfriend, you know. That takes up a lot of my time." She looks at my father and smiles. *We know. We ALL know.*

Juliet's mom's eyes dart to her husband at the word "boyfriend," and my mom glances at my father, then takes a big gulp of water.

It's worth noting that my dad agreed to this gathering. Which is crazy, obviously, and probably speaks more to his love for my mother than his interest in any kind of reconciliation.

Juliet has said barely two words to me, which suits me just fine. I don't have much to say to her, either—besides, you know, "Thanks for stealing my best friend."

"Richard has been so busy with work," Juliet's mom says. "You're never home, are you, darling?"

"Shocking," my father says, and I can practically feel my mother kicking him underneath the table, even though I'm sitting two seats away.

"He's been back and forth to DC almost *constantly*."

I look at Juliet, really look at her. I think about the rumors at school, how she's supposed to be crazy and suicidal. But she doesn't look like either of those things. She just looks gorgeous, and smug.

"Eat, darling," Juliet's mom says to her. "You haven't touched your pasta." She looks at my mother and smiles like, *You know, kids.*

My mom is twirling her spaghetti, but she stops and winks at me. The wink seems to say, *It's okay, we're family, and this night won't last forever.* It's like Charlie's hand squeeze. *I'm here.*

Juliet is sitting across from me, next to my mom, and I see her catch the wink. She narrows her eyes at me.

"So what's keeping you so busy, Uncle Richard?" I ask.

"Humph," he says. He's gruffly shoveling the bread bowl into his mouth, until he chokes, sputters, sips water, and then does it all over again. "We're in the midst of some—" He looks at his wife. "Bullshit."

Juliet's mother taps him on the shoulder. "Now is not the time," she says.

"Why not? There are no secrets here."

My aunt pinches the bridge of her nose with two fingers.

Juliet pushes her chair out and storms off toward the kitchen. Her mom tries to reach out and stop her, but Juliet shakes her off.

"She took it hard," my aunt says. "I think especially with Rob and all." She looks at my mom, explaining. "But we had to tell her. We didn't want her to find out from the news. And people have been sniffing around. We think Richard is going to have to go public about the affair."

My mom nods. My dad says nothing. I know he's thinking, like I am, about the Montegs. About what this is going to mean for Rob's family. For his little brothers.

"When?" my mom asks.

"A week, tops," Uncle Richard says. "Probably not even that."

My mom passes Juliet's father more pasta. He takes it noisily. My dad has gotten up to pour himself a drink in the living room. He takes a bottle out from under our television cabinet—a stash I never knew we had.

Slowly I stand up and round the corner into the kitchen. I expect to see Juliet fuming by the refrigerator, or stampeding past me, but instead I find her melted in a corner, her head on her knees, crying quietly. The sight of her like this, so small and so human, makes me stop in my tracks. Not before she sees me, though.

"What do you want?" she says, her tone bitter and tinged with anger.

"Are you okay?" I bend down to where she is and am surprised that she doesn't flinch away.

"Why do you care?" she says through her hands.

"Honestly?" I say, sliding down next to her. "I don't know."

"For once, honesty in this family."

It's so ridiculous, it almost makes me laugh. "I mean, wouldn't you?"

"Be sitting here on the floor with you?" Juliet says. "Definitely not."

I have to ask her. I can feel the words bubbling up and out, and I know if I don't say it now, I never will. "Why did you do it?"

She lifts her head up, and her eyes are red, her cheeks streaked with tears. "Come on, Rose. Isn't it obvious?"

"No," I say, "or I wouldn't be asking."

She puts her hands on her temples and presses. "You always had what I wanted," she says. "This great, loving family. Parents who cared about you. And Rob was always your best friend." She shakes her head, fresh tears somersaulting down her face. "I wanted to take something from you. I wanted to get back at you."

"For what?" I say. "I never did anything to you."

"Yes, you did," she says. "You never called me after I left, not once. You didn't come and visit until two months had gone by."

"I was seven," I say. "I didn't exactly drive." Not that I do now, but whatever.

"Your mom would have taken you," she says. "In a second if you had asked. You didn't. You didn't when you got older, either. You went along with everything. Being impartial doesn't make you innocent, Rose."

I sit back against the cabinet. It's not even worth telling her how wrong she is. The past is so beside the point. "It didn't have to be like this," I say.

"It's been like this for a really long time. We're only here because my dad was getting into trouble in LA. Same thing." She gestures to the dining room. "You don't know what it's like to have parents who barely even talk to each other."

"You could have asked for my help," I say. "When you guys got here. Instead of doing what you did."

She scoffs. "And you would have given it?"

I take a deep breath and look at her, and for a moment I see the girl I used to know. The one who used to crawl in bed with me during sleepovers and fall asleep with her head on my shoulder, and I'm sorry that I lost her, that I was stupid enough all these years to think she was gone. "I still would."

She holds my gaze. "Don't tell Rob."

"He doesn't know?"

"I didn't tell him anything," she says. And then, matter-of-factly: "And neither will you."

"We don't talk anymore," I say. "In case you hadn't noticed."

"He cares about you," she says.

I almost feel like laughing. "That doesn't mean a lot, coming from you."

"Just promise me you won't tell him." There's something else in her voice now. Something a little desperate. "Promise me you won't say anything."

"I won't," I say, "but from what your parents were saying out there, he might find out soon enough anyway."

She looks down at her hands, and I see that they're shaking. "He still thinks he has the perfect family," she says. "I don't want to take that away from him."

She looks up at me, and there are new tears in her eyes, but they aren't bitter or angry. They're filled with something else entirely. Something like love. And I think, for the first time in ten years, that we might be alike after all.

Scene Five

We all gather in the PL on Monday morning, cranky and bleary-eyed. After Juliet and her parents left last night, I stayed up listening to my parents' hushed tones. Even after they went to bed, sometime in the single digits, I couldn't sleep. I just kept thinking about Juliet's words—*being impartial doesn't make you innocent*—and the look on her face when she asked me not to tell Rob.

Charlie and Olivia are arguing lightly over who discovered the particular brand of jeans they have on, and the rest of the seniors wandering around are fairly quiet, whispering in small groups or tooling around on the Internet.

"Rose, you were there," Olivia says, not looking at me. "We went to Bloomingdales,' didn't we? Tell her."

Lauren and Dorothy are in a corner, scrolling through something on Lauren's iPhone, and they look up and glance at me. I smile and toss some mumbled version of "I dunno" in Olivia's direction. Then John Susquich comes strolling in, the *San Bellaro News* in his hand, and he looks at me before sitting down. "Damn, Caplet," he says, and then flips open his paper.

And then my stomach drops like it's an elevator unhinged. Because I know what they're reading, and I can't believe I didn't see it before. Everyone's eyes are on me, darting like laser beams. I don't have to see the headline ROCKED BY SCANDAL or the old photographs of Juliet's dad and Rob's mom kissing by a car and outside a hotel, or the photos of Uncle Richard groping some woman outside the Capitol. I already know what's in there. I guess Uncle Richard didn't have to announce it, after all.

"Jesus CHRIST." Charlie grabs John's paper and shoves it in my face. "Have you seen this? Are you seeing this?" She flaps it wildly so the pictures blur.

"Yes."

"This is massive. Does Rob know? Rosaline!" Charlie knocks the back of my head, my answer finally dawning on her. "You *knew*?"

Juliet ducks into the PL, her sunglasses secured tightly to her face. The entire room turns, gawks, and falls silent. It's one thing for this to be about your uncle. It's another entirely for it to be about your dad.

She looks small, or it could just be that she's alone. It's been weeks since I've seen her at school without Rob suctioned to her side. But now Rob's suspended and her family is the subject of a sex scandal. I feel sorry for her. Especially after last night.

"No way," Charlie says, like she's having a conversation with my thoughts. "Don't go there. This serves her right. Karma's a bitch."

"Yeah, it is." And it's been a bitch to all of us. I lost my best friend and my cousin, she lost her parents, and somewhere in there we all lost each other. That's the thing about free will: Every decision we make is a choice *against* something as much as it is *for* something else.

Juliet turns to us briefly, and then she leaves the way she came.

"We're going to be late," Olivia says.

Charlie tucks the paper under her arm and cups my elbow. "Rose, let's go."

"Hang on." I make a move to follow Juliet, but Olivia steps in front of me.

"Not happening," she says.

"What?"

She looks at Charlie, who nods like she's giving her permission for something. "You're quick to forgive," Olivia says. "You always have been. You forgave Charlie when she forgot your birthday two years ago." Charlie looks down at her feet, rolling her sparkling water in her hands. "You forgave me when I decided the Belgian was more important than that piano concert you wanted to go to. And that's one of the best things about you, because it means you're willing to look past things and to give people second chances. But the thing is, Rose, some people don't deserve them."

"She's right," Charlie says.

"She's family," I say.

"Says who?" Olivia says. "So you share a last name? Big deal! Your family are the people who know you, the people who are there for you. Rose, *we're* your family. Not Juliet."

I think about everything that's happened, about there being no right choice. And there's one thing I can't stop, regardless of what choice I make, because it's no longer up to me.

"Rob is going to find out," I say.

"Yeah, he is," Charlie says. She puts an arm around my shoulder as she leads me out of the PL. "But it's not your problem to deal with. All of this"—she flaps the paper in the air—"is somebody else's story."

"I don't see why you don't just quit," Charlie says that afternoon. We're sitting out in the courtyard even though it's been drizzling off and on since this morning, and we're talking about the school play. Charlie has a bottle of nail polish balanced on her palm, and she's applying a coat of Tough as Nails to her fingertips—a grayish-blackish color she picked up at the mall last weekend. She makes a face at a group of freshmen ogling us, and they take off toward Cooper House, running.

"Because my entire bio grade is depending on this."

"It's not like Stanford cares about bio," Charlie says. She picks one hand up and blows on her nails. "And I'm sure the dean would fully understand if you told him that the price of admission was you watching your evil cousin prance around the stage with your ex."

"Rob's suspended," I correct her.

"For now," she says.

I catch a glimpse of Len across the courtyard, and it's like I'm right back at that piano bench with him. My entire body lights up, electrified. He's talking to Dorothy and he's wearing a short-sleeved shirt. I can't remember the last time I saw him in one. One time, in eighth grade, Charlie and I ran into him on the beach, but I don't even think he had one on then.

"Cute, huh?" Olivia says, following my gaze.

"Who?" I ask, feigning ignorance.

Olivia rolls her eyes, but she's smiling. "Go talk to him," she says, nudging me in the ribs.

Charlie is swatting her fingers through the air like she's trying to get rid of gnats, and when I say, "I'll be right back," Olivia gives me a small thumbs-up and Charlie just nods.

I cross the courtyard slowly, but when I get about halfway, Len looks up, smiles, and motions me over. Dorothy gives me a little wave and darts into the cafeteria.

"Look who's in short sleeves," I say, trying my best to sound cool when my entire body feels like it's on fire. His black eye has faded, and I can only make out tiny yellowish marks, little fingerprints on his face.

"I'm just trying to be on level with the people," Len says, making a fuss of gesturing around. He smiles, and it makes me look away. I'm thinking about being in my house alone together and, despite the fact that everyone is watching, part of me wants to reach out and touch him, to run my fingers through his hair and put my hands on either side of his face.

I take a deep breath. I want to bring up that date, to tell him I think I might want to go, but I'm not sure how.

"You going to be at rehearsal today?" I ask instead.

Len tucks his hands into his pockets. "I pretty much don't have a choice," he says. "Without me, there is no lighting crew.

No offense or anything." He looks at me under his lashes. "But you kinda suck."

I laugh nervously. "Sadly, that's true."

He holds up his hands. "So how was the rest of your weekend?"

"Eventful."

"Interesting."

"Have you read the paper?"

"I told you I was politically informed," he says.

"So are you going to say anything?"

"Like what?"

"Like 'Your family's really screwed up'?"

He laughs, shaking his head. "You're a trip, Rosaline, you know that?"

I shrug. "That's something."

"Your uncle's kind of a misogynist. And at one point your parents had a hard decision to make. But so what? My parents got divorced when I was five, and now my mom lives with a guy who's been to jail twice, and this morning my twelve-year-old sister broke her arm on the back of her boyfriend's motorcycle. Just because a newspaper doesn't write articles about us doesn't mean we aren't totally fucked."

"I'm sorry," I say. "I didn't know."

"This is life," he says. "We have to take it as it comes, because even though some things are really shitty, there's a lot of really great stuff too." For a moment his eyebrows cinch in tight. But it's not a frown. It's that intense look he gets. The look I saw when he was playing the piano. The one he gets when he really cares about something. And right now he's looking at me.

Scene Six

I've just stubbed my toe, hard, and I'm trying not to scream, but the effort is causing me to sweat up in the wings. Juliet and the Belgian are flitting around stage. I think they've gotten better, but it's hard to tell. The Belgian is still mispronouncing things, and we're only a week away from opening night.

"Can you hand me the script?" Len whispers.

I've been sitting on it, and when I pluck it off the bottom of my chair, the first page sticks stubbornly to my leg. I arch back and try to yank it off, and when I do, I see Len staring at me, this twinkle of laughter in his eye.

"Pretty attached to this performance, huh?"

"Very funny."

Mrs. Barch calls an intermission break, and Juliet collapses into a seat and picks up a water bottle, like she's a sidelined athlete.

Len is fiddling with some fixture, but the words are out before I even have a chance to filter myself. "About that date," I blurt out, all at once. Len squints down at me but doesn't say anything. "You know, how you said Friday night, at the piano."

Len straightens up. "I haven't forgotten," he whispers, "but remember what I said about patience being a virtue?" He's smiling, the corners of his mouth turned up quirkily at the sides.

"I think it's overrated."

"Oh yeah?" Len asks, raising his eyebrows. "What's made you change your mind?"

I have to think hard before I speak, about constructing coherent, sensible sentences, because being this close to him is making all the words rush out of my head like water back into the ocean in one big, sweeping *whoosh*.

"You're wearing a T-shirt," I sort of explain.

"It's my biceps," he says. "I can't let them out too often. Too many people want tickets to the gun show." He sweeps the curl out of his eyes and looks at me. "So," he says, "does this mean I can take you out tonight?"

"Tonight?"

"You said it: Patience is overrated."

He puts his hand on mine, and instantly I feel it again, that electric shock. Except this time it doesn't make me pull away. It makes me move closer. His hand is still on mine, and it's sending a current through my arm and up into my chest. "You do not hold strongly to your beliefs," I say.

"Not the ones that need changing." He looks at me, dead-on. It makes my breath catch in my throat, and I have to kind of blow it out and start all over again.

"Okay," I say. "Pick me up at six?"

"I'll be there," he says. He lifts up my hand and touches it to his cheek. "I'll be right back. I have to grab something from Cooper House."

I watch him go, with a gigantic smile plastered on my face. Like I'm wearing a set of those wax lips Rob and I used to have when we were younger. And there's nothing I can do about it. There's nothing I *want* to do about it. In fact, I'm so caught up in Len that it takes me another minute to realize someone is screaming.

Rob has lobbed himself onto the stage like a tennis ball, and he's standing in front of Juliet, his hands clenched into fists at his sides. The Belgian has disappeared and so has Mrs. Barch. Besides a few cast members hanging around the sides of the auditorium, they're the only ones in sight.

"Did you know about this?" he asks. Screams.

"You're not supposed to be here," Juliet says. Her voice is quiet, tired, and she's still sitting down.

"Did you know about this?" he yells again.

Juliet covers her face with her hands, the same way she did on my kitchen floor last night. I want to run between them, to gather her up and protect them both from each other.

"Answer me," Rob bellows. I can see the veins of his neck bulging out. He has this one vein by his left ear that pops out when he gets angry. I've only ever seen it once, when we got into a fight about whether or not white was a primary color. Completely stupid, but he got so worked up about it, the vein practically disconnected. It makes me almost scared for her.

"I'm sorry," Juliet says. It's just above a whisper, but it's so quiet in this auditorium, you could hear a pin drop.

"I should have known," he says. "I thought I could trust you. I believed in us, despite everything that people said. But they were all right. You're just a crazy liar."

Juliet exhales, picking her head up. "Let's talk about this," she says.

"What's to talk about? You betrayed me."

"I was trying to protect you."

"From what? From the truth?" He steps back and holds his head in his right hand.

"Your family—" Juliet starts, but Rob cuts her off.

"Don't do that. Don't talk about my family like you know them." His face is screwed up tight, like if he lets go, he will unravel completely.

And then Juliet stands, and even though I know she's a good foot shorter than him, from up here they look like they're nose to nose.

"I'm sorry," she says. "I'm sorry I don't know your family better. I'm sorry I can't be there for you the way you need. I'm sorry I'm not *her*."

"This isn't about her," Rob says. He looks a little self-conscious now, and he's glancing around the auditorium.

"Of course it's about her," Juliet says, her voice rising. "You're still in love with her."

There are a million thoughts bouncing around in my head at once. Juliet is talking about me, I know that much, but I've also realized something else, too. Rob is in love with Juliet. He's angry and hurt because he actually cares. If she can't see that, maybe she really is crazy.

"Don't go using this as an excuse to do something stupid again," Rob says through clenched teeth.

Juliet's eyes get wide, and she takes a step back. Rob reaches out and grabs her shoulder. "You can't just walk away."

Juliet is looking straight ahead, and when Rob's hand reaches her shoulder, I see her close her eyes, briefly. "Let me go," she says, and then she leaves, her feet picking up speed as she races out of the auditorium.

Rob slumps down into a seat, his face in his hands. A few of the underclassmen start to giggle, trying to defuse the tension that has just swept across the room. They look like little bobble-head dolls in the wings. Different heads, same bodies. Like all of them are interchangeable. Like the entire cast could be switched out and no one would even notice.

Then Rob looks up. It feels like our eyes lock, even though I know I'm lost in the shadows up here, the lights making it impossible for him to see me. Rob just keeps looking upward, toward me, almost like he's sending up a prayer. Then he stands, pitching Juliet's chair over, and ducks out of the auditorium after her.

Scene Seven

"I know you're bummed out about Rob, and wrapped up in Juliet's latest circus," Charlie says, "but I hardly think gallivanting around with the class clown is the solution." She's driving me home and gesturing wildly.

I lean across the seat and give her flailing arm a squeeze. "'Gallivanting'? Really?" I tease.

"Affection will not break me," she says, making a halfhearted attempt to swat me off.

"I can still try."

She sticks her chin out at me and frowns. "They may break up over this, you know."

"Maybe."

"I'm just saying, it's a pretty big deal. Not an easy fix."

"Yeah," I say, "I know. I still don't think it's going to happen. He really cares about her." I think about Juliet in the auditorium, so small and almost helpless. I can't help feeling bad for her. It's not like she has any friends to talk to either. It's been her and Rob against the world since she got here.

"Whatever," Charlie says. "It could. What then?"

"So could a white Christmas," I say, "but I don't see anyone running out to buy a sled."

Charlie pulls into my driveway and turns off the car. She slumps in her seat but keeps looking forward. "Maybe. I don't know. It just feels like everything is changing." She sighs and looks at me. "Do you ever feel that way? Like one minute you think you have it figured out, and it turns out you were completely wrong about everything?"

"Have we met?" I ask. "That's the story of my life."

Charlie shrugs. "I used to think I knew what I was doing." Her lower lip starts to tremble, and she bites down on it to hold it in place.

"Is this about Jake?"

Charlie shakes her head, but the motion seems to force the tears up and out, and they start falling down her checks, dotting her T-shirt.

I unbuckle my seat belt and lean over, wrapping my arms around her.

"I just miss her," she says into my shoulder, her words muffled.

"I know," I say. I always take Charlie's strength for granted. I forget sometimes that she can hurt too. Sometimes even more than the rest of us.

She pulls back and dabs the back of her hand over her cheeks. "It doesn't get easier. Sometimes I feel like I'm just right back where I started."

"You're not, though. You're so much stronger."

Charlie rolls her eyes and hugs her arms to her chest. "Maybe," she says. "Who remembers?"

"I do." It surprises me how fiercely the words come out, but there they are, marching from my mouth. "I was there, and I remember how hard it was and how much of a mess you were. It's nothing like that anymore. You stumble and you fall, sure. But now you pick yourself back up. You do that now. You've *been* doing that. And sometimes you pick me up too."

"Thanks." She reaches behind us and pulls up the big CAK tote. There is a Kleenex floating around in the top of the bag, and she wipes her nose with it.

"I mean it," I say. "I guess that's my job as your best friend. To remind you that things are not the way they used to be."

She looks at me and smiles. Even with her face red and blotchy, she's still absurdly beautiful.

"You need a reminder, call me," I say. "I'm always here." Then I take her hand and squeeze it. Twice.

"You know who gave me the nickname Charlie?" she asks me.

"No," I say, shaking my head. "I've never thought about it."

"She did." Charlie's smiling and staring off through the windshield into the distance, like she's paying much more attention to what's happening inside her head than out. "It's what she wanted to name me to begin with. She said she thought that if I could pull it off, I'd be something spectacular."

"Well, you do," I say, "that's for damn sure."

"I know," she says, that familiar ring coming back into her voice. She blinks a few times rapidly and focuses back on me. "Thank *God*."

We both crack up laughing, shoulders shaking, until we're practically holding our sides.

"But it's sort of my real name," Charlie says through gasps, "if you think about it."

"Like Rosaline." I have a thought, briefly, but it leaves with a hiccupped laugh.

"I'll call you whatever you want," she says, "as long as you don't make me call you Len's girlfriend."

"Hey," I say, "I'm making progress here. Moving on."

"I don't think dating Len is progress," Charlie says. And then she sighs, tossing the bag back over the seat. "But if you insist on doing it, at the very least you better make him cut that hair."

The house is quiet when I get home, and empty. I drop my bag by the door and wander into the den and, without thinking much about it, settle down at the piano. There was a time when I used to come here every day after school. When my parents would bring me home and I would race inside, plunk myself down, and play. It was like taking a shower. My muscles would relax and my head would clear and the day would wash away.

I choose a piece from memory. It's something by Tchaikovsky that I've always really liked. A love theme. I'm rusty and I start slow, but my fingers remember the way better than I do, and soon I'm flying, gliding over the keys. The thing I always loved about playing was that there was no room for anything else. From the moment my hands touch the keys, it's just me and the piano. We're the only thing that exists in the entire universe.

In fact, it's almost six by the time I tear myself away, which means I've spent almost two hours here. When I sit back, I half expect Len to be seated next to me, smiling encouragingly. And then I leap up, because Len is going to be here any minute and I still have to get ready.

The thing about growing up in Southern California is that you kind of wear the same thing all year round. Aside from the possible addition of a cardigan or wrap in the winter, wardrobe is pretty standard.

When I get up to my room, I open my closet. It smells like lavender because of these tiny bags of potpourri my mom keeps in my sock and T-shirt drawers, and I breathe deeply, enjoying the momentary lull. After a moment I feel calmer and I consider the possible wardrobe options for this date.

I pull out a few items and look at my choices. There is the dress I bought and wore for Rob's mom's fortieth birthday, the one I took with us to see *Phantom of the Opera* in New York. There is a summer dress that I wore when we rode bikes together last year, and one that still has an ice cream stain from when he dropped his chocolate cone on me two summers ago. Every dress in here seems to tell some sort of story about Rob.

I look again, determined to do better. There's a blue dress hidden in the back that my mom and I bought last spring. It's blue cotton and kind of flowy with little cap sleeves and a hem that hits just above the knee. I've never worn it before, and I slip it on. It's comfortable, and I think it makes me look older somehow. I choose a pair of teardrop earrings Charlie gave me for my sixteenth birthday and put on some blush and mascara. It's not as amazing as the silver dress I wore to Fall Back, but I think this one makes me look like me.

The doorbell rings exactly at six. I didn't expect him to be the kind of guy who shows up on the dot, but Len keeps on surprising me. I throw some cash that's on my dresser into my bag and take one last look in the mirror. I'm excited. Something about knowing that Len is downstairs feels right. Not like a dream, but better. Real.

I can't wait to hold his hand tonight and to maybe even have him kiss me. I can't wait to find out what his favorite color is and what he meant about Juilliard, about not being done here. I want to know more about his sister and whether he's close with his dad. I want to know how he feels about Thai food versus Japanese and what his favorite movie is. The future seems better than the past, bigger and more alive, and as I run down the stairs, the only thing I can think is, *I'm excited for what's to come.*

I open the door a tiny bit breathless, but it's not Len standing on the other side. It's someone in jeans and a familiar green T-shirt. It's Rob. His face is red and he's panting, like he's been running. His breath comes in short, hollow bursts, and he's doubled over, his hands on his knees. And he reeks.

"What are you doing?" I blurt out. I keep the door closed just a little, my hand still on the knob.

"Can I come in?" He frowns and glances behind me. "Just for a minute."

"No. My parents are home," I lie. "What's going on?"

He shakes his head. "I had to see you," he slurs.

"Are you drunk?"

"A little."

"You're a mess," I say.

"My life is a mess."

He looks at me and his eyes are red, cracked. He's been crying.

"My mom lied, Juliet lied, my friends are all liars. You're the only one who ever—" He looks at his feet. "You were the only one who ever made any sense."

"Rob—"

"I miss you."

It's all I've wanted to hear. For months I just wanted him to show back up on my doorstep and say it was all a mistake, that I was the one he really wanted. But now, looking at him, drunk and in shambles, I don't want to fall into his arms. "It's a little late for that, don't you think?"

He blinks and looks at me. "I—I dunno," he stutters. "I think I made a mistake." He runs a hand through his hair.

"Look, Rob," I say, "I don't really know what you want from me."

"I want you," he says softly. "I want you back. I *miss* you. Can't you see that?"

He's looking at me with those brown hot chocolate eyes. The eyes that have watched me sleep and seen my piano recitals and that looked on, steadfast, when I first learned how to ride a bike.

"What about Juliet?"

That vein in his neck twitches. "I don't know. I can't even trust her."

What I say next surprises both of us. "It wasn't her fault, you know. You shouldn't hold her responsible."

He looks taken aback, and it takes him a moment to respond. "She still lied," he manages. He's leaning against the door frame, his limbs buckling.

"She didn't lie. She just kept something from you. She didn't want to hurt you." What I don't tell him is that, regardless of who was responsible at first, we all have a role in this.

"What?" He squints at me, like he's trying to focus on putting the words together, but he ultimately shakes his head and gives up. "Did you hear me? I said I miss you."

I cross my arms. I keep expecting my heart rate to speed up, my hands to start sweating, but they don't. I feel surprisingly calm, actually.

"You already said that."

"I don't want Juliet." He sighs and looks at his shoes. "She's not you. She's never been you. I told her I was coming over here tonight, and she didn't even fight me on it."

"You told her?"

"Yeah," he says. He looks guilty.

"You shouldn't be here," I say. "You guys should"—I swallow—"figure things out." Now my heart is racing. I'm suddenly remembering Rob's words in the auditorium this afternoon. *Don't do anything stupid. Again.*

"What? No." He lunges forward, but I step back. "I want to be with you. We've been friends forever, Rosie. I've known you my whole life."

"Things change."

"We never should have."

"That's life," I say. "Things happen."

"I messed up," he says. "I thought she was something she wasn't, and I lost everything. I want to make it up to you. I'll do whatever it takes." He makes a sweeping gesture with his hand, like he's including the whole world. "It's *you*, Rosie. Please."

In one swift, albeit crooked, motion he takes my hand in his. It's been so long since we've even spoken that I'd forgotten what it's like to just be with him. "Please," he says again.

I look at him, his eyes soft and his forehead sweating. It's Rob. The only Rob there is ever going to be. No one will ever feel so comfortable or remember my life the way he can. Maybe it's worth another chance. Even to see if we could just be friends again.

But then I think about Len. About bio and the play and piano and his hands on mine and eating Twizzlers in my room and the way my head feels like it's humming whenever he's around.

"I need to think about it," I say.

He drops my hand. "I understand," he says, but he looks disappointed. "What now?"

"I think you need to go back to Juliet," I say. "You need to make things right."

He nods. "Can't I just stay with you a little longer? We could watch a movie or something?"

"Not right now," I say. "You need to go home."

"I can't go home," he says sadly. "I don't even know where that is anymore." Rob pinches the bridge of his nose with his thumb and pointer finger. He looks tired, and I notice dark circles under his eyes, the color of charcoal dust.

I reach out and put a hand on his arm, and he pulls me toward him, into a hug. But it doesn't feel like it used to. It doesn't make me feel happy or excited or even comforted. It doesn't really make me feel anything at all.

I slide out of his arms and pull the door closed, sitting down on the floor when I'm back inside. I hear his footsteps down the stairs, and then it's quiet, so still I can hear myself breathing. When I was younger, I used to dread being alone. I would convince myself that something terrible had happened to my parents, that they had been in some kind of car accident or something and they were never coming back. I would sit in the corner of my kitchen, terrified and white-knuckled, and wait for them to pull up the driveway. But right now I want to be alone. I want all the time in the world to think about what Rob has just said and what I should do. Could there ever be an us again?

The doorbell rings again. I sit up with a start, annoyed. I can't believe he's come back. I just told him to give me some space. He has no patience, never has.

I yank the door open, already talking, but of course it's not Rob. It's Len. He's dressed in jeans and a white button-down, and he looks so adorably sexy, I just want to leap into his arms right here.

A bouquet of violets is hanging down by his side, the flowers pointed toward the ground. They're my favorite flowers. I used to pick them in Famke's garden and bring them home to my mom. Rob thinks I like roses best, and I've never corrected him because it's so cute when he says "Roses for Rosie." Except my name isn't really Rosie, and I don't like roses. I haven't liked them since I was pricked by a thorn when I was eight years old.

"Hi," I start, but Len just shakes his head. He's looking at me in that way that tells me that whatever I'm about to say, he already knows what it is.

"You have to think about it?" he says.

His car is parked in my driveway, just over to the side of the house. He's been here the entire time. He heard everything. The realization knocks the wind out of me.

"I'm sorry," I say. "Please understand. It's complicated."

I want to tell him how sorry I really am. How Rob is this force in my life, one I can't turn away from. I want to tell him that it's confusing, especially now. How it was always supposed to be Rob, but being here, with Len, makes me want to forget about that. To leave the past entirely. The problem is, I'm just not sure how to do it.

"It's not, actually," he says. He inhales and looks at me. Sharply. Like his eyes could cut through flesh. "Here's the deal. I care about you. I always have. I see who you are. This amazing girl who's smart and beautiful and intelligent and talented and who cares way too much about what other people think. You wrote me off for years, and then this miracle happened this year and you actually paid attention. Do you know why? Because for one damn minute you weren't thinking about Rob." His eyes narrow but he doesn't stop. His voice is loud and strong but not angry, just firm. "I'm a patient person. I've waited for you for what seems like forever. But I'm not going to stick around and watch you pick the wrong person again. So the thing is, Rosaline, it's actually not that complicated. When you think about it, it's really simple."

He hands me the flowers and walks away to his car. I want

to call after him, to tell him to stay, but my feet are cemented to the spot. Instead I just stand on my front steps, holding his violets, my violets, thinking about what he just said as I watch him leave. It's not until he's gone and I'm alone that I realize that this time, it's not what I want at all.

Act Five

Scene One

"Wait up!" I call. I'm flapping my arms and legs wildly, but he's so much faster than I am, it feels like I'm not even moving, just staying afloat.

"Hurry up, slowpoke," he calls, flipping over onto his back and doing the high kicks like those synchronized swimmers in the Olympics.

"No fair," I say. "You got a head start."

"Early bird gets the worm!" he says, but it comes out as "worrrr" because he's flipped over and has a mouthful of water. He's coughing and choking, and I paddle over, a little alarmed, but when I get there, his cheeks are wide and he spits at me, sending water into my eyes and all over my face.

"Stop!" I yell, and then he's making a beeline away from me, kicking so forcefully I am lost in his splashes.

"Come and find me," Rob says, and then disappears beneath the water.

I've heard people say that when something really big happens, the whole world stops and you become frozen in time, but that's not how it happens for me. Instead I'm being catapulted through time, yanked by my navel, back, back, back to before any of this began. The only thing I can think of is that summer at Camp Kwebec. Of Rob and me splashing around in our bathing suits. Of the sun and the promise of lemonade and his voice under the water. *Come and find me.*

I know before my parents tell me. I know the second they walk into my room to wake me. Maybe I dreamed it. Maybe it has something to do with the fact that Rob was here last night, asking to be with me, and when I said I didn't know, I changed the course of things. Whatever it is, I'm not surprised. I don't fight them on it the way they expected me to. I don't even scream "No" or "Why" or any of the things people usually do in movies. Instead I just lie there quietly. I'm already being pulled back to the pool. So far, in fact, that their words sound muffled and their faces look distorted. Like I'm watching them from underneath the water.

Rob is gone, they tell me. But not the way he was yesterday. Not at all. This time he's gone for good.

Car crash. Alcohol. The Cliffs. The words come at me like tiny flashlights piercing the darkness, blinding and brilliant.

I don't look at my mother's tear-streaked face or my father's somber expression. Instead I look up at my ceiling.

It's littered with stars, the stick-on kind that glow in the dark, and because it's five a.m., and therefore not light out, they are shining up there. Rob and I used to collect them when we were little from the vending machines outside our local grocery store. My ceiling isn't extraordinarily high or anything, but we couldn't reach it just by standing on the bed back then, so we used to jump, with the star sticky side up in our palms. We got them all up there that way. There must be hundreds.

Images of Rob come to me in crystal detail. My memory is perfectly clear; it's the present I'm having trouble with.

I see Rob standing in my driveway, yelling at me to take the training wheels off my bike. Rob and me on our back porch, making s'mores. Rob and me standing in line at the Macy's counter, trying to sneak fake jewelry into my mom's purchase.

"We're going to go over to the Montegs', to be with his parents," my mother says. All of a sudden I snap up and awake. Juliet. Who called her? How is she taking this?

"Where is Juliet?" I finally ask. But then I see the way my

mother is looking at me, and I realize—she's gone too. Juliet was in the car with Rob. They're both dead.

For some reason the force of this sends me sitting up, straight up. My mom's sitting there, and my dad's standing over us. The clock reads 5:25. I was born at 5:25, and my mom says that for the first ten years of my life it was the time I would always wake up, like it was the time I was meant to reenter the world.

Neither Rob nor Juliet will ever reenter my world. He will never show up on my front steps. He'll never watch a movie with me or hold me close to him. She'll never be my friend again. She'll never forgive me.

I remember thinking in September, at Olivia's party, that it was like he might as well have died, that death would be easier, because at least I wouldn't have to see him. I was wrong. Death is completely different, final in a way I can't fully grasp. Rob is nowhere on this planet. Not in Italy with his parents or gone at summer camp or even with Juliet. He doesn't exist anymore, and he's never coming back.

"Do you want to come with us?" I hear my mom ask.

"Can I call Charlie?" I feel like a little kid, asking my parents' permission to buy an ice cream, but I'm not sure what to do. What is the proper protocol on this? When your best friend and your cousin die, what are you supposed to do?

"Of course," my mom says. "Whatever you want."

But this isn't what I want. What I want is for today to unfold the way it was supposed to. For us to be at school. Today we are supposed to be having a dress rehearsal for the play. Rob and Juliet are supposed to be on the stage, and Len and I are supposed to be up there, adjusting lightbulbs.

Len.

I can feel something slashing through the grief, gnawing its way closer and closer until it's right at my chest, reaching for my heart. It's guilt, so much of it that it catches in my throat and makes it difficult to breathe.

I should never have agreed to that date with Len. I should have said yes to Rob. I should have pulled him straight inside and made him get into the shower and comforted him and told him I was there. He was drunk and hurting. How could I have turned my back on him?

I grope for the phone on my nightstand and furiously punch in Charlie's number. She picks up on the first ring.

This is something I love about her. She always has her phone on. Never on silent or vibrate or even quiet. Always on full blare. One time we got kicked out of seeing some chick flick because her phone kept blaring—Jake kept calling—and she wouldn't shut it off. She's available. No matter the time of night or morning, and for a second I am more grateful for that than I've ever been for anything else in my whole life.

"Hey, baby," she says, like she isn't sleeping. Like she isn't even tired.

"Can you come over?"

"Duh," she says. "You think I'd abandon you to the wiles of driving? Not a chance."

"Can you come over sooner?" I ask. My mom touches my leg underneath the covers, and I blink back tears. The sound of Charlie's voice and my mom's touch all at once like that feel like too much. "Please."

"Yeah," she says, and I can see her nodding, already out of bed. "What happened?"

"Just come over."

Charlie and I became friends in the sandbox the first day of first grade, but we met before then. We didn't know this until last year, though. We were looking through old photo albums at her house, and there was a picture of us as toddlers dressed in swimsuits at the beach with our moms. There are other people there too. This girl Asara Dool, who moved before high school, and a few more, so it's clear this wasn't a playdate for the two of us, but there we are, in a picture together. Charlie had a second copy made and gave it to me in a frame last year. She had written on the back in gold Sharpie one word: evidence.

I think about that now. About her dress hanging in my closet and my earrings in her drawer and the Swedish Fish on my desk and the million little pieces that remind us that we've been friends since before we can even remember, that she was there before I even knew who she was.

"She's coming over," I tell my mom when I hang up. I say it firmly, deliberately, like it's somehow going to change things. Like all that needs to happen is that Charlie needs to know.

I look at my dad. He's been quiet, his hand on his forehead and his arm across his chest. Usually when things get tense he makes a joke. My mom says she can always count on him to lighten the mood, even when she doesn't want it lightened, but today there is absolutely nothing to say to make things better.

Our phone rings, and for a second I think it's Charlie, but I haven't even put down the receiver. Time is doing something funny. Doubling back on itself so that it's hard to tell when things have occurred. It feels like my parents have been sitting on my bed for years, like there was never a time before I knew Rob was dead. Which would mean—and I can't even believe I'm thinking this—that there was never a time he was alive.

At the same time, I expect him to come waltzing through my door. To suggest we skip the last day and go see a movie.

My mom stands up, and for the first time I realize she is

dressed. Fully dressed. She has on black pants and a cream sweater and even pearls, which she never wears. I imagine her getting dressed this morning, choosing an outfit that would be able to take her through whatever today might bring. She doesn't look like herself, and I know she put these clothes on after she heard. That she took the time to look presentable, that she needed to pull herself together in order to stare down the pain she was about to cause me. Before she came in here and told me that Rob was dead.

"I'll get that," she says, and she looks at my dad. She puts a hand on his shoulder and squeezes, and he stands up.

"I'll come with you," he says.

My mom looks from me to my dad, and I can tell she's nervous about leaving me alone.

"I'm just going to get dressed," I say. "Then I'll come downstairs."

My mom looks relieved, but not much, and she kisses me once on the cheek before she disappears with my dad down the hallway.

When I'm alone, it starts to sink in, to bear down on me from all directions so that it feels like I'm suffocating, drowning. I once read somewhere that if you are in a burning building, you should drop to your hands and knees because the air is cleaner down there, or something. I do that now. I'm on the ground in my room, coughing and sputtering, when Charlie steps inside.

"Oh, God," she says, in my doorway, and then she's on the ground next to me, gathering me into her arms.

Scene Two

The funerals take place three days later. Rob's is in the morning, Juliet's in the afternoon. We're not invited to Juliet's. My uncle calls and tells my father he doesn't want him there. They blame Rob's family for the accident. And, by association, mine.

Juliet's parents are the only ones who think it was Rob's fault, though. There are huge skid marks on the road by the Cliffs where Rob's car went over, and no evidence of any oncoming traffic. The rumors at school are that Juliet grabbed the wheel and led them off the road, free-falling to the water. Tormented, tragic love. Or at least that's what Olivia said. The worst part is, the rumor keeps building on itself, picking up tiny kernels of truth and spinning them into unrecognizable form. Juliet couldn't stand that Rob still had feelings for me. She found out we were seeing each other. If she couldn't have him, no one would. . . .

Charlie helps me pick out a dress. A black one from Macy's that feels like plastic when I put it on. Tight and hot and sticky.

"You look nice," Charlie says with a sad smile. She has basically lived at my house since she came over the other morning. I think she left once to get a toothbrush and change of clothes, but that's about it.

"Thanks." I smile wanly. I wonder if Rob would like the dress, and then I push the thought out. I can't think about that. I can't think about anything.

When we arrive at the church, everyone is already sitting. My parents go to the front. They sit right behind Rob's parents, and I can see my mom with her arms around Rob's mother's shoulder. Just the way I would sit with Charlie. I wonder what my parents think. Whether they suspect suicide too. Rob's little brothers sit beside them, their hands in their laps and their faces blank. I motion for Charlie to slide into the back pew, and she does. She doesn't ask why I don't want to move more forward, and she doesn't suggest something different. She just sits. A few seconds later Olivia sits down next to us.

Everyone is dressed in blacks and grays, and it's impossible to tell anyone apart. I know that somewhere in here are John

Susquich and Matt Lester. I know that Lauren is probably here too, and Dorothy Spellor and maybe even Brittany Fesner. I know that Becky Handon will be here, and Taylor too, and probably even Jason. Mr. Davis and Mrs. Barch and Mr. Johnson. But I can't tell anyone from anyone else. It reminds me of the first morning of school, of sitting in the back of senior seats with Rob and seeing everyone, and noticing how connected we all were. Except no one feels connected here. We're not a spiderweb, not even close. We're just tiny particles of anonymous dust drifting past each other in the darkness. We're lucky to ever even knock each other off course.

The service is nice enough. Jake gets up and says some things. I'm actually surprised at how well he speaks. It's like he's a different person up there, and I wonder why he doesn't act like this all the time. Why usually he peppers all his sentences with so many words that mean absolutely nothing. But maybe it takes something like death to wake someone up.

My mom asked if I wanted to say anything today. I assume Rob's parents suggested it, but maybe she thought of it on her own, I don't know. Either way, I told her no. It's not that I don't have things to say. I just don't know which ones to share. Which stories, I mean. I guess I'm not sure how to remember him. Was Rob my best friend or the guy who broke my heart? Was he my boyfriend or the boy next door? I want to get up there and talk about how he was the one, the person I was supposed to spend forever with. But I can't do that. They died together; they'll always be remembered together. It's decided, once and for all. He was hers. The rumors don't matter; they'll fade. The circumstances and the details will have no relevance after a year or two. People may remember it was suicide, but my name won't be attached. It will just be the two lovers, fused together forever. Sitting in the church, listening to Jake talk about Rob, I can't help but keep asking myself this question: How do you mourn something that never really belonged to you?

I feel Charlie reach for my hand, but I tuck it underneath my leg. I don't want to be that close to anyone right now. The thought of her squeezing my hand twice makes me inexplicably angry. It was fine when we were just talking about heartbreak or book bags, but those traditions shouldn't carry over into something this serious. None of our theories apply to death. . . . Wasn't she the one who first figured that out?

"That was nice," Charlie says when we're outside. It's sunny today, too sunny for a funeral. Everyone is wearing sunglasses, like we're at the beach or something. Olivia is off comforting Ben, and it's just the two of us standing there.

"Nice?" I didn't mean for it to come out icy, but as soon as it does, I realize I'm not sorry. Everyone is acting like this is so sad, so tragic. No one has said how wrong this is. How it never should have happened.

"I just mean," Charlie starts, "that Rob would have liked it."

"It was his funeral," I shoot back. "I don't think he would have been so psyched."

Charlie, oddly, is not wearing her sunglasses, and she squints at me in the sun.

"I didn't mean that," she whispers. "I'm just trying to say—"

"Save it."

We're standing by the edge of the cemetery at the Cliffs. If I look over my left shoulder, I can see the two boulders hanging over the ocean. The rocks where Rob and I spent so many nights. The rocks where he kissed me. The rocks where he died. For a second I want to go over to them and jump, to hurl my whole body off that cliff too. I was right to be so scared of falling. There are a million things in this world that can end you, that can in one tiny second obliterate the life you work so hard to keep alive. Our entire lives are structured around not dying. Eating, sleeping, looking both ways before you cross the street. It's all, all of it, to keep us safe from the thing that we know is going to get us anyway. It doesn't even make sense, if you think about it. It's the world's biggest joke. Our entire lives are set up around not dying, knowing all the while that it's the one thing we can't avoid.

But death shouldn't have come so soon.

The one thing I could have done to save Rob, I didn't do. I could have invited him in. I could have listened when he said he missed me. I could have paid attention to the rumors about Juliet. I could have gotten help. Maybe then they wouldn't have been in the car that night. He wouldn't have been driving drunk. They wouldn't be dead.

"This isn't your fault," Charlie says beside me. Her arms are crossed around her body, and I can see the goose bumps on her pale, freckled skin. "I don't care what happened in the car that night or what it had to do with you. It's not your fault."

"How the hell would you know?"

Charlie recoils as if I've just slapped her, but she doesn't say anything at first. She just looks down at the grass underneath us and shakes her head. "You think you could have stopped this? That you pull the strings?" She looks at me, hard, and for a minute I'm reminded of the Charlie that I love. The fierce, powerful, won't-take-crap-from-anyone Charlie.

Maybe it's because of that that I tell her. "He came back to me."

She doesn't look surprised. She doesn't even uncross her arms. "So what?"

"So what?" I can feel my voice rising. Something in the back of my throat is breaking. Like a guitar string that has just snapped. "He asked to be with me, and I said no. He should have been home in my house that night. He shouldn't have been driving."

Charlie shakes her head, but the movement is almost imperceptible, it's so slight. "It wouldn't have mattered," she says.

"Because Juliet grabbed the wheel?" I dare her.

"Not quite."

"So you don't believe that? You heard he was in love with me, right? That it drove her to take both their lives?" I'm hissing now, spitting venom. "Why don't you explain to me how it wasn't my fault? Because any way you spin this, I could have told him to stay."

She blinks and glances at the church, then back at me. "Look, you think I like history because I'm fascinated with the possibilities, with how it could have happened, but you're wrong. I like it because it's the one thing we actually know in life. The past is the only thing we can count on. The present? The future? They're anyone's guess."

"What's your point?"

"My point is that there are some things that are out of our control. Some things that are just *supposed* to *happen*. We can't stop them. There's nothing we can do."

"We have choice," I say. I taste the word on my tongue and say it again: "Choice." Not fate or destiny but free will.

"Yes," Charlie says, "but not about everything."

"About what, then?" I'm not looking at Charlie anymore. The lump in the back of my throat is bubbling up, and I can feel hot tears begin to sting the backs of my eyes. I won't cry, though, not here. I've cried in front of Charlie hundreds of times, but if

I do it now, here, she will be right. If I cry, I'll be admitting he's really gone.

"You can choose to be happy," Charlie says. She offers the words firmly, like she's offering me her hand. "You reminded me of that this week. Happiness is a choice, Rose." I think about sitting in her car earlier on Monday, talking about her mom. It might as well have been years ago. "I think you can choose not to blame yourself too."

"Hey," Olivia says. She and Ben have come up behind us. He has his arm around her, tucking her firmly to his side, and her head is on his shoulder. She's wearing the same black dress she had on for prom last year. I know it has a snag on the zipper from when she couldn't get it up and Taylor pulled too enthusiastically.

Charlie's bottom lip is quivering, and Ben lets go of Olivia, drawing Charlie into a big hug. They stay that way for a while. I forget sometimes that they're related. That everything that happened with Charlie's mom happened to Ben's mom too. It's overwhelming, and for a moment the magnitude of it all, the fact that death has touched all of us, is almost too much to bear.

"Do you guys want to go to Cal Block?" Olivia asks. I expect Charlie to spin around and tell her how insensitive she is being. That we can't possibly order the special *S* like everything is the same, when Rob and Juliet are dead, but she smiles at Olivia. "Sounds perfect," she says. "Rose?"

But I'm not looking at them or thinking about *queso*. I'm watching someone who has just left the church. He has on a black suit and a blue tie, and he's standing by the doors, holding them open as people stream outside.

Len sees me too, and for a moment the world folds in on itself and the ground under us zips us together so that the only thing that exists in the entire universe is the two of us. But he doesn't make a move to come over to me. He doesn't even wave. Instead he just tips his head. And that one curl swings down onto his forehead.

Then he turns away and walks back in the direction of the parking lot. I wonder if I'm supposed to feel something, but it's like all the emotion has been wrung out of me. I just feel empty. I squeeze my eyes shut, and when I open them again, Charlie is looking at me. "What do you think?" she asks gently. "Cal Block?"

I shrug to say, *Sure, whatever, I don't care. Nothing matters. Nothing even exists anymore.* But I'm not sure my shoulders are working. I'm not sure I'm even breathing.

"Come on." Charlie puts her hands on my shoulder blades and nudges me forward, toward the cars. My parents are a few paces over, talking to Rob's parents. My father has his hand on Rob's dad's back, and they're nodding, their faces pinched up and tense.

I want to get out of here. I want to go as far away as pos-sible from all of this. From Rob's body and my parents and my dead cousin and even Charlie and Olivia. But I let Charlie lead me over to Big Red. Just like always. I climb into the front seat, and Olivia and Ben get into her car. Just like always. We drive to Cal Block, sit in our corner booth, and order the special *S*. Just like always. Olivia piles her chips and complains about the air-conditioning. Charlie rolls her eyes and orders more sparkling water. Just like always.

"Jake said he wanted to be in the water." Charlie ducks down and takes a long drag through her straw. "He's meeting me later."

"Makes sense." Olivia sighs and looks at me. "How are you?"

"Fine."

Olivia glances at Charlie, then back at me. "I'm so sorry," she says. "For the record, I think it's no one's business to talk about this. We all know Juliet was crazy, but . . ."

Something about the way she looks at Charlie, like she's getting permission or something, makes me seething mad. Hot blood is pounding in my ears so it makes it impossible to keep listening. I've put up with their puppy-dog stares and tears and sensitivity and theories—one routine piled atop another atop another that is supposed to all add up to this being okay. Like if they say the right thing and we wear the right thing to the funeral and we squeeze hands twice and tap our noses and go to the same restaurants and we carry on with our traditions, it will be like nothing ever happened. Like Rob never died.

Except he did, and no amount of special *S* will fix that.

"I'm not hungry," I say. "I'm going to go."

"Can we finish?" Charlie gestures to the plate in front of her with one hand and outside to the car with the other.

"I'm not asking you to drive me."

She sits back against the booth. "Okay."

Olivia is biting down on her nails.

"I'm walking," I announce to both of them.

I stand up, and Charlie stops me with her hand. She puts it entirely over mine, like paper covering rock. "It's going to be okay," she says. My eyes start to water as I leave, and I wish now, more than ever, that I could believe her.

Scene Three

When I leave Cal Block, I walk all the way back to the church. I know it's where I'm going before I start. I didn't fight hard enough for our friendship when we were kids, and I missed out on ten years with her. I didn't try hard enough when she was here, and now there won't be another chance. The least I can do is take it upon myself to say good-bye.

I arrive dusty and sweaty. The parking lot is crowded, and there are photographers outside, trying to catch a snapshot of the grieving family. I slip up to the entrance and jostle my way to the front, where a security guard asks me for my name.

"Rosaline," I say.

"Rosaline what?"

"Caplet. I'm her cousin."

He checks the list and shakes his head. "I'm sorry, miss, there's no Rosaline on here."

"But I'm her cousin," I say.

"I just follow orders," he says. "No one not on this list is allowed in."

I stumble backward, dazed. Inside, women in large sunglasses and black low-cut suits are huddling around each other, clutching their Chanel purses to their hearts like children. These people don't even know her. But then, neither did I.

I take out my cell phone, planning on calling Charlie, my tail between my legs, when I see my father standing outside. He's by a tree about three meters from the church, and he's leaning against it, squinting up into the sunlight.

"Dad?"

He sees me and smiles. "Great minds think alike."

"I'm sorry they didn't let you in," I say.

My dad shakes his head. "It's okay. I don't deserve it."

"Yes, you do. You want to be there."

"Sometimes, cookie, that's not enough." He puts his arm around me, and I lean my head on his shoulder. "I'm sorry about all of this," he says. "How are you holding up?"

"Dandy."

"That's my girl."

"I don't even think it's hit me yet. I just can't believe he's gone."

"I know," he says. "Me either. I think about Rob's father—" He clears his throat. "No one should have to lose a child."

"People think Juliet killed them, you know. That it was suicide."

My dad pauses. "And what do you think?"

Then it hits me, the thing I've been thinking since that night sitting on my kitchen floor with Juliet. And when the words spring up and form, I know they're true. "It was an accident. She'd never do anything to hurt him. She loved him."

My dad nods, then looks at the church. The photographers have settled, and the doors are closed. We stay that way, he with his arm around me, staring ahead, until the first mourners come out. "Sleep sweet," I whisper as we both, in our own way, try to say good-bye.

Days turn into weeks, and still I don't feel like time starts again. I go to school, I go to my classes. I nod and smile and say hello, but I'm not really feeling anything. I'm falling, and I know I should stick my hand out, should try to grab on to something and stop myself, but it's like I can't see. Not blind, exactly. More like my eyes are closed. But no matter how hard I try, I can't seem to figure out how to open them.

Nothing helps except music. It's the only thing that makes me feel like I'm still alive, sitting at the piano after school. While the house is still quiet and my parents are out—at work or running errands—I can lose myself. The notes carry me away from here. Not back in time but somewhere else entirely.

I'm comfortable here. Whole. Like nothing's missing.

Charlie and Olivia come by toting board games and vanilla lattes and bags and bags of Twizzlers. They stay up late and come by early. Sometimes Charlie comes and listens to me play. She thinks I don't know that she sits on the porch and waits for me to finish, but I hear her the second she arrives. She still slams car doors and jingles her keys. She's never been an inconspicuous person. Blending in just isn't her thing.

We don't talk about what people are saying at school. The murmurs in the bathroom, the hushed whispers when I pass by in the halls. It's getting quieter, but slowly. I almost fear the day people stop talking. Like a dull fade to black where Rob won't be seen anymore. Or remembered. I'm not looking forward to the darkness.

"Why don't we go out?" Olivia says. Today she's lying in my bed next to me flipping through a magazine she brought over. Charlie is sitting on my floor, stretching.

"Rose?" Charlie mumbles.

"I don't really feel like it."

"Come on. You've barely left the house in weeks." Charlie pops up from the floor and catapults herself onto the bed next to us.

"This isn't like a breakup," I say. "I don't need to go get drunk to get over it. I'm never getting over it."

"Who said anything about drinking?" Olivia says. "I just meant food. A movie. Something."

"Anything," Charlie adds.

"Fine, a movie. No food."

"Not even popcorn?" Olivia asks, but I can tell she's kidding, and even I have to smile.

"If it's synthetic, we don't have a problem."

"What's playing?" Charlie asks as we tromp our way downstairs.

"Who cares."

My parents are in the kitchen sipping coffee.

"We got her up," Charlie says to my mom. "Where's our medal?"

My mom comes over and folds me into a hug. She's been doing that a lot lately. Like if she holds on tight, she can keep me together.

"Well, I'm glad," she says, trying not to look hurt when I pull away. "Have fun."

My dad raises up his mug like he's toasting us, but he looks tired. And sad. I think this has been the hardest on him.

Charlie tries to hold my hand in the car, but I keep my palms planted firmly in my lap. She puts on her iPod, and we all get kind of quiet. A few times Olivia tries to play the "Remember when?" game, but all our stories just remind us of Rob, and we give up quickly. The movie theater is next to Grandma's Coffeehouse, and we park right in front, the way Olivia always does when she runs in on Wednesday mornings. We've been to the coffeehouse all together a few times, mostly when we've had a sleepover the night before, but I don't think I've been once this year. The same woman is still behind the counter, and as we slam doors and walk up to the theater, I realize I don't know her name. We've been coming here for probably ten years, and I've never bothered to ask.

Olivia buys us all tickets for some movie with the blond girl from that vampire show she's obsessed with. Charlie gets popcorn and two different kinds of candy, and we take seats in the back on the left-hand side. It's where we've been sitting since the seventh grade, when we started going to movies together alone, without our parents. I stuff my hand into the popcorn and shove a few kernels into my mouth, but they just taste like cardboard. The candy has no taste either. Even the movie looks dull. Like it's in black and white instead of color. I sit low in my seat and let the screen carry me away, lull me, so at least for the next two hours I'm only half conscious.

When the movie is over, I tell Charlie and Olivia I'll meet them outside. I use the restroom and splash some water onto my face. I shouldn't recognize myself. It's been weeks since I looked in the mirror and even longer since I've had a proper shower, but here I am. Rosaline, just like always. Even Rob's dying couldn't make me disappear.

I'm walking out of the bathroom when I see them buying tickets. Len and Dorothy. She is laughing and smiling, and he's paying. Are they on a date? She holds up a bag of popcorn, and he sticks his mouth in, tongue first, and flicks a kernel up. The rational part of me knows they are just friends, but the other part of me, the part that trusted him, is seething angry. He hasn't even said he was sorry. He didn't even call after Rob died. He didn't even ask if I was okay. We've barely spoken during bio, going through the activities like strangers, and we haven't talked about what happened at my house. He's barely registered my existence.

He sees me but immediately looks away. Great, so he's ignoring me again. Just like he did at the funeral. It's not like everyone else at school isn't treating me the same way. Except I thought Len was different. I trusted him. And he's proven to be exactly like everyone else.

I storm over to them and grab his arm. Hard.

"Hi," I say.

"Hey," he says, looking from my hand to my face and back down.

"Were you going to say hello? Or were you just going to keep ignoring me?"

Dorothy laughs nervously next to him, but he doesn't look at her. He just keeps looking at my hand on his arm.

"I thought we were friends," I continue. "I thought you'd care."

He looks up, and his eyes search mine. "I do," he says.

"Well, my friend just died. My cousin just died." I cough the words out like they're rotten.

"I know," he says. "I was there."

"Oh, you mean at the funeral? Could have fooled me. You didn't even say hello."

Len shakes his arm free from my grasp. "Honestly," he says, "I thought I'd be the last person you'd want to hear from." His voice is quiet, and he's holding his arm close to his chest. "That's why I haven't said anything. In school or otherwise. I didn't think you'd want me to."

"Well, you thought wrong," I say. And then, before I walk out to the car, I add, "Not that it matters anymore anyway."

"Do you want us to come in?" Charlie asks.

I shake my head. "It's fine. I'm tired."

Charlie nods, and Olivia squeezes my shoulder from the backseat. "We're here," she says. "We love you."

"Yeah."

"You have to let us help," Charlie says. "Please."

"Thanks," I say. "Talk tomorrow."

I unbuckle my seat belt and grab my purse. I slide out of the car and shut the door.

"I'll miss practice today," Charlie calls through the window. She's smiling, her red hair catching the last sinking rays of sun.

"You're a stalker," I say.

"And you're really good, Rosie. You know I wouldn't sit around and listen to half-baked talent." Her lips blow kisses as she swings out of the driveway, chauffeuring Olivia home.

I see a letter on the porch when I get closer. My mom has sorted the mail and left it out. I pick it up and walk inside. There is no return address, but the handwriting is familiar. I sit down on the stairs and thread my finger under the envelope flap, wiggling it from side to side until the seal pops. A photo slides out. It's yellowed on the back, and the corner is ripped off, like it's been torn out of an album.

It's a picture of two children, a boy and a girl, sitting at a piano. They are seated on the bench, facing away from the instrument. She's wearing a pink-and-white dress and he has on khakis and a collared shirt. The two children aren't looking at the camera but instead at each other, oblivious, lost in their own conversation.

And they each have a Twizzler dangling out of their mouths. The little girl is me and the little boy is Len. It's a picture from a recital at Famke's.

I turn the photo over, and there is a note on the back, scrawled in the same handwriting I now know so well. From hours spent in the bio lab, homework assignments, and corrected quizzes.

Rosaline,
I'm sorry for those things I said. I meant some of them, but
not all. I still care about you. I'm here, whenever you want
me to be.
Always,
—Len

I take the picture and stand up. Then I climb the stairs, walk down the hallway, and go into my room. It's not until I'm in bed that I realize I have the picture pressed up against my heart.

Scene Four

My birthday this year comes too quickly. It's January first before the calendar can right itself from stumbling over Christmas. The morning usually begins with my mom making pancakes in the kitchen. Banana and chocolate chip. We've been having them since before I can remember. She makes hot cocoa with espresso and we all sit around in our bathrobes and pretend it's snowing outside, which it never is.

"Just once, I'd love to have a white Christmas," my dad says every year, "but I'd be just as happy for it to show up on your birthday."

That's how I feel about Rob. I half expected him to come over on Christmas. Usually I wake up before six. It's one of those habits left over from childhood. The excitement to see what I've gotten and what kind of gifts are under the tree. I went downstairs and just stood in the living room, looking out to our lawn through the double glass doors over toward his house. I stood there for hours, until my mom came and wrapped a blanket around me and forced me back to the couch. I was convinced, somehow, that if I stared long enough, I'd see him. That if I waited long enough, the universe would get tired and let him slip back to me.

I have a habit of waking up early on my birthday, too, but today I wake up at nine. It's dark in my room, and if it wasn't for my clock on my nightstand, I'd have no idea what time it is at all. My phone is flashing on the floor beneath me—three new text messages.

Two are from Olivia. She wrote the text of a birthday card and got cut off. The third, I know before I read it, will be from Charlie. She always sends me the same thing every birthday morning: *Happy birthday, bisnatch. Time to party.*

The familiarity of the text sends me back flat against my pillows. Previous birthdays come sweeping in like leaves blown in the wind. Images and memories swirling around me. Charlie's text and Rob's visit, always in time for pancakes. Hot cocoa with my family. Presents and laughter and always the promise of more. Playing with our Christmas gifts from the previous week and running around on full stomachs. Dinner together and sometimes even the slight champagne headache from New Year's Eve the night before. A new semester of school. Times in which for-ever just seemed like a given. In which time seemed like a stroll on Olivia's beach in Malibu: casual and unrushed.

Last year on my birthday Rob came over for brunch. My mom made her traditional pancakes, and we all sat around and joked about how long it would take my dad to set up the new DVR my mom had bought him for Christmas. Afterward my parents started cooking some elaborate birthday dinner, and Rob and I drove over to Olivia's house. Charlie and Ben were there, and Jake, too, and the six of us spent the afternoon baking brownies and watching *Casablanca*. We ended up burning the first batch because we forgot about them in the oven, but the house smelled like chocolate for the rest of the day. I remember lying on Olivia's couch and thinking there was nowhere else in the world I'd rather be. It was perfect.

My mom knocks softly on my door and comes inside. She sits down on the edge of my bed and then moves closer, placing one hand on my forehead.

"Happy birthday, baby. Are you coming down?" She starts running her hand through my hair the way she used to do when I was little and sick.

"Yeah," I say. "Just thinking."

She nods and motions for me to sit up. I slide until my back is flat against my headboard.

"Look, Rosaline." Usually my mom only uses my full name like that when she's mad at me, but it's my birthday, and something about the way she says it makes me think of Len.

"You never call me that."

My mom dips her chin down and kisses me on the forehead. "It's your name, sweetheart. It's who you really are." She smooths my hair with the back of her hand. "Sometimes things happen in life that we don't understand. That are unreasonably cruel." She stops and touches my cheek. Her hands are warm. She probably already started cooking. "But that doesn't mean you curl up and give in. Do you understand?"

I blink back tears, and she stands up, going over to my window. She pulls back the blinds, and light comes pouring into my bedroom.

"There are still some surprises left," she says. "Come and see."

"What?"

She doesn't respond; she just keeps looking outside. I toss back the covers and realize it's kind of cold in my room. I wrap my robe around me and go to stand behind her. When I get there, I gasp.

All across our lawn down below, covering our outdoor furniture and lining our deck, is a delicate white blanket of snow.

"It's beautiful," I say.

"So are you," my mother says. She puts her arm around me, and this time I let her. I lean my head on her shoulder. I'm as close to anyone as I have been since Charlie collected me from my floor weeks ago, and maybe because I feel protected, for just a moment, it slips out.

"It was my fault," I whisper. I'm blinking, my eyes struggling to adjust to the influx of light. "I know Juliet didn't pull the wheel. It was Rob. He was drunk. He came to see me, and I turned him away. He should never have been in the car. It was my fault he died."

"Is that what you think?" My mom takes her arm away from me and crosses it against her chest.

"It's just true," I say. "He should have been with me. I could have stopped this."

"No," my mom says, "that's not how it works." She wanders away from the window and over to my desk. She picks up a picture and sets it back down. "I realize I don't know exactly what happened between the two of you. And there was all that stuff with Juliet. . . ." She loops her finger in the air a few times like she's trying to hurry herself up. "But one thing I do know is that we don't get to choose when we leave this world. And we don't get to choose when others leave either."

She drops her hands to her sides and sighs. "Honey, think about your dad. He didn't speak to his brother for ten years." She closes her eyes like she's trying to get the words right. "That was a choice," she says, "and he missed out on getting to know his niece. We all did."

"I just didn't think it would happen like this."

"I know, baby," she says, "but this is life. We can't plan it; it just happens. The only thing we get to choose is how we react to it."

I think about Charlie and what she told me. *We can choose to be happy. You can choose not to blame yourself.* Then I get it. And there's one more thing I think we can choose too.

I take out my phone and text her back. *Dinner at my house? Love you.* I get one back immediately: *DUH. Luv u 2, Rosebud.*

"So are you going to join us downstairs for your birthday?" my mom asks.

"In a few minutes. First there's something I have to do." She nods and smiles at my dad, who's just come in. He's holding a big white envelope.

"Happy birthday, cookie," he says. "In the midst of everything, we forgot to give you this."

They look at each other and then at me as my dad slides the envelope onto the bed. Embossed on the front is the Stanford logo. Of course. I'd forgotten to check online.

"Go ahead," my dad says. "See what's inside."

I pick it up and turn it over. I've been waiting for this moment for ten years. Longer, even. I always imagined how it would go. I would call Rob, excited and breathless, and he would come over. We'd sit on the floor in my bedroom and I'd put a hand over my eyes and hand him the envelope. "I can't do it," I'd say. "Just tell me."

He'd open it and read it to himself with a straight face, nodding soberly. Then he'd look up with a blank expression and say, "Rosie, here's the deal." He'd pause, and my heart would be beating out of my chest. Then his face would crack into a gigantic smile and he'd say, "You got in!" He'd thrust the paper into my hands, and I'd read with completely shaking fingers, the letter flapping everywhere.

But now it's just me and the envelope. No Rob. No nerves, even. I turn it in my hands, just holding it, and then I set it back down on the bed.

My dad frowns and looks at me, but my mom is smiling slightly, that little smile that says she just *knows*. "We'll be here when you're ready," she says, and ushers my dad outside.

Something is coming back, some life force I've been missing since Rob died, maybe even before. Probably before, actually, because it feels like my entire life I've been just floating along, anticipating one thing and then another, like my life was a checklist and I just kept ticking items off. I used to think that was safe, comfortable. Like nothing bad could happen if I just stuck to the list. Now I realize it was downright constricting. I don't want to live like I know what's coming.

I throw myself into my bathroom. I run a brush through my hair and gargle with some mouthwash. I've looked better, but I just don't care. I'm buzzing now, humming with the excitement of what I'm about to do.

I jump into some jeans and pull a long-sleeved T-shirt over my head. Then I throw on a sweater. After all, it's snowing outside. For the first time I kind of understand what my mom's been talking about. That it's my birthday and the start of a new year. It's cool, really, that I get this chance to do things differently. That one day, one moment, can mark the beginning of all kinds of change.

My parents are hanging out in the kitchen when I get down-stairs. They actually went over to Juliet's parents' house the other night. I don't know if they will fix things, but I think they've started to try, and for just a moment I'm grateful for that, for the fact that sometimes things turn out the way they do, and even if unthinkable things happen, there is good buried under-neath. Feuds can end. Families can reunite. Friends can change and grow, sometimes even with you. The possibilities of life are unknown and endless, and the staggering reality of that, of how much things can change in a moment, suddenly seems less scary and more full of hope. Overwhelming, but tinged with excite-ment. Like the edges don't recede away into oblivion, stretching out forever, but instead are lit on fire. Energized, somehow. Like life isn't something that happens *to* us but through us and by us. Like we're a part of something. Like we have choice. Because having a plan is great, but sometimes you realize that the thing you really want, you forgot to write down.

"I'll be back later," I say, and shout good-bye. I pull on boots and slip outside. My car is parked in the garage, where it always is, and for a second a familiar fear catches in my throat, but today I push it to the side. It's now or never, and I don't want to wait anymore. I tap my unused license in my palm as I climb inside and put the keys into the ignition. When the car starts, I just keep telling myself that I can do this, that I'm not afraid, that it will all be okay.

And it is. As soon as I start driving, the fear begins to melt away. My hands relax on the steering wheel and I'm cruising down the highway. Effortlessly. Past Grandma's and Charlie's house and school and the place where I fell last year while biking with Olivia and skinned my knee, and where Jake and Rob used to go surfing at the cove. And just like that, I need a new seven. Because not driving is no longer the thing that defines me. And I'm not so sure anymore that there is one thing that defines any of us. Because the fact that Lauren does SAC or that Olivia likes purple or that Charlie has Big Red doesn't really tell us anything about them. Or if it does, it doesn't tell us nearly enough. Their sevens should be that Lauren picks up any responsibility, without ever asking for any credit, and that Olivia stands up for her friends when it really matters, and that Charlie is resilient and strong and that she will hold you up when you can't do the same for yourself. Those are the things that define us. The way we love the people around us, and the choices we make to show it. That's what makes us who we are.

As I keep on driving, it's like a huge gravitational force is pulling me by my belly button toward the Cliffs, tugging me closer and closer so that it feels almost like I'm on autopilot. I don't need to think. Something else, something bigger than me, is doing it for me now.

When I pull into the parking lot, it's empty. For a moment I'm disappointed, wondering if maybe I was wrong, but then I see a figure over to the side, by the rocks. I slam the door and walk closer. He looks just like I thought he would. Shirt and jeans, familiar and exhilarating. I approach him from behind. He's busy bent over something, studying it. I want to go and put my arms around him, bury my head in his shoulder and tell him how I knew I'd find him here. That if he was anywhere, he'd be here, of course. With me. And that there's something I really need to tell him.

"Hey," I say. He stops what he's doing, but he doesn't immediately turn around. He straightens up, runs a hand across his forehead. "I knew you'd be here," I say.

Then Len spins around, slowly, and when he does, I'm reminded of all the times I've been here before. How much has happened in this exact spot. And in the time it takes him to face me, I realize I'm happy to be here, now, like this. That I'm *choosing* to be happy. And that that choice is the best one I have ever made in my life.

"Hey," he says. "How did you know where to find me?" He's frowning, and it throws me off. I thought he'd be smiling. I thought just by seeing me he'd understand.

"Grass," I mumble, because it's the only thing I can think of. "You were doing a project on grass."

His face softens. "You came here to talk about grass?"

"No," I say. "I wanted to tell you something."

"Yes?" he says. He crosses his arms and looks at me.

"I—I—" I stammer, "I understand now. You were right."

"About what?" he asks. He's moved closer to me now, and I can feel the warmth of him. I want to press myself up next to him, to have him put his arms around me, but I force myself to stay still and finish what I have to say.

"You told me something months ago. Something about letting go."

Len uncrosses his arms, and when he does, that curl swings down onto his forehead. This time I don't stop myself. This time I reach over and sweep it away, and at the same time I say, "You were right. He wasn't meant for me. And not just because he's no longer here."

I can feel Len inhale, my hand still on his forehead. I let my hand trace back through his hair. It's soft, like the cashmere sweaters my mom keeps wrapped in tissue paper in her closet. "But you were wrong about something too."

"Oh yeah?" he says. He has inched closer to me too, and one of his hands reaches up to touch my arm. The contact sends sparklers off down my spine. Even though it's snowing, he's not wearing a jacket, and I reach for his arm too, and slowly trail my fingers down his birthmark, along one of the many wonderful things that makes him *him*.

"Yeah."

"What's that?" he whispers. His lips are inches from mine, and I have to bite my lip to keep from reaching out and pulling his face down right this instant.

"It's not the hardest part of letting go. The hardest part is just making the choice to do it. Everything after that is easy."

Len nods. "So is that what you've done?"

"Yes," I say.

"And what have you chosen?" His voice is low and deep, and when he talks, it feels like the vibrations of his words are humming through me like music.

"You."

I can't be sure who moves first, but all of a sudden our lips meet, and when they do, it's like the entire world has been turned off because all the light in the universe is existing just between us. Like fireworks on the Fourth of July. So much light you can even hear it.

When we break apart, we're both breathing hard. Len keeps one arm around me, and with the other he points up to the sky.

"Do you see that?" he says.

"There's nothing there," I whisper. "Just clouds."

Len shakes his head. "It's Andromeda," he says. "A princess from a Greek legend. She was chained to a rock in the ocean to die, and Perseus saved her. It's a spiral galaxy, just like the Milky Way."

"But it's not night yet," I say. "The stars aren't out."

"Of course they are." He smiles and pulls me closer. "Just because you can't see things sometimes doesn't mean they're not there."

I think about the things I haven't seen. How much has changed. How six months ago I thought I had everything figured out. I was so sure of how things were going to unfold. I think about Len saying he wasn't finished with high school yet, and I think I know what he means now, because I'm not either.

"I got my letter from Stanford."

He smiles. "They paying you to go?"

"I don't know. I didn't open it. I don't even know if it's what I want anymore."

Len considers this, running a hand gently through my hair. "You know, NYU has a great music school," he says. "And it's not too late to apply."

I lean back and look at him. "This wouldn't have anything to do with the fact that Juilliard is in New York, would it?"

He scoffs and rolls his eyes. "Please," he says. "I have better things to do than sit around and think about us spending our college years together, playing music, sitting in coffee shops . . ."

"We probably wouldn't even see each other," I say, teasing. "I'm sure we'd be very busy."

"Plus, there's that girl with the tattoos I need to date in order to properly rebel." He laughs. "Still and all, I think we could make it work."

"Yeah?"

He looks down at me and touches his forehead to mine. "We're here, aren't we?"

Here. This place that has seen a beginning and an ending and now a beginning again. He pulls me toward him, and when our lips meet, the possibility of life seems to explode outward, and the astounding energy of the universe, of how alive the roots and the leaves and the stars and even the delicate, white, precarious snow is, makes me smile against his lips.

"So what happens now?" I ask.

He kisses my nose, and I can see his dimples dancing. "Anything you want, Rosaline," he says. "Absolutely anything."

Epilogue

Olivia was right. The point of the Choose Your Own Adventure books was just that: choice. It wasn't about where you ended up; it was about the decisions you made to get there. And I don't want to skip to the end anymore. Because in real life there is no way to know, anyway. There are no guarantees. You can start down one road and figure out it wasn't the one you really wanted to be traveling down at all. Or you could switch courses just to realize this new path leads to the exact same place as the old one. And, see, that's where choice comes in. Because while you can't know where you'll end up, you can, even in the last act, alter the course you're taking. You can veer off to the left, swing right, and find yourself somewhere you thought you'd never be. I guess the thing I've realized is that fate and destiny only get you so far. Because they decide beginnings, not endings. Destiny might drop you off somewhere, but it's your job to get where you're going, to decide your own ending, what moment you choose to close the curtain on. So I guess Shakespeare didn't get it wrong, after all. The truth is that there are many different endings to the same story.

This one is mine.

Acknowledgments, and thanks . . .

First and foremost to my stupendous agent, Mollie Glick. Thank you for your belief, your commitment, and your mad iPhone skills. You make me feel supported, challenged, and excited every single day. I have the best job in the world because of you.

To my incredible editor, Anica Rissi, who loved Rosaline from the get-go. Thank you for fighting for this book; for the chocolate; for your genius, ridiculously awesome editorial guidance; and for always, always making me feel like the coolest kid on the block.

To Brad and Yfat Gendell, who, from my first minute here, have made New York home. Yfat, none of this, not one single part, would be possible without you. Thank you for seeing something in that girl that I didn't yet, and thank you for making me family.

For Hannah Brown Gordon, there is not enough gratitude. Thank you for helping me understand that this was my story, and for holding my hand as I figured out how to tell it. Between the two of us we use a lot of words, but we need only one: love.

To my wacky buddy cop, writing partner, and wonderful friend, Leila Sales, who stood next to me and sat across from me during this entire process. You showed me that this extraordinary dream was possible, and you challenge me every day to be worthy of it.

To Melissa Seligmann, who lived through this and many other books with me. I was never alone, because I had you.

To everyone at Pulse who made me feel so welcomed from day one. Bethany Buck, Mara Anastas, Jennifer Klonsky, and Guillian Helm, thank you. I couldn't imagine a better place to call home.

To Katie Hanson for sharing her apartment with me every Sunday and for celebrating these triumphs as her own.

To all of my friends, you know who you are: I love you.

To Yes Giantess, for helping me write my way in. Check them out: www.myspace.com/yesgiantess.

A big thank-you to everyone at Foundry, in particular

Stephanie Abou and Stephen Barbara. Stephen, thank you for introducing me to the wonderful world of children's literature. I will always be grateful.

And finally to my parents, to whom this book is dedicated. You always believed, even when I didn't. I am so blessed to have you both.

About the Author

REBECCA SERLE is a full-time writer, which means she gets to wear pajamas to work. She went to the University of Southern California, then got her MFA from the New School in NYC. (She likes New York much more than LA, but don't tell anyone that.) Rebecca loves shiny hair, coffee, yoga, and pretending to be British. She, too, experienced heartbreak once. It worked out okay, though, because she turned the experience into this book. *When You Were Mine* is her first novel. Find out more at rebeccaserle.com.